Beginnings of the American People

Carl L. Becker

Table of Contents

CHAPTER I

THE DISCOVERY OF THE OLD WORLD AND THE NEW

We come in search of Christians and spices.
Vasco da Gama.

Gold is excellent; gold is treasure, and he that possesses it does all that he wishes to in this world, and succeeds in helping souls into paradise.
Christopher Columbus.

I

Contact with the Orient has always been an important factor in the history of Europe. Centers of civilization and of political power have shifted with every decisive change in the relations of East and West. Opposition between Greek and barbarian may be regarded as the *motif* of Greek history, as it is a persistent refrain in Greek literature. The plunder of Asia made Rome an empire whose capital was on the Bosphorus more centuries than it was on the Tiber. Mediæval civilization rose to its height when the Italian cities wrested from Constantinople the mastery of the Levantine trade; and in the sixteenth century, when the main traveled roads to the Far East shifted to the ocean, direction of European affairs passed from Church and Empire to the rising national states on the Atlantic. The history of America is inseparable from these wider relations. The discovery of the New World was the direct result of European interest in the Far East, an incident in the charting of new highways for the world's commerce. In the thirteenth and fourteenth centuries Europeans first gained reliable knowledge of Far Eastern countries, of the routes by which they might be reached, above all of the hoarded-treasure which lay there awaiting the first comer. Columbus, endeavoring to establish direct connections with these countries for trade and exploitation, found America blocking the way. The discovery of the New World was but the sequel to the discovery of the Old.

From the ninth to the eleventh century the people of Western Europe had lived in comparative isolation. With half the heritage of the Roman Empire in infidel hands, the followers of the Cross and of the Crescent faced each other, like hostile armies, across the sea. The temporary expansion of the Frankish Empire ceased with the life of Charlemagne, and under his successors formidable enemies closed it in on every hand. Barbarian Slav and Saxon pressed upon the eastern frontier, while the hated Moslem, from the vantage of Spain and Africa, infested the Mediterranean and threatened the Holy City. Even the Greek Empire, natural ally of Christendom, deserted it, going the way of heresy and schism.

Danger from without was accompanied by disorganization within. In the tenth century the political edifice so painfully constructed by Charlemagne was in ruins. The organization of the Roman Empire and the Gregorian ideal of a Catholic Church, now little more than a lingering tradition, was replaced by the feudal system. Seigneurs, lay and ecclesiastic, warring among themselves for the shadow of power, had neither time nor inclination for the ways of peace or the life of the spirit. Learning all but disappeared; the useful arts were little cultivated; cities fell into decay and the roads that bound them together were left in unrepair; the life of the time, barren alike in hovel and castle, was supported by the crude labor of a servile class. To be complete within itself, secure from military attack and economically self-supporting, were the essential needs which determined the structure of the great fiefs. The upper classes rarely went far afield, while the "rural population lived in a sort of chrysalis state, in immobility and isolation within each seigneury."

But the feudal régime, well suited to a period of confusion, could not withstand the disintegrating effects of even the small measure of peace and prosperity which it secured. Increase in population and the necessities of life liberated those expansive social forces, in politics and industry, in intellectual life, in religious and emotional experience, which produced the civilization of the later Middle Ages; that wonderful thirteenth century which saw the rise of industry and the towns, the foundation of royal power in alliance with a moneyed class, the revival of intellectual activity which created the universities and the scholastic philosophy, the intensification of the religious spirit manifesting itself in such varied and perfect forms,—in the simple life of a St. Francis or the solemn splendor of a Gothic cathedral.

Of this new and expanding life, the most striking external expression was embodied in the Crusades. Strangely compounded of religious enthusiasm and political ambition, of the redeless spirit of the knight-errant and the cool calculation of the commercial bandit, these half-military and half-migratory movements of the twelfth and thirteenth centuries mark the beginning of that return of the West upon the East which is so persistent a factor in all modern history. Christendom, so long isolated, now first broke the barriers that had closed it in, and once more extended its frontier into western Asia: Norman nobles, establishing the Kingdom of Jerusalem and the Latin Empire, enabled the Church to guard the Holy Sepulchre, while Italian cities reaped a rich harvest from the plunder of Constantinople and the Levantine trade.

The Latin Empire and the Kingdom of Jerusalem did not outlast the thirteenth century, but the extension of commercial activity was a permanent result of vital importance for the relations of Orient and Occident. The swelling volume of Mediterranéan trade which accompanied the crusading movement depended upon the growing demand in the West for the products of the East. Europe could provide the necessities for a simple and monotonous life, without adornment or display. But the rise of a burgher aristocracy, the growth of an elaborate and symbolic ritualism in religious worship, the desire for that pomp and display which is half the divinity of kings, created a demand for commodities which only the East could supply,—spices for flavoring coarse food, "notemege to

4

putte in ale," fragrant woods and dyes and frankincense, precious stones for personal adornment or royal regalia or religious shrines, rich tapestries for bare interiors, "cloths of silk and gold."

All these products, and many more besides, so attractive to the unjaded mind of Europe, celebrated in chronicle and romance from the thirteenth to the fifteenth century, were to be found in those cities of the Levant—in Constantinople, in Antioch or Jaffa or Alexandria—which were the western termini to long established trade routes to the Far East. Wares of China and Japan and the spices of the southern Moluccas were carried in Chinese or Malay junks to Malacca, and thence by Arab or Indian merchants to Paulicut or Calicut in southern India. To these ports came also ginger, brazil-wood, sandal-wood, and aloe, above all the precious stones of India and Persia, diamonds from Golconda, rubies, topaz, sapphires, and pearls. From India, the direct southern route lay across the Indian Ocean to Aden and up the Red Sea to Cairo or Alexandria. The middle route followed the Persian Gulf and the Tigris River to Bagdad, and thence to the coast cities of Damascus, Jaffa, Laodicea, and Antioch. And by the overland northern route from Peking, by painful and dangerous stages through Turkestan to Yarkand, Bokhara, and Tabriz came the products of China and Persia,—silks and fabrics, rich tapestries and priceless rugs.

From the twelfth century Italian cities grew rich and powerful on the carrying trade between western Europe and the Levant. Venice and Genoa, Marseilles and Barcelona, whose merchants had permanent quarters in Eastern cities, became the distributing centers for western Europe. Each year until 1560, a Venetian trading fleet, passing through the Straits of Gibraltar, touching at Spanish and Portuguese ports, at Southampton or London, finally reached the Netherlands at Bruges. But the main lines to the north were the river highways: from Marseilles up the Rhone to Lyons and down the Seine to Paris and Rouen; from Venice through the passes of the Alps to the great southern German cities of Augsburg and Nuremburg, and thence northward along the Elbe to the Hanse towns of Hamburg or Lubec; or from Milan across the St. Gothard to Basle and westward into France at Chalons. The main carriers from the North of the Alps were the merchants of South Germany; while the Hanse merchants, buying in southern Germany, or in the Netherlands at Bruges and Antwerp, sold in England and France, in the Baltic cities, and as far east as Poland and Russia.

II

Before the middle of the thirteenth century no Italian merchant could have told you anything of the "isles where the spices grow," or of the countries which produced the rich fabrics in which he trafficked: he knew only that they came to Alexandria or Damascus from Far Eastern lands. For from time immemorial the Orient had been the enemy's country, little known beyond the bounds of Syria, a half-mythical land of alien races, of curious customs and infidel faiths, a land of interminable distances, rich and populous, doubtless, certainly dangerous and inaccessible. But in the thirteenth century the veil which had long shrouded Asia in mystery was lifted, discovering to European eyes countries so rich in hoarded

5

treasure and the products of industry that the gems and spices which found their way to the West were seen to be but the refuse of their accumulated stores.

The discovery of Asia in the thirteenth century was the direct result of the Mongol conquest. Before the death of Jenghis Khan in 1227, the Tartar rule was established in northern China or Cathay, and in central Asia from India to the Caspian; while within half a century the successors of the first emperor were dominant to the Euphrates and the Dniester on the west, and as far south as Delhi, Burma, and Cochin China. The earlier conquests were conducted with incredible ferocity; but the influence of Chinese civilization moderated the temper of the later Khans, who exhibited a genial and condescending curiosity in the people of Christendom. Diplomatic relations were established between Tartar and Christian princes. In the Paris archives may still be seen letters written from Tabriz to the kings of France bearing official Chinese seals of the thirteenth century. For the first time Europeans were welcome beyond the Great Wall. Kublai Khan sent presents to the Pope and requested Christian missionaries for the instruction of his people. Traders and travelers were hospitably received, clever adventurers were taken into favor and loaded with benefits and high office.

It was in 1271 that two prosperous Italian merchants, Maffeo and Nicolo Polo, at the invitation of Kublai Khan, left Venice, taking with them Nicolo's son, the young Marco, destined to be the most famous of mediæval travelers. Going out by way of the Tigris River to Hormos, they turned eastward, and after many weary months journeying across Persia and China arrived at the city of Cambulac, now known as Peking. Here they remained for twenty years, favored guests or honored servants at the court of the Grand Khan. Henceforth Maffeo and Nicolo retire into the background; we catch occasional glimpses of them, shrewd Venetians, unobtrusively putting money in their purses, while the young Marco occupies the center of the stage as royal favorite, member of the Privy Council, or trusted ambassador to every part of the emperor's wide domains. A happy chance enabled them to return at last; and by a route no European had yet taken: from Peking to Zaiton; thence by sea through the famous Malacca Straits to Ceylon and India; up to Hormos and across to Tabriz and Trebizond; and so, by way of the Bosphorus, home to Venice, with a tale of experiences rivaling the Arabian Nights, and a fortune stitched up in the seams of their clothes.

The fortune, in "rubies, sapphires, carbuncles, diamonds, and emeralds," was straightway turned out before the admiring gaze of friends; while the story was told, to friends and enemies alike, many times over, and presently, in a Genoese prison, set down in French—*The Book of Ser Marco Polo the Venetian concerning the Kingdoms and Marvels of the East*. It was only one of many books of that age describing the countries of the Orient, for Marco Polo was only the most famous of the travelers of his time. Diplomatic agents, such as Carpini, the legate of Innocent IV, or William de Rubruquis, the ambassador of St. Louis; missionaries, such as John de Corvino, Jordanus de Severac, or Friar Beatus Oderic, laboring to establish the faith in India and China; merchants, such as Pegalotti and Schiltberger, seeking advantage in the way of trade:— these, and many more besides, penetrated into every part of Asia and recorded in letters, in dry and precise merchant hand-books, in naïve and fascinating narrative accounts, a wealth of information about this old world now first discovered to Europeans.

For the revelations of the travelers amounted to a discovery of Asia. In the age before printing news spread from mouth to mouth. Reading had not yet replaced conversation, and a narrative of events was alike the duty and the privilege of every chance visitor from far or near. What a celebrity, then, was the Asiatic voyager, returning home after many years! It is said of Marco Polo that even in Genoa, where he was held a prisoner, "when his rare qualities and marvelous travels became known there, the whole city gathered to see him. At all hours of the day he was visited by the noblest gentlemen of the city, and was continually receiving presents of every useful kind. Messer Marco, finding himself in this position, and witnessing the general eagerness to hear all about Cathay and the Grand Chan, which indeed compelled him daily to repeat his story till he was weary, was advised to put the matter in writing." And certainly those voluble Italians were not men to remain silent. Thousands, who never read the book of Ser Marco or the charming narratives of Rubruquis or Friar Oderic, must have heard many of their wonderful stories as they were carried by the merchants and priests, students, minstrels, and high diplomatic agents who went up and down the highways of Europe in the fourteenth century.

And the tale was marvelous, indeed, to the unaccustomed ears of Europe,—a tale of innumerable populous cities and great rivers, a tale of industry and thrift and glutted markets, above all a tale of treasure. What was doubtless heard most eagerly and told again with most verve were the accounts of cities with "walles of silver and bulwarkes or towers of golde," palaces "entirely roofed with fine gold," lakes full of pearls, of Indian princes wearing on their arms "gold and gems worth a city's ransom." In that country, says Rubruquis, "whoever wanteth golde, diggeth till he hath found some quantitie." Oderic tells of a "most brave and sumptuous pallace" in Java, "one stayre being of silver, and another of golde, throughout the whole building"; the rooms were "paved all over with silver and gold, and all the wals upon the inner side sealed over with plates of beaten gold; the roof of the palace was of pure gold." As for the Grand Khan, he had, according to Marco Polo, "such a quantity of plate, and of gold and silver in other shapes, as no one ever before saw or heard tell of, or could believe." And so freely did the returned traveler discourse of Kublai Khan's millions of *saggi* of revenue, that he was ever after known in Italy as Ser Marco Milioni.

In contrast with this country, how small and inferior is Europe! Such is the most general impression conveyed by the accounts of the travelers. Do you think you have some powerful kings here?—they have always the air of asking— some great rivers, populous and thriving cities? But I tell you Europe is nothing. "The city of Quinsay," says Oderic, "hath twelve principall gates; and about the distance of eight miles, on the highway unto each one of the said gates, standeth a city as big by estimation as Venice and Padua." And this trade of the Levant, profitable as you think it, is but a small affair. On a single river in China, the greatest in the world, "there is more wealth and merchandise than on all the rivers and all the seas of Christendom put together." Of that great wealth, very little, indeed, ever comes to the Levant: "for one ship load of pepper that goes to Alexandria or elsewhere, destined for Christendom, there come a hundred, aye and more too, to this haven of Zaiton"; while the diamonds "that are brought to our part of the world are only the refuse of the finer and larger stones; for the flower of the diamonds, as well as of the larger pearls, are all carried to the Grand Khan or other princes of these regions: in truth, they possess all the great treasures of the world."

What a reversal of values for that introspective mind of Christendom, so long occupied with its own soul! And what an opportunity,—all the great treasures of the world possessed by people who welcome merchants but "hate to see soldiers"; being themselves "no soldiers at all, only accomplished traders and most skillful artisans." Here was the promised land for Europeans, wretchedly poor, but good soldiers enough. Here was Eldorado, symbol of all external and objective values which so fired the imagination in that age of discovery; presenting a concrete and visualized goal, a *summum bonum*, attainable, not by contemplation, but by active endeavor; fascinating alike to the merchant dreaming of profits, to the statesman intent on conquest, to the priest in search of martyrdom, to the adventurer in, search of gold.

III

And who was not in search of gold? "Gold is excellent; gold is treasure, and he who possesses it does all that he wishes to in this world, and succeeds in helping souls into paradise." So thought Columbus, expressing in a phrase the motto of many men, and conveniently revealing to us an essential secret of European history. For gold, so abundant in the East, was scarce in the West. The mines of Europe have never been adequate to the needs of an expanding industrial civilization. Importation of expensive Eastern luxuries, normally overbalancing exports, produces a drain of specie to the Orient, that reservoir to which the precious metals seem naturally to flow, and from which they do not readily return; so that to maintain the gold supply and prevent a fatal appreciation of money value has been a serious problem in both ancient and modern times. During the Roman Republic the supply of gold was maintained at Rome by the systematic exploitation of Syria and Asia Minor. But after Augustus reformed the government of the provinces, the accumulated treasure of the West began to return to the Orient: the annual exportation of 200,000,000 sesterces in payment for the silks and spices of India and Arabia, of Syria and Egypt, was one of the causes of economic exhaustion and the collapse of imperial power. "So dear," says Pliny, "do pleasures and women cost us."

During the age of feudal isolation, this ever-recurring problem did not exist; and in the twelfth and thirteenth centuries it seems not to have been pressing. Imports from the Orient were nearly balanced by exports to Syria, for which the crusading movements and the Kingdom of Jerusalem created an abnormal demand. The rise of trade in the West was accompanied by an expansion of the credit system centering in the banking houses of Florence; while the supply of metals was more than maintained by the plunder of Asiatic cities, paid over by crusaders in return for supplies and munitions of war, or brought home by returning princes and nobles, by priests and merchants, by Knights of St. John or

8

of the Temple. Between 1252 and 1284, the ducat and the florin and the famous gold crowns of St. Louis made their appearance,—the sure sign of an increased gold supply, rising prices, and flourishing trade.

But in 1291 the Kingdom of Jerusalem was overthrown; successful crusading ceased, and the plunder of Syrian cities was at an end. Yet the volume of Oriental trade was undiminished; normal exports were insufficient to pay for imports; and from the end of the thirteenth to the middle of the fifteenth century the drain of precious metals from Europe was followed by the inevitable appreciation of gold. Prices fell; many communes were bankrupt; kings, in desperate straits, debased the coinage and despoiled the Church. It was in 1291 that Edward I forced his "loan" from the churches; and Philip IV, in 1296 forbidding the export of gold and silver from France, set about with unparalleled cunning and cruelty to destroy the Templars in order to appropriate the wealth which they had accumulated in the Holy Land.

It was in this very fourteenth century, when gold was appreciating and prices were falling, that the immense wealth of the Orient was first fully revealed to Europeans. All the commodities which Arab traders sold at high prices to Venetian merchants in the Levant were now known to be of little worth in the markets of India. In that country, all the reports agreed, "they have every necessity of life very cheap"; and every luxury as well—forty pounds of "excellent fresh ginger for a Venice groat"; "three pheasants for an asper of silver"; five grains of silver buying one of gold; three dishes, "so fine that you could not imagine better," to be had for less than half a shilling. It was the Arab middlemen that made the difference: the enemies of Christendom, intrenched in Jerusalem and Egypt, guarded the easy highways to the East and took rich toll of all its commerce. What a stroke for State and Church if Europe, uniting with the Ilkhans of Persia, could establish direct connections with the Orient, eliminate the infidel middlemen, and divide with Mongol allies the fruits of Indian exploitation!

Such projects, drifting from court to court in the early fourteenth century, form the aftermath of the great Crusades. In 1307 Marino Sanuto, Venetian statesman and geographer, presented to Clement V an elaborate plan for the revival of the old conflict with Islam. But Sanuto contemplated something more than the recovery of the Holy Land. Sketching with sure hand the trade routes from India to the Levant, he demonstrated that the Arabs were enriched at the expense of Christian Europe. Yet beyond the narrow confines of Syria were the Mongols, well disposed toward Christians, but enemies of Mohammedan Arab and Turk. First weaken the Moslem powers, said Sanuto, by an embargo on all exports of provisions and munitions of war to Syria and Egypt, and then overthrow them by a combined attack of Christian and Mongol armies. The great end would thus be attained: a Christian fleet on the Indian Ocean, subjugating all the coast and island ports from India to Hormos and Aden, would act as convoy for Italian merchants trading directly with the Eastern markets by way of Alexandria and the Red Sea, or down the Tigris River to the Persian Gulf.

The project of Sanuto, anticipating the achievements of England in our own day, was doubtless as vain as it was splendid. For the times, in fourteenth-century Europe, were out of joint. Clement V and his successors at Avignon, scarcely able to hold the Papal States, were little inclined to attempt the conquest of Syria. The Empire had lost its commanding position. Italian cities, released from imperial control, warred perpetually for existence or supremacy. England and France were preparing for the desolating struggle that exhausted their resources for a hundred years. "All Christendom is sore decayed and feeblished, whereby the Empire of Constantinople leeseth, and is like to lese," for lack of the "Knights and Squires who were wont to adventure themselves," but who adventure themselves no more.

In 1386, when this naïve plaint was addressed to Richard II by the dispossessed King of Armenia, conditions in Asia, even more than those in Europe, were such as to make the plans of Sanuto forever impossible. Johan Schiltberger, journeying to the Orient early in the fifteenth century, encountered dangers and difficulties unknown to Marco Polo a hundred years earlier. The successors of Kublai Khan no longer ruled in China; while the Ilkhans of Persia, having long since adopted Mohammedanism, were now as ill-disposed as formerly they had been friendly toward Christian states. Eastern and central Asia was indeed once more closing to Europeans: its rulers no longer sought alliance with Christian princes; no longer requested the service of papal missionaries; no longer welcomed traders and travelers. And in the Levant itself ominous changes were portending: the Ottoman Turks, pressing upon the Greek Empire from Asia Minor and the Balkan Peninsula, were already well advanced upon their career of blighting conquest which was destined to throw Christendom upon the defensive for more than two centuries. At the opening of the fifteenth century, although the trade routes had not been closed by the Turks, the *Drang nach Osten*—the hope of cutting through the Moslem barrier in order to establish direct connection with India—was at an end. Unless a new way to the East could be found, the better part of the treasure of the Orient was lost to Europe.

IV

Long before the fifteenth century many men had thought it possible to reach India by sailing around Africa. Since classical times geographers had both asserted and denied the possibility. During the Middle Ages the Ptolemaic theory was in the ascendant; but the observations of thirteenth-century travelers gave powerful support to the ideas of Eratosthenes. Europeans who had sailed from Malacca to Hormos, or had read the book of Marco Polo or Friar Oderic, knew well that no impenetrable swamp guarded the southern approaches to Asia; while those who had seen or heard of Arab ships clearing from Calicut for Aden could scarcely avoid the inference that a wider sweep to the south might have brought the same ships to Lisbon or Venice.

This inference, the alert and practical Italian intellect, unhampered by scientific tradition or ecclesiastical prejudice, had unhesitatingly drawn. The famous Laurentian *Portolano*, a sailing chart constructed in 1351, was precisely such a map as Marco Polo, had he turned cartographer, might have drawn: the first map in which Africa appears familiar to modern eyes; with the point of the continent foreshortened, and the Atlantic and Indian Oceans joined at last, it held out to all future explorers the prospect of successful voyages from Venice to Ceylon. Sixty years earlier, even before Polo returned from China, the heroic attempt had been made; Tedisio Doria and the Vivaldi, venturous Genoese seamen, passing the Rock of Gibraltar, pointed their galleys to the south in order "to go by sea to the ports of India to trade there." They never returned, nor were ever heard of beyond Cape Non in Barbary, but the memory of their hapless venture was perpetuated in legends of the fourteenth century which credited them with sailing "the sea of Ghinoia to the City of Ethiopia."

To go by sea to the ports of India was an undertaking not to be achieved by unaided Italian effort, or in a single generation. The skill and daring of many captains might find the way, but discovery was futile unless backed by conquest, for which the support of a powerful government was essential. Not from Italian states, weak and distracted by inter-city wars, or absorbed in established and profitable Levantine trade, was such support to come, but from the rising nations of the Atlantic, which profited least by the established commercial system. Lying at the extreme end of the old trade routes, the merchants of France, England, Spain, and Portugal were mulcted of the major profits of Oriental trade. Here prices were lowest and money most scarce. Yet the future of these countries, consolidated under centralized monarchies in alliance with a moneyed class, depended upon a full royal treasury and thriving industry. "The king," said Cardinal Morton, addressing the English Commons, "wishes you to arrest the drain of money to foreign countries. The king wishes to enrich you; you would not wish to make him poor. Consider that the kingdoms which surround us grow constantly stronger, and that it cannot be well that the king should find himself with an empty treasury." To replenish the royal treasury by enriching the *bourgeois* class was the basic motive which enlisted the Western monarchs in maritime exploration and discovery.

Yet not to the greater states of the West was reserved the honor of first reaching the Indies by sea. The Kingdom of Portugal, first to venture, was first to reach the goal. Looking out over Africa and the South Atlantic, effectively consolidated under King John of Good Memory while its neighbors were still involved in foreign wars or the problems of internal organization, the little state enjoyed advantages denied to England before the accession of Henry Tudor, or to Spain before the conquest of Granada. And to these advantages the fates added another, and greater. For at an opportune moment it was given to Portugal to possess one of those great souls, of lofty purpose and enduring resolution, whose fortune it is to gather the scattered energies of many men and with patient wisdom direct them to the attainment of noble ends. To Prince Henry the Navigator, who raised the endeavors of the nation to the level of an epic achievement, it is chiefly due that Portugal became, in exploration and discovery, the foremost country of the age.

In origin, the Portuguese search for India was but the sequel to the century-old conflict with the Moslem, a more subtly conceived crusade. Losing their hold on the Spanish Peninsula, the Moors were still intrenched in Africa; and in 1415 a Portuguese fleet, crossing to the northern point opposite Gibraltar, took and plundered the fortress and city of Ceuta. It was on this occasion, and subsequently in 1418, that Prince Henry gained from Moorish prisoners reliable information of the rich caravan trade from the Senegal and Gambia Rivers, and from the Gold and Ivory Coasts on the Gulf of Guinea, to Timbuctoo, and across the desert to Ceuta and Tunis: information which strengthened, if it did not inspire, the guiding motive of his life. For enriching Portugal and undermining the Moorish power in Africa, how much more effective than the plunder of Ceuta would be the conquest of the Guinea Coast! Once round the shoulder of Africa and the thing was done! And who could say what lay beyond the Gulf of Guinea? Prester John, perhaps, or the shining treasures of India.

And so, returning from Africa in 1418, the Prince retired to the famous Sacred Promontory in the Province of Algarve, where he gave the best energies of forty years to the task of African exploration. Backed by the resources of the state, commanding the best scientific knowledge of the day, patiently enduring "what every barking tongue could allege against a Service so unservicable and needlesse," he sent out year after year the most skillful and daring sailors of Italy and Portugal, and inspired them anew, as often as they returned baffled and discouraged, with his own perennial enthusiasm. Between 1435 and 1460, famous captains in his service—Gil Eannes, Denis Diaz, the Venetian Cadamosto—made those crucial voyages round the Point of Bojador, past the desert to Cape Verde, and beyond as far as Sierra Leone. After 1443 the labors of the Navigator were no longer thought to be wasted; for when the rich traffic in slaves and gold was opened up to Portugal, the greed of gain was added to scientific interest as a motive for exploration:—"Gold," says the chronicler, "made a recantation of former Murmurings, and now Prince Henry was extolled."

When Prince Henry died in 1460 no ship had sailed beyond Sierra Leone; but the nation had caught the spirit of the master, and in the next generation the search for India replaced the exploration of the Gulf of Guinea. Escobar crossed the Equator in 1471, and fourteen years later Diego Cam sailed a thousand miles beyond the mouth of the Congo River. It was in 1486 that Bartholomew Diaz, third of that family to forward African exploration, left Lisbon determined to reach the Indian Ocean. Having passed the farthest point reached by Diego Cam the year before, he put out to sea and ran before the strong northern gale for fourteen days. Turning eastward in search of the coast, and then north, land was at last sighted to the west. The northerly trend of the coast, as they pushed on four hundred miles farther, assured Diaz that he was, indeed, in the Indian Ocean. The valiant captain would have gone on to India, but the crew forced him to turn back. It was on the return voyage that he first saw the southernmost point of Africa—object of so many notable ventures: the Tempestuous Cape, as Diaz would have named it; but no, replied the king, may it rather prove the Cape of Good Hope.

Among those for whom the voyage of Diaz was of vital importance was an unknown Italian map-maker, already possessed with the one idea that was to make him more famous than Diaz, but which as yet had brought him only poverty and humiliation. Christopher Columbus, son of a Genoese wool-comber, sailor and trader and student of men and of maps from the age of fourteen, had

12

come, about the year 1477, from London to Lisbon, where he married in 1478 Felipe Moñiz de Perestrello, whose father had been a captain in the service of Prince Henry and first governor of Porto Santo. Student of cartography and professional map-maker, expert sailor himself, who had probably been to the Gold Coast, associating with captains and sailors in this seaport town of Lisbon, Columbus must have picked up all the common sailors' gossip of the age, and all the best-known scientific speculation. With the Greek tradition that the Indies might be reached by sailing west from the Pillars of Hercules, he was probably familiar, even if he had not read the famous statement of Aristotle in Roger Bacon's *Opus Majus*, or in the *Imago Mundi* of Pierre d'Ailly; familiar also he certainly was with the persistent mediæval legends of islands in the western Atlantic,—Atlantis, and the Seven Cities, and Isles of St. Brandan.

Here in Lisbon, poring over old maps, by fortunate miscalculation underestimating the size of the earth, noting, as expedition after expedition returned, the indefinite southern extension of the African coast, Columbus became convinced that the Portuguese had chosen the longer route to the East, and that "the Indies in the east might in the Earth's Globositie be as readily found out by the west, following the sun in his daily journey." To reach the Indies by sailing west, and to discover, for the king who should authorize him, such new lands as might fall his way, became henceforth the consuming ambition of his life. It was a project which he had already, about 1484, laid before the King of Portugal. Repulsed, and at the same time betrayed, he went to Spain, where he was encouraged by the Count Medina Celi and the Cardinal Mendoza, only to have his plan rejected by the Council to which it was referred. The queen was not unfavorably disposed, but the Moorish wars occupied her days and depleted her treasury. Weary with following the court about, it must have been with profound discouragement that Columbus heard of the success of Diaz in 1488. For the time was short; Diaz had all but reached the goal, and one more voyage might bring the Portuguese to India before Columbus could induce the Spanish sovereigns to try the better plan.

But the Portuguese did not follow up their advantage, and after four more years of waiting, when the Moorish wars were successfully concluded by the conquest of Granada, Columbus at last obtained a favorable hearing from Ferdinand and Isabella. By the King and Queen of Spain Christopher Columbus was authorized to "discover and acquire certain islands and mainland in the ocean"; to appropriate for himself a tithe of the precious metals which might be found there, and to be "Admiral of the said islands and mainland, and Admiral and Viceroy and Governor therein." Within three months all was ready, and on Friday, August 3, 1492, the famous expedition, about ninety men in three small ships, with compass and astrolabe for determining direction and altitude, but no log for the dead reckoning, left Palos for the Canaries. It was not with adverse winds or a rough sea that the admiral had to contend, but with a superstitious crew often moved to mutiny,—terrified by the strange variation of the needle, questioning whether the steady trade winds that bore them on would ever permit them to return, certain that the Sargasso Sea would prove that impenetrable marsh of which they had heard. With unfailing resourcefulness, with patience

13

and tact, with the compelling force of a masterful character, the great commander vanquished fear and superstition, never doubting that since "he had come to go to the Indies he would keep on till he found them by the help of God."

It was on the 11th day of October, seventy days out from Spain, and none too soon, that land was sighted; and on the following morning Columbus, bearing the cross of the Church on the banner of Castile, set foot on one of the minor Bahamas, the present Watling's Island. For two months and a half he cruised in these waters, seeking gold and spices, and the evidence of great cities, "still resolved to go to the mainland and the City of Quinsay, and to deliver the letters of your Highness to the Grand Can, requesting a reply and returning with it." He did not find Quinsay or the Grand Khan, but he discovered Santa Maria, and Hayti, where the first Spanish colony in the New World was established, and Cuba, which was taken to be the mainland. Resting in this belief, the admiral set out for home, reaching Palos February 15, 1493. And it was straightway reported in Europe that the Genoese captain had "found that way never before known to the east."

The East, yet not the desired part of it,—not Cipango, or the city of Quinsay, nor yet the rich Moluccas. These, however, Columbus never doubted, would be easily found. Others were less sanguine. The Spanish sovereigns seemed scarcely convinced that the islands of Columbus were parts of Marco Polo's Indies; while King John suspected that they were really within the southern Guinea waters belonging to Portugal. Therefore the Portuguese King hastened to secure, by papal bulls and the Treaty of Tordesillas with Spain in 1494, the famous Demarcation Line which reserved to Portugal, for exploration and discovery, the regions lying east, and to Spain the regions lying west, of a meridian three hundred and seventy leagues west of the Cape Verde Islands. And five years later, when Vasco da Gama at last reached Calicut by the eastern route, no one could longer maintain, so it seemed to the Portuguese King, that the Spanish explorers were in Indian waters. In July, 1499, the news of Da Gama's success reached Lisbon; and Emanuel, with pleasant malice, hastened to inform the Spanish sovereigns that the real Indies had been visited "by a nobleman of our household," and that he had found there, what every one expected to find, what Columbus had nevertheless not found, "large cities, and great populations"; as evidence of which he had brought home "cinnamon, cloves, ginger, nutmeg, pepper, also many fine stones of all sorts; so that henceforth all Christendom in this part of Europe shall be able, in large measure, to provide itself with these spices and precious stones."

The conclusion which the Portuguese King so eagerly accepted was meanwhile confirmed by every western voyage. Beyond the islands which Columbus had discovered, an interminable barrier everywhere blocked the way. In 1498, the admiral himself had touched the mainland near Trinidad, and in 1502 he explored the Bay of Honduras. Hojeda and Pinzon, in 1499 and 1500, sailed along nearly the whole northern coast of South America, while in 1501 Americus Vespucci followed the eastern coast from the point of Brazil as far as 35° south latitude. It could no longer be doubted, by those at least who had seen

14

the great mouths of the Amazon and the Plate Rivers, that behind this long stretch of coast lay an immense continent; a projection of Asia, doubtless, separated from it by some narrow strait, perhaps, or possibly by an unknown sea: at any rate, a "boundless land to the south," as Columbus reported; and which "may be called a new world, since our ancestors had no knowledge of it," as Vespucci thought; "a fourth part of the world," said Waldseemüller in his *Introduction to Cosmography*, published in 1507, "which since Americus discovered it may be called Amerige—i.e., Americ's land or America." In 1506 Bartholomew Columbus prepared the earliest extant map showing this *Mondo Novo*, represented as a projection of southern Asia and extending three fourths of the distance to the shoulder of Africa.

This new world of America, a seemingly impenetrable barrier, lay between Spain and the Indies—the real Indies from which the Portuguese were yearly bringing home a rich freightage of gems and spices. In 1509 their ships first reached Malacca; two years later that "golden Chersonese" was taken by Albuquerque; and in 1512 D'Abreu returned with the first cargo of cloves from Amboina and Banda, the very "isles where the spices grow." To find a passage through the *Mondo Novo*, which Columbus had discovered, became therefore the aim of future Spanish exploration—inspiring the second voyage of Pinzon in 1508, the expedition of Balboa across the Isthmus in 1513, the fatal last cruise of Solis to the mouth of the Plate River, and the final triumphant venture of Ferdinand Magellan.

For the world was not so large but that the spice islands, three thousand miles east of Calicut, must be in Spanish waters. Firm in this belief, the Portuguese Fernam Magalhaes, who had been with Albuquerque at Malacca, offered to King Charles of Spain his services in search of the western passage. It was in 1519 that this man, "small in stature, who did not appear in himself to be much," yet withal a "man of courage and valiant in his thoughts," set out in five worn-out ships, manned by Spanish officers and a treacherous crew, to achieve the greatest feat of navigation ever recorded in the world's annals. Undaunted by an almost fatal mutiny or the terrors of an Antarctic winter, he pushed on through the dangerous straits which bear his name, north and west over that sea which, pacific as it was found to be, he would scarcely have attempted had he known its vast extent. Sailing on month after month, the crew depleted by sickness and death, living at last on rats and biscuit worms and roasted soaked leather thongs, the little expedition finally reached the Philippine Islands. Here the heroic commander lost his life; and but few of those who left Spain ever returned. One ship only out of five, the Victoria, crossed the Indian Ocean and at last, September 7, 1522, three years out from Spain, sailed with eighteen survivors into the port of St. Lucar.

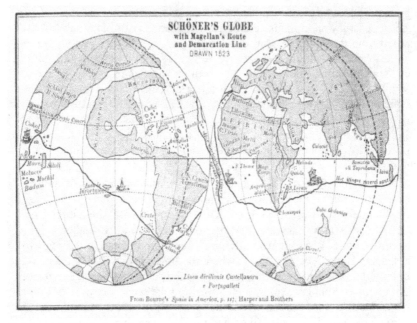

Schöner's Globe, with Magellan's Route and Demarcation Line; Drawn 1523

For the first time a single ship had circled the round earth. And through all the vicissitudes of that notable voyage, the object which during fifty years had inspired so many fruitless ventures was not forgotten. The little Victoria had shipped at Moluccas, and now deposited at St. Lucar, twenty-six tons of cloves. Yet few ships would ever again, in the way of trade, sail west from Spain for the spice islands; for between the Indies of Columbus and the Indies which he had hoped to find lay an uncharted and boundless ocean which reduced the Atlantic to the measure of familiar inland waters; and between the two seas, dimly perceived as yet, stretched the continent which was indeed a *Mondo Novo*—the New World of America.

BIBLIOGRAPHICAL NOTE

An excellent brief account of the discovery of America is in Channing's *History of the United States*, I, chs. I-II. For the relations of Europe and Asia, and the Portuguese explorations, see Cheyney's *European Background of American History*, chs. I, II, IV. An excellent brief sketch of the life of Columbus is in *Ency. Brit.*, 11th ed. Marco Polo is most conveniently found in *Everyman's Library* (Dutton). The standard edition is that of Henry Yule, 2 vols., London, 1903. Azurara's *Chronicle of the Discovery and Conquest of Guinea* is printed by the Hakluyt Society, 2 vols., London, 1896. Chapter VII gives five reasons for Prince Henry's interest in African exploration. In recent years Henry Vignaud has maintained with much learning and critical ability that the famous Toscanelli letter is a forgery, and that Columbus's first voyage to the west was for the purpose of discovering new countries, but that he had no

16

intention of reaching the Indies. The first point he has probably established, but as much cannot be said for the second. See Vignaud, *Toscanelli and Columbus*. Dutton, New York, 1902.

CHAPTER II

THE PARTITION OF THE NEW WORLD

The time approacheth and now is, that we of England may share and part stakes, both with the Spaniard and the Portingale, in part of America, and other regions yet undiscovered.

Richard Hakluyt

I

No feeling of exultation accompanied the discovery of America. The Portuguese alone were well content to see rising on the western horizon a new continent blocking the way to India. It was more than thirty years before the Spanish explorers found the rich cities which Columbus sought; and a century after the voyage of Magellan the vain hope of reaching the South Sea by some middle or northwest passage still inspired the activities of French and English adventurers. In 1534 Verrazano, in the service of Francis I, skirted the coast from Cape Fear to Sandy Hook seeking the way to China. Fifty years later Sir Humphrey Gilbert's *Discourse of a North West Passage* led to the voyages of Frobisher and Davis. Undismayed by their failures, the excellent Hakluyt assured the queen in 1584 that the passage to "Cathaio may easily, quickly, and perfectly be searched oute as well by river and overlande as by sea." And as late as 1669, when Virginia had been settled for half a century, Sir William Berkeley still had faith "to make an essay to doe his Majestie a memorable service, which was to goe to find out the East India Sea."

Yet before the middle of the sixteenth century America took on a value of its own, and ceased to be regarded as a mere obstacle, in the path of trade. After the conquest of Mexico and Peru, the New World, found to be rich in silver and gold, was thought to be a new Indies indeed. To the idealizing mind of the age America already spelled opportunity; and in the sixteenth and seventeenth centuries the maritime states of Europe established their spheres of influence there—still seeking, through its trackless forests, a waterway to the South Sea, still seeking gold, falling back at last upon the prosaic business of colonization and the exploitation of its less attractive resources. The Spaniards found no lack of treasure, but in North America gold ever turned to ashes, and the great South Sea receded like a mirage before every advance. Yet the failure of many voyages to the frozen North, and of many inland expeditions ending in disaster and death, could not quench the optimism which the gentlemen adventurers caught from the men of the Renaissance and bequeathed to the colonist, and which for two hundred years the frontiersman has preserved as a priceless heritage of the New World.

When Columbus returned from his first voyage of discovery in 1493, he brought home some gold trinkets which the Indians had readily exchanged for glass beads. The transaction is symbolical of two centuries of South American history. The achievements of the Conquistadores have scarcely a parallel in the annals of conquest; but it was the desire for treasure that led them on; and the treasure they discovered became the foundation of the Spanish Empire. In exchange for their gold and silver, Spain imposed upon the native races of America an enlightened despotism and the benefits of Christian civilization.

From Hispaniola as the first center, the Spaniards soon extended their dominion over the islands of Cuba, Porto Rico, and San Domingo, and to the mainland of North America. Seeking gold and the fountain of perpetual youth, Ponce de Leon explored Florida in 1513, and in 1521 and 1525 Allyon and Gomez skirted the eastern coast as far north as Labrador. They found no fountain of youth, nor any passage to the South Sea, nor treasure. It was twenty-five years after Columbus's first voyage, when Velasquez reached Cozumel off the coast of Yucatan, that the Spanish explorers first encountered a people advanced beyond savagery, and came upon evidences of that wealth which determined the future of their empire. Two years later Hernando Cortez, the greatest of the Conquistadores, was given command of the expedition which ended in the capture of Mexico and the overthrow of the Aztec power. The simple Mexicans, who had never seen a white man, first welcomed Cortez as the long expected Culture God, and the hapless Montezuma gathered as a present for the invader treasure equal in present value to the sum of six and a half million dollars. Most of this was lost in the lake during the fatal retreat from the city; but when the conqueror returned to Spain in 1528, he brought with him, to that very port of Palos where Columbus had landed in 1493, three hundred thousand *pesos*[1] of gold and fifteen hundred marks of silver.

The silver mines of Mexico were not exploited until many years later, but the conquest gave an immense impetus to further exploration. It was the hope of rivaling the brilliant success of Cortez that inspired those fruitless expeditions through what is now the southern part of the United States. Cabeza de Vaca and three companions, sole survivors of Narvaez's ill-fated expedition to conquer an empire in Florida, wandered for many years over the country between the Mississippi and the Gulf of California. Picked up in 1536 by Spanish slavers, De Vaca's report of the vast country to the north induced Mendoza, the Governor of New Spain, to send out Friar Marcos from Mexico in 1539 to find the famous Seven Cities. The friar found no cities, but during the next three years the search was continued by Coronado, who penetrated as far north as the present State of Kansas. It was also in 1539 that De Soto, who had accompanied Pizarro in the conquest of the Incas cities, set out from Florida in search of another Peru. After three years of untold hardship he died of swamp fever in the region of the great river which he discovered and in which he lies buried. The only result of all these expeditions was to establish the claims of Spain to an immense territory; and it was not until 1565 that the Spaniards founded, at St. Augustine in Florida, the first permanent European settlement north of the Gulf of Mexico.

18

"To the south, to the South," cried Peter Martyr, "for the riches of the Aequinoctiall they that seek riches must go, not into the cold and frozen north." It was a judgment justified in the event. Francisco Pizarro, having verified the report of rich kingdoms to the south, received in 1528 from the Emperor Charles V a commission to conquer the country of the Incas in Peru. With reckless daring equaled only by cunning treachery and unspeakable cruelty, the little band of adventurers that followed Pizarro made its way to the city of Cuzaco. The Incas were more civilized than the Aztecs, their defense less resolute, their wealth more abounding. The ransom of Atahucellpa and the plunder of the capital, when melted down into ingots, measured nearly two million *pesos* of gold. And to the south of the capital city were the inexhaustible silver deposits of the Andes. In 1545 the Government registered the mines of Potosi, the main source of the treasure which, flowing in ever-increasing volume into Spain, so profoundly influenced the history of Europe and America.

It is said of the Emperor Charles V that his eyes "sparkled with delight" when he gazed upon the vases and ornaments wrought in solid gold which Hernando Pizarro, returning from Peru in 1534 with the royal fifth of the first fruits of plunder, displayed before him. Yet the profit and the burden of the empire which Charles established in America fell mainly to his son, Philip II. And a great revenue was as essential to Philip as to Charles; for, although he did not succeed to the imperial title, he aspired no less than his father to the mastery of Europe. Circumstances seemed not unfavorable. With the close of the Council of Trent in 1563, the policy of conciliation was at an end, the Jesuits were in the ascendant, and the forces of the Counter-Reformation were prepared to do battle with the heresies that disrupted Christendom. In this death struggle the King of Spain was well suited to be the leader of Catholicism. Crafty in method and persistent in purpose, sincerely devout, unwavering in his loyalty to the true faith, never doubting that God in his wisdom had singled him out as the champion of the Church, Philip identified his will with truth and saw in the extension of Spanish power the only hope for a restoration of European unity and the preservation of Christian civilization. To set his house in order by extirpating heresy and crushing political opposition was but the prelude to the triumph of Church and State in Europe. Germany and France were rent by dissension and civil war. England was scarcely to be feared; without an effective army or navy, half Catholic still, governed by a frivolous and bastard queen whose title to the throne was denied by half her subjects, the little island kingdom could by skillful diplomacy be restored to the true faith or by force of arms be added to the Empire of Spain.

For an ambition so inclusive, the American revenue was essential indeed. And in the second half of the century it reached a substantial figure. The yearly output of the mines rose to about eleven million *pesos* per annum, and the amount which the king received for his share, between the years 1560 and 1600, was probably on an average not far from one and three quarters millions, while at the same time other sources of revenue from America became of considerable importance. It was a goodly sum for those days, but it was not enough for the king's needs. When Charles abdicated, the imperial treasury was indebted in the sum of ten millions sterling; and much of the bullion which was carried by the treasure fleets that plied regularly between Porto Bello and Cadiz was pledged to German or Genoese bankers before it arrived, while some of it found its way into the pockets of corrupt officials. What remained for the king, together with the last farthing that could be wrung from his Spanish and Italian subjects, was still inadequate, to his far-reaching designs; and Philip II, reputed the richest sovereign in Christendom, was often on the verge of bankruptcy.

It was a disconcerting fact, indeed, that although Spain and Portugal had divided the world between them, the thrifty Dutch seemed to reap the major profits of their discoveries. Within half a century Antwerp had risen to be the chief *entrepôt* and financial clearing-house of western Europe. English wool was marketed there, and there English loans were floated. There Portuguese spice cargoes, purchased while still at sea, were brought to be exchanged at high prices for the gold and silver that found its way into the hands of Spain's creditors in Germany, Italy, and France. A wealthy people were these Dutch subjects of Philip II; subjects, yet half free, escaping his control. It was intolerable that the Netherlands, infested with heresy, drawing their wealth from the enemies of Spain, and from Spain itself, should not contribute their share to the service of the empire.

To control the Netherlands and to divert the profits of Dutch trade into the Spanish treasury was thus an essential part of Philip's policy. When the Duke of Alva left for Brussels in 1567 he promised to make the Netherlands self-supporting and to extort from them an annual revenue of two million ducats. But the methods of Alva were destined to failure. He was a better master of war than of finance, and by ruining Dutch trade he killed the goose that laid the golden egg. The Southern Netherlands were finally conciliated by a more skillful policy than any known to Alva; but the city of Antwerp never recovered from the ruin which Philip's unpaid soldiers inflicted upon it in 1576, and when the war was over, the commercial and industrial activities which had made it prosperous were to be found in Amsterdam in the independent Netherlands, and in London across the Channel.

Yet if the Netherlands escaped the direct control of Philip, their wealth might be appropriated at its source. The Portuguese were still intrenched in the East, and Dutch prosperity was in no small part founded on privileges granted at Lisbon. Philip's opportunity came in 1580 when a disputed succession to the throne opened the way to intervention and the rapid conquest of Portugal. At a stroke the Portuguese dominions in Africa and the East Indies were added to Spain's American possessions. Throughout Europe Philip was thought to have played a winning card; for the most desired sources of the world's wealth were at the disposal of the Catholic king if he could but police the sea. But so complete a monopoly was not to be endured by his rivals; and France, Holland, and England, as a necessary prelude to their colonizing activities in the New World and in the Old, gathered their forces to dispute the maritime supremacy of Spain.

II

It was well understood that the power of Philip II depended upon his American treasure, and his treasure upon his control of the sea. "The Emperor can carry on war against me only by means of the riches which he draws from the West Indies," cried Francis I when Verrazano brought home some treasure taken from Spanish ships in Western waters. And Francis Bacon expressed the belief of the age when he wrote that "money is the principal part of the greatness of Spain; for by that they maintain their veteran army. But in this part, of all others, is most to be considered the ticklish and brittle state of the greatness of Spain. Their greatness consisteth in their treasure, their treasure in the Indies, and their Indies (if it be well weighed) are indeed but an accession to such as are masters of the sea."

It was not for France to contest the maritime supremacy of Spain in the sixteenth century. The wars of Francis I and Charles V bred a swarm of corsairs who harassed Spanish trade and penetrated even to the West Indies; but before 1559 the resources of the French Government were mainly devoted to resisting the Hapsburgs in Europe, and after 1563 the country was distracted by civil war. The Mediterranean proved, indeed, an attractive field for French commercial expansion. The common enmity of French and Turk toward the Hapsburg found expression in the commercial treaty of 1536 between Solyman and Francis I, and in the following half-century the "political and commercial influence of France became predominant in the Moslem states." But in Western waters the activity of France was slight. Without the naval strength to resist Spain, she could not afford to offend Portugal, who was her effective ally. Francis I interdicted expeditions to Brazil because the Portuguese King protested, and Coligny's Huguenot colony in Florida was destroyed by the Spaniard Menendez in 1565. Breton fishermen plied their trade off the Grand Banks; but in this century the only French expedition having permanent results for colonization was undertaken in 1534 and 1535 by Jacques Cartier, who sailed up the St. Lawrence as far as Montreal, and in the name of Francis I took possession of the country which was to be known as New France.

The Dutch did yeoman service against the navy of Philip during the war of independence, but the task of breaking the maritime power of Spain fell mainly to England in the age of Elizabeth. Cabot's notable voyage was without immediate result. Neither the frugal Henry VII, who gave "£10 to him that found the new isle," nor his extravagant son, who was engaged in separating England from Rome and in enriching the treasury with the spoils of the monasteries, coveted the colonies of Spain or greatly feared her power in Europe. But Elizabeth, seated on the throne by precarious tenure, confronted at home and abroad by the rising fanaticism of the Catholic reaction, found the ambition of Philip a menace to national independence. And she knew well that Spain must be met in the Netherlands and on the sea. Yet the task which confronted her was one for which the naval resources of the state were inadequate, and the politic and popular queen turned to the nation for assistance in the hour of need.

And not in vain! For year by year the national opposition to Spain gathered force. Products seeking markets and capital seeking investment were increasing, while opportunities for profit abroad were diminishing. Merchant and capitalist were everywhere confronted by the monopoly of Spain and Portugal, and thus the maritime and commercial supremacy of the queen's chief enemy was at once

21

a national menace and a private grievance. English Protestants, driven into exile in the days of "Bloody Mary," returned in the time of Elizabeth, bringing back the spirit of Geneva, and imbued with an uncompromising hatred of Papists which was fanned to white heat by the Jesuit plots, supposed to be inspired by Philip himself, against the queen's life. The rising opposition to Spain thus took on the character of a crusade: for statesmen it was a question of independence; for merchants a question of profits; for the people a question of religion. And so it happened that in time of peace the ships of Spain were regarded as fair prize. When piracy wore the cloak of virtue there were many to venture; and the queen was ready to reward the buccaneer for the crimes that made him a popular hero. Cautious in her purposes, devious in her methods, too frugal and too poor to embark on great undertakings or open hostility, Elizabeth encouraged every secret enterprise and every private adventure which had for its object the enrichment of her subjects at the expense of the common enemy.

John Hawkins will ever be memorable as the man who first openly contested the double monopoly of Spain and Portugal, and taught English merchants "how arms might signally help the expansion of trade." Descended from seafaring ancestors, his own apprenticeship was served in voyages to the African coast. Negroes were plentiful there, and laborers scarce in the West Indies. Well considering that the slave trade would insure the salvation of the benighted heathen and redound to the profit of thrifty planters, the devout Hawkins set about serving God and mammon for the advancement of his own fortunes and the glory of England. With capital supplied by City merchants, three vessels were equipped; and in 1562 Hawkins sailed for Sierra Leone, where he procured by force or purchase three hundred negroes, who were exchanged with no great difficulty at Hispaniola for a rich cargo of merchandise. An enterprise which netted sixty per cent profit was not to be abandoned, and in 1564 a second voyage was made, with greater profit still. But the third voyage, in 1567, came to grief at San Juan de Ulloa, where Hawkins fell in with the Spanish plate fleet. The fleet might have been plundered, but the naïve Hawkins, relying in vain upon the pledged word of the Spaniards, was treacherously attacked and his ships mostly destroyed, while he himself barely escaped with his life.

Accompanying Hawkins on this voyage, and escaping with him from San Juan de Ulloa, was "a certain Englishman, called Francis Drake." Reared in a Protestant family which had felt the effects of the reaction under Queen Mary, he had an instinctive hatred of the Roman Church, and his experience at San Juan de Ulloa inspired him at the age of twenty with a lifelong animosity toward all Spaniards. Renouncing the semi-peaceful methods of Hawkins, Drake devoted his life to open privateering, never doubting that in plundering Spanish ships he was discharging a private debt and a public obligation. And of all the gentlemen adventurers who made plunder respectable and raised piracy to the level of a fine art, he was the greatest. He carried himself in the "pirate's profession with a courtesy, magnanimity, and unfailing humanity, that gave to his story the glamour of romance." No other name struck such fear into Spanish hearts, or so raised in English ones the spirit of adventure and of contempt for the queen's enemies. He is known in Spanish annals as "the Dragon," and before he died the maritime power of Spain had passed its zenith.

Three years after the disaster at San Juan de Ulloa the trend of events favored the bolder course. In 1570 the Pope's Bull deposing Elizabeth from the English throne was nailed to Lambeth Palace; and in 1572, not without the tacit approval of the Government, and backed by the rising national hostility to Spain, Drake set out for the Indies, where he operated for two years, planning attacks on Cartagena and Nombre de Dios, or rifling the treasure trains as they came overland from Panama. Henceforth the watchfulness of Spain was redoubled in the West Indies; but the Pacific, which Drake had seen from the Peak of Darien, was still regarded as a safe inland lake. Into the Pacific, with its coasts unprotected and its ships scarcely armed at all, he therefore determined to venture. Authorized by the queen and with Walsingham's approval, he set out in 1577. Quelling a mutiny as his great predecessor had done at St. Julian, he passed the Straits of Magellan, and sailed northward along the coast, harming no man, but taking every man's treasure until the ship was full. He would have returned home by some northeast passage, but failed to find any, and so at last crossed the Pacific—the second to circumnavigate the globe. We are told that the queen "received him graciously, and laid up the treasure he brought by way of sequestration, that it might be forthcoming if the Spaniards should demand it."

It is not recorded that the treasure was ever restored, but it is known that Drake was knighted by the queen on the deck of the Golden Hind. And it is recorded that in 1588 Philip prepared the Invincible Armada, which appeared in the English Channel to demand the submission of England. It was a decisive moment in the history of America; and it is doubtful what the issue might have been had the queen been dependent upon the royal navy alone. But round the twenty-nine ships of the royal navy there gathered more than twice as many of those privateers who in a generation of conflict had become past masters in dealing with the ships of Spain. Manned by sailors seasoned to every hardship, equipped with the best cannon of the day, rapid and dexterous in movement, the English ships, outnumbered though they were, sailed round and round the unwieldy galleons of the Armada, crippling them by broadsides and destroying them with fire-ships, without ever being brought to close quarters. And so the "Invincible navy neither took any one barque of ours, neither yet once offered to land but after they had been well beaten and chased, made a long and sorry perambulation about the northern seas, ennobling many coasts with wrecks of noble ships; and so returned home with greater derision than they set forth with expectation."

The defeat of the Armada was followed by a carnival of conquest. Within three years eight hundred Spanish ships were taken; and in 1596, shortly after the deaths of Drake and Hawkins, Sir Thomas Howard of Effingham captured the city of Cadiz and returned home with ships full of plunder. It was the last great operation of the war, and the beginning of the end of the Spanish Empire; for the way was now clear for the maritime and colonial expansion of her rivals. The Dutch, with independence assured, organized those India companies through which they ousted the Portuguese from the spice islands, and established, at the mouth of the river discovered by Henry Hudson in 1608, the colony of New Netherland in America. With the civil wars of religion happily closed, France was free to complete the work of Cartier. In 1603 Champlain, in the service of a St. Malo merchant, sailed up the St. Lawrence to Montreal; and five years later he established a post on the Heights of Quebec, destined to be the capital of the great inland empire of New France. And England, whose ships now sailed the sea unchallenged, began to build a more lasting empire in America and the Orient. It was in 1607 that Virginia was planted; and three years later Captain Hippon, in the service of the East India Company, established an English factory at Masulipatam in the Bay of Bengal.

III

A notable result of the struggle with Spain was the growth of an active interest in colonization. Knowledge of the wide world, which Richard Eden had freshly revealed to Englishmen in the reign of Mary, was greatly enriched by the voyages of the Elizabethan seamen. John Davis, returning from the Far East, made known "as well the King of Portugal his places of Trade and Strength, as of the interchangeable trades of the eastern Nations among themselves"; and Cavendish, who was the third to "circompasse the whole globe of the world," brought to the queen "certain intelligence of all the rich places that ever were known or discovered by any Christian." By the side of Drake and his followers, whose ambition it was to destroy the power of Spain in the New World, stand the brilliant Gentlemen Adventurers, who labored to plant there the power of England: Frobisher and Davis, the gentle and heroic Gilbert, and Raleigh, poet and statesman, the very perfect knight-errant of his age, whose faith in America survived many failures and is registered in words as prophetic as they are pathetic—"I shall yet live to see it an English nation." The adventurous and pioneering spirit of the time is forever preserved in that true epic of the Elizabethan age, the incomparable *Voyages* of Richard Hakluyt; and in the *Discourse on Western Plantinge*, which he wrote at the request of Raleigh for the enlightenment of the queen, as well as in the general literature of the next fifty years, are revealed to us the ideas, mostly mistaken and often naïve, which gave to America the glamour of a promised land.

Of the motives which inspired the colonizing activity of England at the close of the sixteenth century, the desire to spread the Protestant religion was no unreal one. The war for independence, having taken on the character of a crusade, had touched with emotional fervor the Englishman's loyalty to the national faith. Religion became a national asset when it was thought to be served by an extension of the queen's domain. The pride of patriotism, as well as the sense of duty, was stirred by the fact that whereas Spanish Papists had been "the converters of many millions of infidells," English Protestants had done nothing for "thinlargement of the Gospell of Christe." It was felt to be the duty of Englishmen to take on this "white man's burden," and for the sake of the true faith plant "one or two colonies upon that fyrme, learn the language of the people, and so with discretion and myldeness Instill into their purged myndes the swete and lively liquor of the Gospell."

24

Yet the religious motive was buttressed by others more material and less disinterested. Until well into the seventeenth century, when much bitter experience had proved the contrary, America was still thought to be a land of wealth easily acquired—"as great a profit to the Realme of England as the Indies to the King of Spain." Many credible persons, said Hakluyt, had found in that country "golde, silver, copper, leade, and pearles in aboundaunce; precious stones, as turquoises and emaurldes; spices and drugges; silke worms fairer than ours of Europe; white and red cotton; infinite multitude of all kindes of fowles; excellent vines in many places for wines; the soyle apte to beare olyves for oyle; all kinds of fruites; all kindes of oderiferous trees and date trees, cypresses, and cedars; and in New founde lande aboundaunce of pines and firr trees to make mastes and deale boards, pitch, tar, rosen; hempe for cables and cordage; and upp within the Graunde Baye, excedinge quantitie of all kinde of precious furres." So that one may "well and truly conclude with reason and authoritie, that all the commodities of our olde decayed and daungerous trades in all Europe, Africa, and Asia haunted by us, may in short space and for little or nothinge, in a manner be had in that part of America which lieth betweene 30 and 60 degrees of northerly latitude."

Little wonder that the New World of America, thus portrayed in heightened colors, proved attractive to gentlemen adventurers dreaming of personal dominion, to merchants intent upon profit, or to kings seeking revenue and prestige. The colonizing activities of the time were but incidental to the larger movement of commercial expansion and the extension of political power. The founding of the East India Company in 1600 and of the Virginia Company in 1609 were but two expressions of the same purpose: America was but one of the two Indies whose exploitation would redound at once to private advantage and to national welfare. That the individual and the state had a common and inseparable interest in the expansion of commerce and the settlement of colonies is, indeed, one of the most characteristic and significant ideas of the time: characteristic, since it pervades the literature of the period; significant, because it is an index of those profound political and economic influences that were transforming the old into the new Europe.

For at the opening of the seventeenth century the old order was fast disappearing. The ideal of a single Christian community, so long symbolized by the Holy Roman Empire and the Holy Catholic Church, was losing its hold upon the minds of men as the result of the differentiation of European culture on lines of racial or national distinction. In politics this movement was embodied in the rise of the centralized national state; and the sixteenth century ushered in the era of international wars, of which the struggle between Elizabeth and Philip II was one, and one of the most important. When such conflicts were always impending, it was essential that the resources of the nation should be at the disposal of the Government. The national state could, therefore, neither share authority with the Pope at Rome, nor endure independent feudal or municipal jurisdictions within the realm; and in its military and administrative organization, feudal officers, since the thirteenth century in France and England, had been steadily replaced by paid agents appointed by the king, whose hostility to the Pope was chiefly inspired by the desire to secure from the Church the money necessary to maintain them. A well-filled treasury was thus the first need of the sixteenth-century state, and so it fell out that in western Europe the middle class—the merchant and the capitalist and the money-lender—was the chief resource of kings in conflict with feudal or ecclesiastical privilege. The prosperity of the trading class and the efficiency of the Government were thought to be inseparable; and that commerce should be regulated in the interest of the state was, therefore, the unquestioned maxim of the age.

Two things above all the interest of the state demanded: that the supply of precious metals should not diminish; and that the nation should not be dependent upon rival countries for staple commodities. The supply of gold and silver actually present in the king's coffers, or within the radius of his tax-gatherers, was of far greater moment then than now. The issues of war, in an age when credit was relatively undeveloped, were likely to depend upon it. Scarcely less important was the question of staples. To be dependent upon rivals for necessities was thought to threaten at once the prosperity of the trading class and the strength of the Government: giving hostages to the enemy in time of war and a diplomatic advantage in time of peace; carrying off the supply of gold and silver; and likely, therefore, by raising the value of money, to disorganize industry and deplete the sources of the state's revenue. To be economically self-sufficing in order to be politically independent was the cardinal doctrine. "That Realme is most compleat and wealthie which either hath sufficient to serve itselfe or can finde means to exporte of the naturall comodities [more] than it hath occasion necessarily to import," said an English writer, expressing in a phrase the essential principle of mercantilism, which, indeed, was only the old feudal or municipal ideal adapted to the needs of the national state.

A theory which crystallized the practice of two centuries must have been more than "an economic fallacy." And, indeed, in the time of Elizabeth and the first Stuarts it was a condition and not a theory that confronted England. Many essential commodities had long been imported from countries which, toward the close of the sixteenth century, were disposed to place obstacles in the way of English trade. From Baltic lands came naval stores, and potash so necessary to the woolen industry. Mediterranean countries furnished salt, dried fruits, sugar, and the staple luxuries wine and silk. Dyes, saltpeter, and spices from the Far East were sold to English merchants by the Portuguese or the Dutch; and at exorbitant prices, for the thrifty Hollanders no sooner got control of the spice islands than they raised the price of pepper from three to eight shillings per pound. And it was the Dutch, intrenched in the European fisheries partly through favors granted by Elizabeth, who imported into England two thirds of the fish so extensively consumed by the nation.

While England was dependent upon rivals for many necessities, the foreign markets for her own products were now becoming inadequate. Apart from wool, England exported little; but the confiscation of the monasteries, the ruin of Antwerp, the rising prices resulting from the influx of silver from New Spain, contributed to stimulate English industry and to increase in some measure the volume of commodities seeking markets abroad. Yet the markets were closing in some places and becoming less accessible in others. "It is publically knowne that traffique with our neighbor countries begins to be of small request, the game seldom answering the merchant's adventure, and foraigne states either are already or at the present are preparing to inriche themselves with wool and cloth of their own which heretofore they borrowed of us." English traders were persecuted in Spain; English exports were checked by tariffs in France and by Sound dues in Denmark; privileges formerly enjoyed in German towns were being withdrawn in retaliation for the exclusion of Hanse merchants from advantages long enjoyed in London; and as for Flanders, heretofore the great mart for English wool, the civil wars had, as Hakluyt says, "spoiled the traffique there."

The desire to change this untoward condition of things was what inspired the unwarranted enthusiasm of the time for American and Indian colonization. The voyages of Willoughby and Frobisher, seeking some northeast or northwest passage, were but the prelude to the later voyages by way of the Cape of Good Hope and to the foundation of the East India Company, the specific purpose of which was to procure the products of the Orient independently of the Dutch and at lower cost. The colonization of America it was supposed would serve a similar purpose. It was still thought to be rich in precious metals; its soil well adapted to commodities now purchased in the Levant. Its waters would furnish England with the herring now purchased of the Dutch, and its forests would make her independent of the Baltic countries for naval supplies. Once gain a footing in India and America, and the commerce of England, now so largely foreign, would be diverted into national channels to the benefit of all concerned: "Our monies and wares that nowe run into the hands of our adversaries or cowld frendes shall pass into our frendes and naturall kinsmen and from them likewise we shall receive such things as shall be most available to our necessities, which intercourse of trade maye rather be called a home bread traffique than a forraigne exchange."

The identification of the industrial and political interests of the nation with the fortunes of the centralized state was necessarily accompanied by a marked change in the character of international trade. The national king, whose power rested so largely upon the industrial class, could not leave in the hands of municipal councils the control which they had formerly exercised; while long ocean voyages, and traffic with countries inhabited by alien and often hostile people, required the combined capital of many men and a more powerful backing than any municipal council could furnish. Individual trading, therefore, gave way to corporate trading; the joint-stock company, assisted or controlled by the state, replaced the individual merchant operating under municipal encouragement and protection. It was accordingly in the age of Elizabeth, when English merchants were lamenting the want of markets, and when English ships were pushing into every part of the world, that such chartered trading companies made their appearance in rapid succession, taking their names from the distant regions in which they obtained a monopoly—Cathay, the Baltic, Turkey, Morocco, Africa. Of these, and of all subsequent organizations of a similar character, the most famous in England was the East India Company. By the

27

charter, which bears date December 31, 1600, two hundred and fifteen knights and merchants were incorporated into a self-governing association competent to acquire property in land, and enjoying a monopoly of English trade with all countries lying east of the Cape of Good Hope as far as the Straits of Magellan. The laws of the company were required to conform to those of England, and its officers to take the oath of allegiance to the Crown. Encountering many obstacles and some serious reverses, the Company soon established a thriving trade in the Indian Ocean; its great East Indiamen acquired a fame unique in the annals of commerce; and the corporation itself, with privileges confirmed and extended by Charles II, was destined in the eighteenth century to be the chief instrument in the establishment of England's Indian Empire.

IV

When English knights and merchants set out to establish colonies in the New World, two familiar institutions were convenient to the purpose—the proprietary feudal grant, and the chartered trading company; noblemen ambitious for personal dominion turned naturally to the former, while merchants intent upon profits turned as naturally to the latter. The first hapless ventures in American planting, dominated by the idealistic and militant temper of the Elizabethan age, were initiated and directed in the spirit of the gentleman adventurer: in the spirit of Sir Humphrey Gilbert, who identified America with the fabled Atlantis and lost his life in a pathetic attempt to establish an English colony in Newfoundland; in the spirit of Sir Walter Raleigh, whose famous lost colony, settled in the year 1587, exhausted his fortune and disappeared at last, leaving no trace. These men were less interested in profit than in reputation; less intent upon commercial expansion than on the extension of the queen's dominions. But their resources were too limited, their ideals too little practical for the realization of their dreams. The patents to Gilbert and Raleigh took the form of a grant of lordship by feudal tenure; and from the papers left by the former we can create again, even to details, his vision of a transformed wilderness, America's future state: an America of extensive proprietary domains; an America reproducing, in its lords and landed gentry surrounded by freeholder and tenant, in its counties and boroughs and parishes, the social and political aristocracy of old England.

The proprietary feudal grant was destined to play its part in the colonization of America, but the resplendent vision of Gilbert did not survive the reign of Elizabeth. Raleigh was the last of the great Elizabethan adventurers, and with the accession of the pedantic James I the New World was beginning to be regarded in the dry light of a commercial opportunity. To the knights and merchants who had witnessed the vain efforts of Gilbert and Raleigh, the chartered company seemed better adapted to their purposes than the proprietary grant. The methods that had proved fortunate in the Old World would doubtless prove equally so in the New; and in the year 1609, men who were already netting one hundred per cent profit from their investments in the India Company were prepared to venture something in a solid business scheme to exploit the resources of America.

A tentative scheme, failing for want of efficient organization, had already been set on foot. Three years earlier, in 1606, James had been induced to license sundry of his loving subjects "to deduce and conduct two several colonies or plantations in America." Among those active in the undertaking were Bartholomew Gosnold, recently returned from a Western voyage, Richard Hakluyt, Sir Thomas Gates, Sir George Somers, and Edward Maria Wingfield, a London merchant. Though not incorporated, the patentees were formed into two companies, the London Company, so called because its members were mainly London merchants, and the Plymouth Company, consisting mainly of merchants from Plymouth and the west of England. Each company was permitted to establish one colony having a jurisdiction one hundred miles along the coast and one hundred miles inland; the London Company anywhere between 34° and 41°, the Plymouth Company anywhere between 38° and 45°, north latitude; provided only that no colony should be located within one hundred miles of one already established. The patent provided that there should be in each colony, for managing its affairs, a resident council of thirteen members which was to take instructions from the Royal Council for Virginia, a body of fourteen men— afterwards enlarged—residing in England and appointed and controlled by the king. The patentees were permitted to trade freely within the limits designated by the grant, and to enjoy the customs dues exacted from other Englishmen and from foreigners who might wish to compete with them.

After a single vain attempt to establish a colony at Sagadahoc, the Plymouth Company confined its activities to trade and exploration within the region to which John Smith in 1614 gave the name of New England. Sir Fernando Gorges was one of the patentees actively interested in these ventures; and in 1620 he procured, for himself and associates to the number of forty, a charter which transformed the old company into a close corporation under the title of the New England Council or Corporation for New England. Upon the patentees the charter conferred the sole right to trade, to grant title to land, and to establish and govern colonies within the region between 40° and 48°, north latitude, in America. The New England Council possessed neither the capital nor the popular support necessary for engaging in colonizing ventures; and during the fifteen years of its existence it did little but sublet to others the rights which it possessed. Of the council's land grants, of which there were many both to individuals and to corporations, and which, often conflicting, furnished the grounds for innumerable future disputes, four only are important as the basis of permanent colonies in New England. The territory at Plymouth was granted to the Pilgrims in 1621; in 1628 the territory between the Merrimac and the Charles Rivers was conveyed to the Company of Massachusetts Bay; and two grants made in 1629, of territory between the Merrimac and the Piscataqua to John Mason, of territory between the Piscataqua and the Kennebec to Fernando Gorges, mark the beginnings of the colonies of New Hampshire and Maine. All its ventures profited the New England Council nothing. February 3, 1635, the territory within its jurisdiction was parceled out among the patentees, and on June 7, its charter of fruitless privileges was surrendered.

It was reserved for the London Company to begin the planting of the first American commonwealth; but it was by happy chances rather than by wise foresight in the promoters that the colony outlived the company. The first comers, who were set down at Jamestown in 1607, would soon have perished but for the harsh good sense of the redoubtable Captain John Smith; and two years' experience with the wilderness and the Indian, with dissensions among settlers and councillors, demonstrated that the patent was unsuited to the purposes for which it had been granted. More colonists were needed in the colony, more capital required to transport and maintain them, more authority to direct and control them. To meet these needs, a charter was obtained in 1609 which created an incorporated joint-stock company under the title of "The Treasurer and Company of Adventurers and Planters of the City of London for the First Colony of Virginia." Shares were offered for subscription, to be paid for in money by the adventurers who remained in England, and in personal service by the planters who went to the colony. Each shareholder, whether adventurer or planter, was a member of the company, and was to receive such dividends as his shares might earn. The undertaking was widely advertised; and when the charter passed the seals, shares had been subscribed by 659 individuals, including 21 peers, 96 knights, 58 gentlemen, 110 merchants, and 282 citizens, and by 56 of the companies of the City of London.

The affairs of the new company were to be managed by a treasurer and council, resident in England, and appointed and controlled by the freemen assembled in general court. The little colony in Virginia was but an adjunct to the company, and its management was left, without other than conventional and perfunctory restrictions, to the treasurer and council, subject to the approval of the freemen. The first treasurer was Sir Thomas Smythe, who was also the first president of the East India Company, a great merchant in his day, whose influence in Virginia was a predominant one until he was succeeded as treasurer by Edwin Sandys in 1618. Smythe and his associates were little interested in the transmission of English institutions to the New World. They did not regard Virginia, as the historian is apt to do, in the interesting light of an experiment in constitutional liberalism, or conceive of the company as the mother of nations. Their object was to pay dividends to the shareholders, and the colonist was expected to exploit the resources of Virginia for the benefit of the company of which he was a member. Virginia was in fact a plantation owned by the company; its settlers were the company's servants, freely transported in its vessels, fed and housed at its expense, the product of their labor at its disposal for the benefit of all concerned.

With these ideas in mind, and enlightened by past experience, the company appointed Sir Thomas Gates to be "sole and absolute Governor," and sent him out in 1609, together with five hundred settlers in nine ships. Two vessels were wrecked, and what with plague and fever less than half the new colonists ever reached Virginia. The governor was himself stranded on the Bermudas; and when he finally arrived after nine months, sixty starving settlers were found scattered along the James River. Men who had been reduced to eating their dead comrades or the putrid flesh of buried Indians were scarcely good material for regenerating a feeble plantation. Sir Thomas Gates, therefore, decided to abandon the colony. But by a happy chance, as he was sailing with the survivors down the river, he met Lord de la Warr come from England with fresh supplies and new recruits; whereupon he turned back, still hoping to retrieve the desperate fortunes of Virginia.

The decision proved wise in the event. But it was doubtless due to the drastic measures of the company that the misfortunes of previous years were not repeated. The governor returned to England, leaving the colony in the hands of De la Warr, who governed in the spirit of the instructions issued to Gates at the time of his appointment. Popularly known as "Dale's Laws," the regulations under which Virginia was finally made self-supporting were published by Gates after his return in 1611, under the title of "Articles, Laws and Orders, Divine, Politique, and Martial for the Government of Virginia." The new code was based upon the military laws of the Netherlands, and was enforced in the spirit with which the experience of Gates and Dale had made them familiar. From blasphemy to disrespect, from murder to idleness or embezzlement of the common store, the company's servants were liable to meet the knife, the lash, or the gallows at every turn. Until 1618 the régime of martial law was maintained; and the settlers stood guard or marched to the fields at the word of command, scarcely aware, doubtless, that they had been granted all the liberties enjoyed by men "born within this our realm of England."

The military régime which made Virginia self-supporting did not make it prosperous, or profitable to the company. In December, 1618, after an expenditure of £80,000 sterling, there were in the colony "600 persons, men, women and children, and cattle three hundred att the most. And the Company was then lefte in debt neer five thousand pounds." The hard-headed Smythe saw little prospect of the dividends which the shareholders were demanding; and he was ready to give way to any one who still had faith to sink yet more money in the enterprise that for a dozen years had disappointed every expectation. Such an idealist was Sir Edwin Sandys. Son of a Puritan Archbishop of York, he had studied at Oxford under Richard Hooker, whose famous book he had read in manuscript. The *Ecclesiastical Polity* had perhaps confirmed Sandys in a republican way of thinking; and in the year 1618 he was probably a nonconformist—a "religious gentleman," as Edward Winslow called him: at all events, a man of humanitarian and anti-prerogative instincts; a friend of the Earl of Southampton, and leader of those in the company who were in sympathy with the rising tide of liberal sentiment in English politics.

The liberal policy which Sandys favored in England, he was now prepared to adopt for the management of Virginia. Convinced that the military and joint-stock régime, even if it had ever served a useful purpose, was retarding the development of the colony, Sandys and Southampton determined to reverse the policy of their predecessors by instituting private property in land and conceding a measure of self-government. A popular assembly was accordingly established in 1619; restrictions on conduct and religious opinion were relaxed; and land grants, both to individuals and to corporations, in small and large tracts, were made on easy terms. It was hoped that an appeal to self-respect and to self-interest would encourage immigration and foster thrift and industry. When Sandys became treasurer in 1618 the time seemed propitious; for it had already been discovered that Virginia tobacco could be sold at a profit in London; and it

31

was the expectation of Sandys, by obtaining for the company its fair share of the profit arising from the importation of tobacco into England, to repay to the shareholders the long-delayed interest on their investments.

The scheme was not without great possibilities, and the company spared neither money nor effort to make it a success. Within three years more than thirty-five hundred emigrants crossed to Virginia. In 1621 the expenditures of the company had reached a total of £100,000, and in 1624 the amount had been doubled. Yet, quite apart from the high death-rate which depleted the colony, or the Indian massacre of 1622 which threatened its existence, all the efforts of Sandys ended in failure. Drawn into the main current of English politics, the Virginia Company was unable to live in those troubled waters. James regarded with little favor the liberalism which Sandys and Southampton were promoting in England as well as in America. On high moral grounds he disliked the use of tobacco, and for economic and fiscal reasons was opposed to its cultivation in Virginia. He was determined, at all events, that such profits as might arise from its importation should enrich the royal exchequer rather than a powerful corporation controlled by men who were carping at the king's prerogative. And the king found support in the company itself; for Smythe and Warwick turned against the corporation and furnished pretexts to prove that it had betrayed its trust and should forfeit its rights. In 1624 the charter was accordingly annulled, and Virginia became a royal province.

Thus ended the most serious attempt of a commercial company to make profit out of American planting. Famous and successful in the annals of colonization, it proved a complete disaster as a financial speculation. During the reign of Charles I, merchants were therefore but little disposed to venture their money in enterprises of that kind. Nor was Charles himself, who guarded the royal prerogative more jealously even than James had done, likely to look with favor upon the creation of corporations which would prove useless in case of failure and might prove dangerous if they succeeded. The rough sea of politics in the time of the second Stuart was unsuited to floating successful colonial ventures of any kind under governmental sanction; but in so far as he was disposed to further the development of America, it was natural enough for Charles, who found that his usurping Parliament was backed by the mercantile interest, to frown upon colonial corporations, and to make use of the proprietary feudal grant as a means of rewarding the courtiers and nobles who supported him. The very year that the New England Council surrendered its charter, Archbishop Laud was urging the king to recall that of Massachusetts Bay. It was a few years later that Fernando Gorges was made Lord Proprietor of Maine; a few years earlier that Lord Baltimore, a loyal supporter of the House of Stuart, received a feudal grant after the manner of the Durham Palatinate of that part of Virginia which was to be known as the Province of Maryland.

BIBLIOGRAPHICAL NOTE

The best accounts of early exploration and settlement in America are in Channing's *History of the United States*, I, chaps. III-VII; and Bourne's *Spain in America*, chaps, VI-IX. An admirable account of the activities of English seamen in the sixteenth century is given by Walter Raleigh in volume XII of his edition of Hakluyt's *Voyages*. An interesting contemporary narrative of Drake's voyage around the world is in Hakluyt's *Voyages* (Raleigh ed.), XI, pp. 101-33. Hakluyt's *Discourse on Western Plantinge* is in the Maine Historical Society Collections, series II, vol. II. For the rise of the chartered trading companies, and their connection with early American colonizing companies, see Cheyney's *Background of American History*, chaps. VII-VIII. The best discussion of the English interest in colonization at the opening of the seventeenth century is in Beer's *The Origins of the British Colonial System*, chaps. I-III. The most elaborate and learned account of the colonies in the seventeenth century is that of Osgood, *The American Colonies in the 17th Century*, 3 vols. Macmillan, 1904. The most readable account of the founding of Virginia is in Fiske's *Old Virginia and Her Neighbours*, I chaps. I-VI. John Smith's account of the settlement of Jamestown is in his *True Relation*, printed in Arber, *Works of Captain John Smith*. Birmingham, 1884.

FOOTNOTES:

[1] *Pesos*=approximately $3.00.

CHAPTER III

THE ENGLISH MIGRATION IN THE SEVENTEENTH CENTURY

They are too delicate and unfitte to beginne new Plantations and Collonies, that cannot endure the biting of a muskeeto.

William Bradford.

To authorize an untruth, by toleration of State, is to build a sconce against the Walls of Heaven, to batter God out of his chair.

The Cobler of Aggawam.

I have often wondered in my younger dayes how the Pope came to such a height of arogancie, but since I came to New England I have perceived the height of that tripple crowne, and also the depth of that sea.

Samual Gorton.

I

Those who looked to America for great financial profit or immediate political advantage were disappointed. The seventeenth century had run half its course before the colonies became an important asset to the English Government: no gold came from them to enrich its treasury, few supplies to furnish its navy, while the revenue, derived from its slowly growing trade was insignificant. Equally deceptive was the New World as a field for corporate exploitation. The sagacity of Thomas Smythe and the idealism of Edwin Sandys were alike unavailing. Before the Virginia Company was dissolved in 1624 it had sunk nearly two hundred thousand pounds in its venture "withoutt returne either of profitt or of any part of the principall"; and in 1660 Lord Baltimore, whose colony was well established, was himself living in straitened circumstances.

Yet within sixty years after the Susan Constant entered the James River, seven colonies were firmly planted on the coast of North America: Virginia and Maryland to the south; Massachusetts Bay and Plymouth, Connecticut and Rhode Island, in New England; and between the two groups of English settlements was the Dutch colony of New Netherland on the Hudson. Within the limits of these colonies dwelt a population of more than seventy thousand people, economically self-sufficing, possessed of well-defined political institutions and clearly marked types of social and intellectual life. The English migration and the founding of the English colonies was in fact due mainly to the initiative of the colonists themselves; and the institutions which they established in America were different from those which statesmen and traders had imagined. The character of colonial life and institutions was determined by the motives which induced the settlers to leave the land of their birth, by the inherited traditions which they carried with them into the wilderness, and by the wilderness itself—the circumstances which, in the new country, closed them round.

The motives which induced many Englishmen to come to America in the seventeenth century must be sought in the profound social changes occurring in the time of Elizabeth and the first Stuarts. The high hopes with which the Virginia Company looked forward to successful colonization were partly inspired by the prevailing belief that England was overpopulated. There was much to justify the belief. The reign of Elizabeth witnessed a striking increase in the number of unemployed, the poverty-stricken, and the vagabond. The destruction of the monasteries left the poor and defenseless without their accustomed sources of relief; while steadily rising prices, due partly to the increased supply of silver from the Spanish-American mines, were not infrequently disastrous to those who were already living close to the margin of subsistence. As never before country roads and the streets of towns were encumbered with the vagrant poor, and the jails and almshouses were filling up, as a result of Elizabethan legislation, with petty thieves, "rogues and sturdy beggars."

That the surplus population would readily flow into the colonies, to the advantage of all concerned, was the common belief. For successful colonization, said the author of *Nova Britannia* in 1609, but two things are essential, people and money; and "for the first wee need not doubt, our land abounding with swarms of idle persons, so that if wee seeke not some waies for their foreine employment, wee must provide shortly more prisons and corrections for their bad conditions." Yet for more than a decade one of the chief difficulties of the Virginia Company was to procure settlers. Reports from Virginia were discouraging. The prosperous preferred to remain at home, and the company had "to take any that could be got of any sort on any terms." Little wonder that the colony for many years barely survived. It survived only by taking on the character of a penal camp, in which the settlers worked for the company that fed them, and ordered their daily routine by the regulations of martial law.

The settlement was doubtless saved from destruction, but it did not greatly prosper, under the military and joint-stock régime; for "when our people were fed out of the common store, glad was he who could slip from his labour or slumber over his task he cared not how." The first step in the abolition of the joint stock was taken in 1616 when Sir Thomas Dale "allotted to every man three acres of land in the nature of farms." It was the beginning of better things, since not even the most honest men, when working for the company, "would take so much pains in a weeke as now for themselves they would do in a day." The first general distribution was made in 1618, and within a few years the communistic system was a thing of the past. Throughout the century the "head right" was the nominal basis for the granting of land: fifty acres were regarded as the equivalent of the cost of transporting one colonist. But in fact the head right was customarily evaded. The payment of from one to five shillings was usually sufficient to secure title to fifty acres, and in 1705 the practice was legalized. Titles so secured were burdened with the payment of a small quit-rent to the state; but the quit-rent was difficult to collect, was often in arrears, and sometimes never paid.

A greater incentive to settlement than free land was the discovery of a crop that could be exported at a profit. Virginia had been founded to raise silk and tropical products, and to supply England with naval stores. But the difficulties were greater than had been anticipated, and in 1616, when John Rolfe, having discovered a superior method of curing the leaf, sold a cargo of native tobacco in London at a profit, the future of Virginia was assured. Neither the plans of the company nor the scruples of the king could prevail against the force of economic self-interest. Twenty thousand pounds were exported in 1619, forty thousand in 1622, sixty thousand in 1624. Tobacco became at once, and in spite of long opposition on the part of the home Government remained, the chief enterprise of the colony. Virginia was founded on tobacco, and like the other Southern colonies, sacrificed everything to the raising of her most important commodity; and for Virginia, as for the other Southern colonies, the conditions necessary for the cultivation of her great staple were of determining influence in the development of her social institutions.

Those who were interested in the Virginia Company loudly proclaimed that the recall of the charter would ruin the colony. But it was population, rather than corporate or royal control, that Virginia needed, and the profits from tobacco proved a more powerful incentive to large families and immigration than all the efforts of king or company. Within a decade after 1624 the number of settlers increased from 1232 to 5000. In 1649 the population had reached 15,000, and in 1670 it stood at 38,000. Land was virtually free to those who could pay for the cost of clearing, and the rich soil of the tide-water bottoms assured an easy living and the prospect of accumulating a competence. As the conditions of life grew easier, the Virginians, with the true instinct of frontiersmen, described America as God's country, abounding in every good thing: "Seldom any that hath continued in Virginia any time will or do desire to live in England, but put back with what expedition they can." The glowing accounts which reached England appealed to those of every class whose straitened circumstances or unsatisfied ambitions disposed them to a hazard of new fortunes. The yeoman farmer, whose income was small and whose children would always remain yeomen; the lawyer and the physician, the merchant and the clergyman, ambitious to become landowners and play the gentleman; younger sons of the country gentry, for whom there were no assured avenues of advancement: these felt the call of the New World. Fretted by social restrictions, or pinched by rising standards of living, they saw Virginia in the light of their ideals, and were willing to exchange a safe but restricted position for the chance of economic and social enfranchisement.

Since the main road to wealth and influence in Virginia was the raising of tobacco, every emigrant with capital to invest at once became a landowner; and the conditions of tobacco-planting disposed him to enlarge his estate as rapidly as possible. It is true that one advantage of tobacco over other products was its high acreage value. But the price ordinarily was low, and many acres were necessary for large net returns. Besides, the soil was soon exhausted, so that the successful planter found it necessary to be always acquiring new land in order to let the old lie fallow. It thus happened that, in spite of the cost of clearing and the danger from the Indians, Virginia was not settled, as its founders had intended, in compact towns modeled upon the English borough, but in widely separated plantation groups, stretching far up on both sides of the James River. The average size of patents granted before 1649 was about four hundred and fifty acres; in the period between 1666 and 1679 the average had risen to nearly nine hundred, while there were ten patents ranging from ten to twenty thousand acres each. By 1685 a total population not exceeding that of the London parish of Stepney had acquired title to an area as large as all England.

For clearing and planting so large an area much unskilled labor was essential. In Virginia, and in all the Southern colonies with the exception of North Carolina, there accordingly existed, side by side with the landowning planter class, and sharply distinct from it, a servile laboring class which formed a large part of the total population. In 1619, we are told, "came a Dutch man of war with 20 negars." The ship was probably English rather than Dutch. In either case the circumstance marks the beginning of African slavery in the English continental colonies; but the importation of slaves was slight until the close of the century, and the laborers who cleared the forests and worked the fields were largely supplied by contract, and were known as "servants." The servant was a person bound over for a term of years to the planter who paid his transportation or purchased the contract right from its original owner. The term of service varied from two to seven years, at the expiration of which the servant became a freeman. Ex-servants sometimes migrated to other colonies, notably to North Carolina after the foundation of that colony, or in the next century to the up-country beyond the "fall line"; but many became renters or tenants on the estates of the large planters, or in time became planters themselves. The servant class included some condemned criminals and political offenders, and some educated and cultured people who had fallen on evil times; but they came mostly from the jails, the almshouses, or the London streets. They were the unfortunate and the dispossessed rather than the vicious—men who were vagabonds because there was nothing for them to do, or petty thieves because they were starving. They were, none the less, an inferior and a servile class. The colonial law made no great distinction between the servant for life and the servant for a term of years; during the term of his indenture, the latter was subject to his master, driven and whipped like the negro slave with whom he worked and ate and with whom he was classed.

Less clearly defined than the distinction between the free and the unfree was the distinction, which began to develop toward the middle of the century, and which was doubtless accentuated by the Cavalier migration from England during the Commonwealth period, between the small and the large landowner. The master of a great estate, enjoying a certain leisure and exercising a political and social influence denied to the average freeman, was set above the mass of the planters much as in England the titled nobility was set above the gentry. Of this small but important class, the first William Byrd was a notable example. Uniting in his ancestry the Cavalier and the Roundhead traditions, he inherited, before the age of twenty, 1800 acres of land and a recognized social position in the colony. Before his death he had built up an estate of 26,000 acres, which his son, in the next century, increased to 179,000 acres. He was at once planter, merchant, politician, and social leader. His caravans of from fifty to one hundred pack-horses penetrated regularly for many years to the Cherokee country beyond the Blue Ridge Mountains. The furs which they brought back, together with the products of his plantation, were exported to England and elsewhere in payment for slaves, servants, or other commodities which were periodically landed at his private wharf to be used on his own estate or retailed from his general store to the small planters roundabout. Before he reached the age of thirty, Byrd became, and remained throughout his life, a leader in his own county and in the colony at large—a colonel of militia, a burgess in the assembly, and member of the governor's council.

From the middle of the century Virginia society thus began to take on the character which it retained throughout the colonial period. The colony was primarily a rural and an agricultural community, combining in curious fashion the democratic spirit of the frontier with the aristocratic temper of an older civilization. The unit of social organization was the plantation, which naturally tended to become, and in the case of the larger plantations often became in fact, relatively complete and self-sufficing—a little world in itself. The planter, surrounded by his family and his servants and cut off from intimate or frequent contact with his neighbors, producing, for the most part in abundance, all the necessities and many of the luxuries of life, was master of his *entourage* and but little dependent upon the outside world. Inevitably the conditions of plantation life developed the aristocratic spirit, the sense of mastery and independence which comes from directing inferiors in an isolated and self-sufficing enterprise.

Influences of environment were strengthened by the traditions which the settlers had inherited. Neither planter nor servant came to America with utopian ideals of society or government. It was discontent not dissent that drove them out. Dissatisfied with their position in the English social system, they were yet well content with the system itself; a system which they were willing enough to establish in the New World in the hope of obtaining in it a more desirable position for themselves. And so it happened that the laborer and the farmer, the small landowner and the master of a great estate, the clergyman and the high official, were disposed to take as a matter of course the position which custom assigned them, and in that position to exercise the authority and render the obedience which was proper to it.

Tradition and environment thus conspired to establish a government in which initiative and leadership fell to the great planters, while the mass of the freemen exercised a restrained and limited supervision. It was a happy accident, rather than any strong popular demand, that gave to Virginia an elected chamber. Sir Edwin Sandys and the Earl of Southampton, who gained control of the Virginia Company in 1618, hoped to put the enterprise on a paying basis by lavish land grants and liberal concessions in respect to religious and political liberty. Governor Yeardley was accordingly sent out in 1619 with instructions to call together "two Burgesses from each Plantation, freely to be elected by the inhabitants thereof." In June of the same year twenty-two burgesses, representing eleven districts, together with the governor and council, assembled in the church at Jamestown and inaugurated representative government in Virginia by passing a body of laws in which the customs of England were adapted to the conditions of a frontier community. After the dissolution of the company in 1624 the appointment of the governor and council vested in the Crown, but the House of Burgesses, elected at first by the freemen, but after the Restoration on the basis of a freehold test, was continued. From the first the assembly, filled by planters, exercised a beneficial influence in giving a practical character to the laws of the province; while on certain occasions, and notably during the period of the Commonwealth, it was the dominant influence in the government of the colony.

But for the most part the assembly was the instrument rather than the source of power. The directing influence was usually in the hands of the great planter who combined the functions of merchant and country gentleman, lawyer and politician and social leader. His knowledge of law and his familiarity with affairs, his social connection and influence, his greater leisure, the traditional authority which hung about his position, all disposed the small planters to accept his initiative and abide by his decisions. It was difficult to defeat his candidate for the burgesses; difficult for the elected burgess not to defer to his opinion. And if the great planters were influential among the burgesses, they were predominant in the council. The home Government expected the governor to manage the affairs of the colony by gathering to his support the most wealthy and influential men in it. Accordingly, the great planters were customarily appointed to the local offices and to the council. Generally speaking, the governor and the great planters established a community of interest on an exchange of favors. The small group of men in the council, related by marriage, ambitious, shrewd, and pushing, already wealthy or bound to become so, supported with reasonable loyalty the royal interests, and found their reward in exploiting, through the political machinery which they controlled, the resources of the colony for their own profit. This compact was the basis of the long régime of Berkeley. But the governor was made aware of the source of his strength when he trespassed upon the preserves of the oligarchy which supported him.

His attempt to control the Indian trade drove men like Colonel Byrd over to the side of Bacon, and the authority of the governor collapsed like a pricked balloon.

Of this oligarchy of politician-planters, Colonel Byrd was indeed the most notable. Already wealthy and influential, in 1687 he went to London and secured, through the favor of William Blathwayt, the office of receiver-general of the customs, to which was attached the office of escheator; offices, among the most important in the colony, which he held until his death. It was the duty of the receiver to receive the quit-rents, and to receive them, at the option of the taxpayer, in tobacco in exchange for certificates at the rate of about eight shillings per hundredweight. Tobacco so received was stored in warehouses, and sold at the close of the year by the receiver-general for the benefit of the customs. The tobacco offered for the quit-rents was naturally of inferior quality. Such as it was, the king favored selling it at auction. But the Virginia assembly preferred to have the receiver dispose of it by "private arrangement"; and in fact Colonel Byrd found it convenient to make such "private arrangements" with burgesses or members of the council, who sometimes paid as much as six shillings for tobacco which would bring ten or twelve in the open market.

Members of the legislature who profited by such practices were doubtless willing to stretch a point in favor of the receiver of the customs. In 1679, before he had become receiver, Colonel Byrd was able to obtain from the assembly, on condition of maintaining fifty armed men to repel Indian attacks on the frontier, a grant of ten thousand acres at the Falls extending on both sides of the James River. The grant was disallowed in England, but other grants of great value were obtained with little difficulty. Patents were easily obtained, but they did not become effective until the land was "settled" by clearing and cultivating a minimum tract. For a poor man this was the chief obstacle to acquiring a great estate; but a rich man was often able to avoid it altogether. In 1688, Byrd secured a patent for 3313 acres. He failed to "settle" it and the title lapsed. But the land could not be granted again until the lapse of title was officially declared in the office of the escheator. Colonel Byrd was fortunately escheator as well as receiver, and the lapse of his own title was not declared until 1701, when the same tract was immediately repatented to Nathaniel Harrison, who straightway transferred it to his neighbor and very good friend, the original patentee. In like manner the colonel preëmpted 5644 acres of land, which he held without improvement for ten years when it was transferred to his son.

The aristocracy, of which Colonel Byrd was a shining light, nevertheless held by a somewhat precarious tenure. The crude and primitive conditions of the wilderness, restricting both the occupations and the diversions of life within narrow limits, inevitably ran the thoughts of men in much the same mould. The routine of work and pleasure was much the same on the great plantation as on the small: clearing and planting, spinning and weaving, dancing and horse-racing, neighborly hospitality which was generous and sincere because the opportunity to exercise it was rare, attendance at church or at the county court, at elections, at the annual muster—it was a range of activities too limited to permit of any deep-seated sense of difference between man and man.

And, indeed, the main basis of distinction in this new world was a purely external one—the possession of wealth; and wealth was in no unreal sense the bequest of nature to capacity. Initiative and industry, rather than the dead hand of custom, marked a man for distinction and preferment. It was the land of opportunity where the servant could become the farmer, the farmer a planter, where the planter, acquiring by skill or happy chance a great estate, thereby entered in with the political and social grandees. There were classes but no castes; not birth or title, but individual enterprise determined rank and influence. And in an undeveloped country the possession of a great estate was not a social grievance, but an evidence of success in the perennial contest with nature, the measure of personal prowess and a test of civic virtue. The enrichment of Colonel Byrd, even by ways that were devious, was viewed with complacence by his neighbors so long as it harmed them not. Yet the submission of the small to the great planter was a convenience rather than a necessity. The wilderness, with the Indian as a part of it, developed a crude and a ruthless spirit, but never a cringing or a submissive one. The gentleman and the magistrate were deferred to, but neither was regarded as sacrosanct; and when, in the régime of Berkeley, special privilege in alliance with official corruption seemed to be narrowing the chances of the common man, the insurgent spirit of frontier democracy, denying the validity of distinctions and demanding fair play, found militant expression in Bacon's Rebellion. The episode was an early instance of that struggle between rich and poor, between exploiter and exploited, of that stubborn insistence upon equal opportunity which have so often characterized the more decisive periods of American history.

II

The origin of New England is inseparably connected with the Protestant Reformation, that many-sided movement of which no formula is adequate to convey the full meaning. From one point of view it was the nationalization of the Church, the subjection of the ecclesiastical to the lay power. In the end the principle of territorial sovereignty everywhere prevailed, in Catholic no less than in Protestant countries: whether Lutheran or Gallican or Anglican, whether completely separated from Rome or retaining a spiritual communion with it, the Church submitted to the principle of *cujus regio ejus religio*, and became an instrument in the hands of kings for erecting the lay and territorial absolutism on the ruins of the universal church-state. James I spoke for all his kind when he cried out, "No Bishop no King!" The lay prince wished not to destroy the Church, but to use it; the sum of his purpose was to transfer the ultimate authority in conduct and thought from the divinely appointed priest to the divinely appointed king.

But the Reformation was far more than resistance to Rome. It did not cease when the king triumphed over the Pope. The "dissidence of dissent and the Protestantism of the Protestant religion" was as incompatible with royal as with priestly authority. In this "reformation of the Reformation" the strength of the movement was everywhere in the towns. It was generally true, and nowhere more so than in England, that Protestantism was the result of a middle-class revolt against the existing régime, a denial of established standards in politics and morality, the determined attempt to effect a transvaluation of all customary values.

The quarrel of the middle-class man with the world as he found it was of long standing. In the feudal-ecclesiastical structure, fairly complete in the eleventh century and to outward seeming still intact in the fifteenth, there was no prepared niche for the *bourgeois*. The peasant to obey and serve; the noble to fight and rule; the priest to instruct and pray:—these, all in their different ways respected and respectable careers, completed the sum of God's purpose in arranging the occupations of men. Yet into this trinity the *bourgeois* had intruded his unwelcome presence. The secret of his rise was the skill of his hand to fashion material things, and his practical intelligence to care for them. Neither personal service nor personal prowess was the source of his power. Untouched by the principle of homage or of *noblesse oblige*, he commanded, or was himself commanded, through the medium of material values. He put money in his purse because it was the measure of his independence, the symbol of his worth; and he kept it there, guarding it as the priest guarded his faith or the noble his honor. Long occupation with the concrete world of affairs had given his mind a peculiar quality; his intelligence was direct and firm, his thinking clear and dry, without atmosphere, unrelieved by poetic imagination or the play of fancy.

Set apart by occupation and temperament, the middle-class man had little in common with either the servile or the ruling class; little in common with the noble who despised his birth, ridiculed his manners, envied his wealth; little with the priest who found him too rigid, too intelligent, too reserved with his money and his soul to be a good son of the Church; little with the peasant who renounced him as a renegade or ignored him as a *parvenu*. All these benefits the *bourgeois* returned in full measure, despising the peasant for his ignorance and servility resenting the inquisitiveness of the clergy and the condescension of the nobility, at the same time that he aspired to the power of the one and the superior position of the other. And from the outside world the *bourgeois* had secured a measure of protection. With his money he had purchased corporate independence and enfranchisement from feudal obligation. The gild, at once an industrial enterprise, a religious association, and a charitable foundation, bound him to his fellows and rounded out his life.

At the close of the fifteenth century many circumstances had contributed to identify the interests of the small country gentry with those of the moderately well-to-do townsman, and to set them both in opposition to the higher nobility and the wealthier merchants and promoters. The control of trade was passing from the master merchant to the capitalist, from the city to the state. Powerful financial monopolists like the Fuggers and the Welsers, in alliance with the territorial prince or the national government, were undermining the industrial independence of town and gild. Exactions of State and Church were increasing. The growing extravagance and immorality of the wealthy, both burgher and noble, was matched by the worldliness of the upper clergy, and accompanied by the decay of spiritual interests, the accentuation of ritual and ceremony, and increased reliance upon external and formal works as sufficient for salvation. From this world of the high-placed favorites of fortune, where corruption

41

flourished unashamed and power was too often exercised without a redeeming sense of obligation, the middle class was already withdrawing at the close of the fifteenth century. The townsmen in Germany found satisfaction for their spiritual and intellectual interests in reviving the religious activities of the gilds, and in the formation of lay religious societies in which a simplified form of worship was accompanied by study of the Bible and the preaching of the unworldly virtues of upright living. It was this separation of the *bourgeois* from the world in which he lived that constitutes the first protest, the beginning of the Protestant movement.

Ideal constructions are doubtless the psychic precipitates of social experience, and the Protestant theory was but the reasoned expression of the middle-class state of mind. Thwarted by the existing world of fact, the leaders employed their practical and dexterous intelligence to create a new world of semblance, a world of the spirit, in which the way was illumined by the light of reason, and the individual rather than the social conscience gave the sense of right direction. Material for such a philosophy was ready to hand. The practice and the thinking of the apostolic churches had been newly discovered by the study of the secular and the sacred past; and the essence of all Protestant thinking was implied in the phrase in which Luther embodied the teaching of St. Paul: "Good works do not make the good man, but the good man does good works." Not the conventional judgments of society, expressed through the commands of Church or State, but the individual conscience, justified by faith in God's purpose, determines a man's merit. St. Augustine's ideal City of God was thus once more set over against the visible secular world of man. Into this intangible community, a house not made with hands, the elect and the select withdrew themselves, abiding there as in a refuge, untouched by the corruptions of a spotted world, seeking with humility the will of God and submitting with all the pride of conscious merit to law.

As the middle-class experience implied the Protestant theory of religion, it implied the Puritan conception of morals and conduct. Puritanism originated in the towns for the same reason that it lingers in the country; it was formerly the townsman rather than the countryman whose ideas and manner of living stamped him as peculiar. The spiritual and social isolation of the townsman is therefore the source of the outward impassiveness of the Puritan, as well as of the intensity of his inner experience: the continued impact of noble or priestly contempt had crusted his nature with a manner that was rigid and resistant and undemonstrative, beneath which smouldered the explosive forces of thwarted ambition and the sense of unrecognized intellectual and moral excellence. Conscious of a worth which society ignored, he transformed his qualities into virtues, and erected his virtues into social standards of value. Prudence and economy, restraint of manner, denial of the sensuous and the sensual appeal, reserve of soul, the unmoved endurance of the pricks of fortune—these became the virtues of the Puritan because they were not the virtues of the world which despised him: by these self-erected standards he justified himself and passed judgment on the society in which he felt himself an alien and a stranger.

Opposition was therefore but fuel to the Puritan flame. Every persecution of society or obstacle of nature encountered in the endeavor to withdraw from the world was a confirmation of its corruption, a device of the devil to tempt him astray, or God's wise method of testing his faith. To persevere was the very proof of his election, the sure evidence of right thinking. The doctrine of eternal torment in hell, said Jonathan Edwards, used to appear "like a horrible doctrine to me. I remember very well when I seemed convinced, and fully satisfied, but never could give an account how, or by what means I was thus convinced." The very painfulness of the idea was doubtless what induced him to accept it. It was not the truth of the doctrine convincing his intellect, but the discipline of the will involved in vanquishing the horror of it, that gave him peace; so that in the end it seemed to him, not so much true, but "exceeding pleasant, bright, and sweet." St. Augustine furnished us one of the keys to Puritanism when he said: "No man loves what he endures, but he may love to endure." The Puritan loved to endure. To expect resistance and to meet it unmoved; to welcome calumny and reviling with a steadfast mind; to transform a hostile verdict of the majority into an unconscious award of merit:—such was the Puritan temper in its most distinguished representatives.

III

In England the Puritan temper was given its effective edge during the latter years of Elizabeth and the reigns of the first Stuarts. The Armada was scarcely destroyed before the queen assumed a less complaisant attitude toward dissent. James I warned the clergy at Hampden Court that he would make them conform or harry them out of the land. The third decade of the century witnessed the triumph of Anti-Christ on every hand: in Germany the success of imperial arms was crowned by the Edict of Restitution; with the capture of Rochelle, the Huguenots in France lost their towns of refuge and found themselves at the mercy of the state; and in England itself the first Charles, more absolutist and more Catholic than his father, was thought to aim at nothing less than the ruin of Parliament and the restoration of the Roman religion. Under the stress of opposition there was accordingly a marked accentuation of the Puritan and the Separatist spirit. To Nonconformist and Independent alike the truth became more clear the more it was traduced and maligned. Year by year there was a deepening sense of being in the world but not of it; and to those who were already spiritual exiles, the idea of removing to America came to seem but the outward expression of an inner fact: "All the churches of Europe have been brought under desolation; it maybe feared that the like judgements are coming upon us; and who knows but God hath provided this place to be a refuge for many, whom he meanes to save out of the generall callamitie."

It was not the Puritan Nonconformists who first sought refuge on American shores, but a less aggressive people, who were called Brownists in derision, but who called themselves Separatists. Robert Browne first formulated the doctrines of the sect; but its origin, and the reasons for its persistence in the face of bitter persecution, are not altogether clear. Poor in purse and feeble in numbers, Separatism found adherents chiefly in London and Norfolk, and among the lower classes of artisans and countrymen. It was in London and Norfolk that many thousand Dutch refugees found homes during the reign of Elizabeth; and it was in Norfolk that a kind of unofficial, lay religion had been for many decades

43

a marked feature of craft gild activities. Dutch influence and the practice of the gilds may have furnished a fruitful soil for the propagation of Separatism; but the leaders who formulated its doctrines and ideals were mainly educated Englishmen, graduates of Cambridge many of them, whose deliberate thinking carried them from Anglicanism to Nonconformity, and from Nonconformity to Separatism. Such was Robert Browne the founder, John Greenwood, Henry Barrowe, and John Penry; and such were the later leaders, William Brewster and John Robinson. These men, like the Puritans, were Calvinistic in doctrine; like the Puritans, they held that true Christians formed an ideal commonwealth, whose ruler Christ was, and whose law was the Bible; like the Puritans, they believed that the test of the true Christian was an inner spiritual condition bearing fruit in right living, rather than external conformity to established custom. But the Separatist was at once less aggressive and more radical than the Puritan Nonconformist. Desiring toleration for himself, he accorded it to others; submitting to persecution, he refused to practice it; and convinced that no purification of the Established Church could make it the true house of God, his cardinal doctrine was the separation of the spiritual and the temporal commonwealths. It was the merit of the Separatist to have caught that inspiring vision which was denied to most Protestant sects—the vision of the day when it belongeth not to the magistrate "to compell religion, to plant churches by power, and to force a submission to Ecclesiasticall Government by lawes and penalties."

When the seventeenth century opened, exile for opinion's sake was no new thing for this despised and persecuted sect; and the little Separatist congregation of Scrooby which John Robin son led out of England in 1608 had doubtless read in Foxe's *Book of Martyrs* of the many early Protestants who had removed in the days of Mary to live unmolested at Basel or Geneva. They themselves could endure persecution with a steadfast heart. But they were unable to prevail against the "errors, heresies, and wonderful dissentions" which the devil had begun to sow even among the elect, and so crossed to Holland and settled in Amsterdam. In Amsterdam they were, indeed, free from persecution; but the conditions of life were unfamiliar there, and the dissensions more bitter even than in England. Therefore they moved on to Leyden, where they were joined by other English congregations, and where they remained, "knit together as a body in the most strict and sacred bond and covenant of the Lord." Yet even there the world compassed them about and was not to be resisted. Of the grinding toil which made them old before their time they could not complain; but their children, associating with foreigners and disposed to marry with them, were losing their language and departing from their early instruction; while the renewal of the war with Spain threatened the liberty they enjoyed in their new home. To preserve the true faith intact, it was necessary to withdraw still more completely from the world; and they turned to America where they would be as isolated in fact as they were in idea. And so they "left that goodly and pleasant citie, which had been their resting place near 12 years; but they knew they were pilgrimes, and looked not much upon these things, but lift up their eyes to the heavens, their dearest countrie, and quieted their spirits."

Of many attempts to withdraw from the corruptions of a complex world of fact in order to dwell in spiritual peace according to the simple law of God or nature, few are more interesting than that which issued in the little colony of Plymouth. But in point of numbers, and in respect to the storm and stress of conflicting ideals which produce great events, Plymouth was soon eclipsed by Massachusetts Bay. The repressive measures of Elizabeth and James I bore less heavily on the Nonconformist than on the Separatist; but during the early years of Charles the activities of the former became the special object of royal displeasure. And from the point of view of the king the Nonconformist who wished to remain in the Church was, indeed, more dangerous than the Separatist who wished to get out of it. The great majority of the Puritans were still of the former type. Men like Cotton and Winthrop, less spiritual and more practical, less unworldly and more resistant, than men like Robinson and Bradford, were not prepared to renounce the land of their birth without a struggle. They wished rather to get control of the Government in order that their own ideas might prevail, and were more disposed to purify a corrupt society by act of Parliament than by passive renunciation and unobtrusive example.

And in the third decade of the century the Puritans were well on the way to the control of Church and Parliament. All over England they were sending to Westminster men of their own stubborn temper for whom political and religious liberty were but two sides of the same shield. They were buying up impropriated tithes and gaining control of appointments to livings. In hundreds of parishes the congregations remained outside while the official reader intoned the service from the Prayer Book, and then entered to hear their chosen minister preach doctrines that boded ill to the cause of royal authority. To the over-sanguine it might have seemed that episcopacy was beginning to break down into congregationalism, and congregationalism laying the foundation for control of Parliament, when Charles I, in March, 1629, pronounced the famous dissolution that marked the beginning of his personal rule. It was then that many Nonconformists, despairing of success at home, began to look to America as God's appointed refuge "from the generall callamitie"; and the ten years from 1630 to 1640, during which the king endeavored with the aid of Wentworth to dispense with Parliament, and with the aid of Laud to crush out Nonconformity, is precisely the period of the great Puritan migration to New England.

In the summer of that very year 1629 a group of Nonconformists, under the lead of John Winthrop, a gentleman of Suffolk whose estate was becoming inadequate to his customary manner of living, convinced themselves that they could best serve God by renouncing the struggle against king and bishop in order to set up in America a "due form of Government both civil and ecclesiastical." And for such an enterprise it seemed that the way had been miraculously prepared. In March, 1628, John Endicott and five associates had obtained from the New England Council a grant of land extending from a point three miles north of the Merrimac River to three miles south of the Charles, and westward from the Atlantic as far as the South Sea. The enterprise had in the mean time been joined by many Nonconformists, and in 1629 the associates obtained from the king a charter which confirmed their rights to the land, and in

45

addition authorized them, under the title of "The Governor and Company of Massachusetts Bay," to establish and govern colonies within the limits of their jurisdiction. All the powers of the company were intrusted to a governor, deputy-governor, and board of eighteen assistants, with the final authority in the freemen assembled in general court. The officers were elected by the freemen of the company, and freemen were admitted to the company by the officers. The charter originally provided for the "election of the Governor and officers here in England"; but before it passed the seals the phrase was omitted: "With much difficulty," says Winthrop, "we got it rescinded." The change was of vital importance for those who were preparing to set up, as free as possible from all outside authority, a "due form of Government both civil and ecclesiastical." Since the charter did not require the company's elections to be held in England, the freemen and officers had but to remove to America to transform a commercial corporation into a self-governing colony.

With this end in view, the offices of the company were transferred to those who signified their intention of removing. In March, 1630, all arrangements were completed, and over a thousand people, including the governor and officers of the company, left England. When they landed at Salem in June the prospect was so disheartening that some two hundred returned in the ships that brought them out; and of those who went on to Boston Harbor two hundred died before December. The unfavorable reports of those who returned discouraged migration for many months; but for ten years after 1632 the repressive measures of Laud and Wentworth produced a veritable exodus, so that in 1643 the population of Massachusetts Bay is estimated to have been not less than sixteen thousand.

The leaders of the migration were substantial and hard-headed laymen like Winthrop and Dudley, and able and conscientious clergymen such as Cotton, Norton and Wilson, Davenport, Thomas Hooker, and Richard Mather. During the eclipse of Parliament and the Country party in England, the former found many avenues of advancement closed, while their estates, even when carefully husbanded, would no longer permit them, as Winthrop said, to "keep sail with their equals." The latter, excluded by their Puritan and evangelical convictions from the profession for which they were trained, turned to America as the most inviting field for service among the elect of God. They were men of ability and conviction—"a chosen company of men, picked out ... by no human contrivance, but by a strange contrivance of God," to be the leaders of a chosen people.

Yet the Puritan colony was not made up of leaders. In firm intelligence, in clearly realized conceptions of Church and State, in moral fervor and spiritual exaltation, men like Winthrop and Davenport were far removed from the rank and file. The great majority of those who first came to Massachusetts were small "merchants, husbandmen, and artificers"; men with little property or none at all; uneducated and home-keeping men whose outlook was bounded by the parish; Puritans by temperament and habit rather than by reasoned conviction: followers in a very real and literal sense. Few of them would have come as individuals; but they came as families and groups of families from the same community, yielding to the call of a favorite minister or trusted neighbor. And few would

46

have come for religion's sake alone. Persecution was the efficient cause, but straitened circumstances frequently gave point to the pricks of conscience. Even Winthrop himself, a man of substantial possessions, tells us that a consideration for his undertaking the New World venture was that "his meanes heer are soe shortened as he shall not be able to continue in that place and employment where he now is." How far more persuasive an appeal was this to common folk! "This lande grows weary of her inhabitants, soe as man is heer of less price amongst us than a horse or sheep. All towns complain of the burthen of their poore though we have taken up many unnecessary, yea unlawfull trades to maintaine them. Children, servants, and neighbors (especially if they be poore) are considered the greatest burthen. We stand heer striving for places of habitation (many men spending as much labour and cost to recover or keep sometimes an acre or two of land as would procure them many hundred as good or better in another country) and in ye mean tyme suffer a whole continent as fruitful and convenient for the use of man to lie waste without any improvement."

Both in a spiritual and a material sense, it was to preserve and not to dissolve the ties of community life that the Puritans, leaders and followers alike, came to Massachusetts. Coming as townsmen seeking land, they settled in towns, to which they often gave the names of the places from which they came—for example, Boston, Plymouth, Dorchester. The town was not originally an industrial center, but a group of agricultural proprietors who procured from the company title to the land which they held individually or in common according to custom, and which they cultivated after the manner with which they were familiar. Free and equal access to the soil was the principle upon which the original grants were made: there were no quit-rents or charges; the allotments were small, and so far as possible equal in value. And happily the ideals of the settlers were suited to the environment in which they found themselves. The soil was adapted to the raising of a variety of farm products; corn and fodder and vegetables, swine and cattle and horses; products requiring neither great estates nor servile labor for profitable cultivation. Thus in New England the unit of settlement was a group of small, free proprietors living together in villages and managing their affairs by concerted action. The town and the town meeting were as natural to New England as the plantation and the county were to Virginia and the other Southern colonies.

But the community in New England was a spiritual as well as an industrial enterprise, and the counterpart of the town was the church. By the leaders especially, settlement was regarded more as a planting of churches than as the founding of towns. In their view the church covenant was the expression of the fundamental social pact, the public confession of membership in the spiritual City of God, the very basis of "that Church-State," that "due form of Government both civil and ecclesiastical," which they had come to the New World to establish.

"We covenant with our Lord and with one another"—so runs the Salem covenant, which may be taken as typical—"we avouch the Lord to be our God, and ourselves to be his people, in the truth and simplicity of our spirits. We promise to walk with our brethren, with all watchfulness and tenderness, avoiding jealousy and suspicion, back-bitings, censurings, provokings, secret risings of spirit against them; but in all offenses to follow the rule of our Lord Jesus, and to bear and forbear, give and forgive, as he hath taught us. We do hereby promise to carry ourselves in all lawful obedience to those that are over us, in church and commonwealth. We resolve to approve ourselves to the Lord in our particular callings; shunning idleness as the bane of any state; nor will we deal hardly or oppressingly with any, wherein we are the Lord's stewards."

Town and church were thus the basis of settlement; but whatever measure of self-direction either might enjoy, neither was regarded as independent. All legal authority was vested in the company and exercised by the officers and freemen assembled in general court. Yet of the two thousand settlers who came over in 1630, less than a score were members of the company. Authority so narrowly confined could not long remain unquestioned in a primitive community. In October, 1630, one hundred and nine persons petitioned to be admitted to the freedom of the corporation. It was a critical moment in the history of this "due form of Government." Without numbers, the colony could not thrive; without restriction of authority, it would be in danger of falling away from the ideals of its founders. The circumstance was one of many to reveal the essential difference, in respect to primary motive, between leaders and followers. The mass of the settlers had migrated primarily to secure economic enfranchisement: too great restraint would drive them to the north, where colonists were desired by Mason and Gorges, or to Plymouth, where the tolerant Pilgrims would welcome them perhaps on easier terms. But Winthrop and his associates had migrated primarily to establish a community that should live by God's law; and to admit all freeholders to share in its direction would end in the defeat of that high purpose.

Weight of numbers prevailed at last; and the history of Massachusetts Bay in the seventeenth century is the story of the vain and pathetic effort of single-minded men to identify the temporal and the spiritual commonwealths. The compromise presently made was the first step in the final surrender. The one hundred and nine petitioners were admitted; but it was shortly voted, in plain violation of the charter, that the rights of the freemen should be confined to the election of the assistants; and, "to the end that the body of the commons may be preserved of honest and good men, it was likewise ordered that for time to come no man shall be admitted to the freedom of this body polliticke but such as are members of some of the churches within the lymitts of the same." In order to preserve the purity of the state still more effectively, it was voted, in 1636, that even church members should be excluded unless the churches to which they belonged had secured the approbation both of the magistrates and of a majority of the churches already established.

The suffrage remained thus restricted until 1684, although a nominal modification was made in 1664. But the freemen were not long content to see their privileges confined to the election of assistants and magistrates. The first protest was characteristically English. In 1632 the minister of Watertown Church, George Phillips, more independent in his manner of thinking than the

48

majority of the clergy, induced his congregation to pass the first resolution in America against taxation without representation: "It was not safe," they contended, "to pay money after that sort for fear of bringing their posterity into bondage." A magisterial reprimand from Governor Winthrop reduced the protestants to the level of an apology; but in 1634 the freemen demanded to see the charter, and when it became generally known that supreme authority was vested in the freemen assembled in general court, rather than in the board of assistants, the latter was forced to concede to the former a share in the business of lawmaking. Since it was inconvenient for all the freemen to attend the sessions of the general court in person, they adopted the custom of sending two deputies from each town to represent them. The assistants, thus overbalanced by the deputies, demanded the privilege of the negative voice, a contention which the deputies were inclined to deny, but which resulted, in 1644, in the separation of the general court into two houses, the board of assistants constituting the upper chamber and the deputies the lower. During the same period the discretionary powers of the magistrates in administering the laws gave the deputies much concern; and their constant protests were not without effect, although the victory was mainly to the magistrates. The results of the first decade of conflict between leaders and followers over the distribution of political power are registered in the famous Body of Liberties which was promulgated in 1641.

In spite of concessions to the freemen, political privilege remained narrowly limited. Between 1631 and 1674 the total number of freemen admitted was 2527, about one fifth of the adult male residents. The suffrage was thus far more exclusive than a freehold test would have made it. In town meeting, voting was not always restricted to freemen; but in deciding important matters non-freemen were usually excluded. And yet the formal restriction of political privilege, narrow as it was, gives no true measure of the real concentration of political power. Deference to the magistrate, no less than the habit of protest against illegal action, was an English tradition. The circumstances of the migration had tremendously accentuated the force of the religious appeal, and the freemen, being church members, were of all the settlers precisely that part most disposed to defer to the wishes of the clergy, and to select for magistrates those whom they approved.

"They daily direct their choice to make use of such men as mainly endeavor to keepe the truths of Christ unspotted, neither will any christian of sound judgment vote for any but such as earnestly contend for the faith, although the increase of trade and traffique may be a great inducement to some."

The freemen sometimes demonstrated their power, but the same men were customarily returned to office year after year. The magistrates and the clergy, a handful of men with practically permanent tenure, men of strong character and of great ability for the most part, virtually governed Massachusetts Bay for two generations.

They governed the colony, these "unmitred popes of a pope-hating commonwealth," yet not without storm and stress; and of all their difficulties, the quarrel with the freemen over the distribution of political power was far from being the most perplexing. In 1681, Roger Williams, a young minister of engaging personality, with "many precious parts, but very unsettled in judgemente," came to Boston. He scrupled to "officiate to an unseparated people," and soon went down to Plymouth, where he "begane to fall into strange oppinions, and from opinion to practise; which caused some controversie, by occasion whereof he left them something abruptly." Returning to Massachusetts, he became minister of Salem Church, which was itself thought to be tinged with radicalism. But the radicalism of Williams went beyond all reason. He maintained that the land of New England belonged to the Indians, and that the settlers were therefore living "under a sin of usurpation of others possessions." And he denied that the state had any rightful authority in matters of conscience, holding with Robert Browne that "concerning the outward provision and outward justice [the magistrates] are to look to it; but to compell religion, to plant churches by power, and to force a submission to Ecclesiasticall Government by lawes and penalties, belongeth not to them." By farmer and magistrate alike the man was regarded as a nuisance, and after three troubled years was banished from the colony.

The ideas of Williams were too relevant not to arouse controversy, but too remote from the spirit of the age to win many adherents. Of another sort was Mistress Anne Hutchinson, a woman of "nimble wit and active spirit," one of those popular village characters who go about among the poor and sick, bringing wholesome draughts of cordial, gossip, and consolation. As a taster of dry sermons there was none better; so that many women of Boston, and not a few men, fell into the habit of assembling at her house, where she discoursed on the latest sermon or Thursday lecture, and by exegesis and comment and criticism made all clear. And her doctrine went straight to the heart and intelligence of the average man in the seventeenth century, as it does to-day and has in all ages. "Come along with me says one of them. I'le bring you to a woman that preaches better Gospell than any of your black-coats that have been at the Niniversity, a woman of another kind of spirit, who hath had many revelations of things to come; and for my part, saith he, I had rather hear such a one that speaks from the mere motion of the spirit, without any study at all, than any of your learned Scollers, although they may be fuller of Scripture." This, indeed, was the secret of Mistress Anne's power, that she spoke the language of the untutored, and infused into the scholastic categories of theology the elemental and familiar emotions of daily life.

The issue raised by Anne Hutchinson soon passed into politics, and the little colony was divided into irreconcilable factions. The good woman had a great following in Boston, including not a few in high places. Wheelwright was her avowed defender; John Cotton was half convinced. The credit of the party was raised by the accession of the brilliant Sir Harry Vane, lately come from England, and destined to return hither to vex a greater than Winthrop. Vane was as radical in politics as Mistress Anne was in religion; and the two made common cause against the magistrates and clergy. Had the issue been confined to Boston the result could not have been doubtful, for the Boston Church was predominantly Hutchinsonian; but the ministers as a body supported Winthrop and Wilson, and the old magistrates were returned in the election of 1637. The victory was a crucial one. The erratic Vane went off to England; Cotton returned to his first allegiance; and when the cause of all the trouble was cited to appear before the court in the fall of the same year, the decree of banishment was a foregone conclusion. Like Luther before the diet, Anne Hutchinson pressed for reasons—"I desire to know wherefore I am banished." It was in the spirit of the Roman Church that Governor Winthrop replied—"say no more; the Court knows wherefore, and is satisfied."

The direct result of the expulsion of Williams and Anne Hutchinson was the founding of Rhode Island, famous as an early experiment in the separation of Church and State. Williams, with his few followers, denied admittance to Plymouth, went on to the south and founded the town of Providence. Into this region there shortly came the much larger group, including William Coddington, who followed Anne Hutchinson into exile. The settlements of Portsmouth and New Port, which they established there, were united with Providence, under a patent procured by Williams in 1643, to form the colony of Rhode Island, where flourished, to the scandal of its neighbors, that "soul liberty" of which Williams was the apostle. Yet not without difficulty. Peopled by those who were too eccentric not to prove troublesome, the history of the little colony was a stormy one—its peace "like the peace of a man who has the tertian ague"; but its fame is secure, and, its founder, condemned by the common sense of his age, will ever be celebrated as the prophet of those primary American doctrines, democracy and religious toleration.

Rhode Island was founded by those who were not allowed to remain in Massachusetts; Connecticut by those who, finding its conditions too restricted, did not wish to remain there. Few facts have been more potent in determining the history of America than the steady migration in search of better opportunities. A decade had not passed before the westward movement began. As early as 1633 many people at the Bay, fired by favorable reports which John Oldham brought back from the Connecticut Valley, began to have "a hankering after it." In 1634 the people of Newtown, under the leadership of Thomas Hooker, asked permission of the general court to remove there, advancing, in support of their petition, "their want of accommodation for their cattle, the fruitfulness and commodiousness of Connecticut, and the strong bent of their spirits to remove thither." The petition was at first denied, but in 1636, permission having at last been obtained, a considerable number from the towns of Newtown, Dorchester, Watertown, and Roxbury migrated to the west and south and settled the towns—Hartford, Wethersfield, and Windsor—which became the nucleus of the colony of Connecticut.

While the fertility of the Connecticut Valley was doubtless attractive, some of the motives which actuated Hooker and his followers lie concealed in the naïve phrase, "the strong bent of their spirits." Thomas Hooker, and to a less extent John Haynes and Roger Ludlow, were men of outstanding ability. But as their towns were second to Boston, they themselves were overtopped in influence by Winthrop and Cotton, Dudley and Wilson. In the compact community of Massachusetts Bay, ideas as well as cattle found accommodation difficult. In religion and politics Hooker was more radical than Winthrop: he was not wholly out of sympathy with Anne Hutchinson; and he defended the proposition that "the foundation of authority is laid in the free consent of the people," whereas Winthrop maintained that the best part of the people "is always the least, and of that best part the wiser part is always the lesser." And so, when the petitioners were permitted to leave, the strong bent of their spirits directed them, not only to the Connecticut, but southward without the limits of the Massachusetts jurisdiction.

While Hooker and his associates, with room for their cattle and their ideas, clear of Boston's shadow and the din of disputes over the negative voice and the covenant of works, were establishing a more liberal Bible Commonwealth on the Connecticut, Theophilus Eaton, a merchant of "fair estate and great esteem for religion," and John Davenport, a dispossessed London minister, were establishing at New Haven a Bible Commonwealth stricter even than that of Massachusetts. They had arrived, with their congregation of well-to-do middle-class Londoners, at Boston in 1637, where they remained during the winter. Winthrop would have retained them permanently; but Davenport found the colony distracted by the Hutchinson episode, and was as much distressed by the concessions which had been made to the "mere democracy" as Hooker had been by the restraints in favor of a "mixed aristocracy." They therefore moved on, accompanied and followed by some inhabitants of Massachusetts, to establish at New Haven a community in which the Scriptures should be the "only rule attended to in ordering the affairs of government." But these "Brahmins of New England Puritanism" did not find the peace which they pursued. The distractions which they left Boston to avoid attended them in the wilderness; and in the end the colony was united with the settlements to the north, where the liberal ideas of Hooker had proved compatible, not only with strict morality and frugal prosperity, but with religious and spiritual concord as well. The charter of 1662 which founded the larger Connecticut embodied the ideas of Hooker rather than those of Davenport, and was so wisely contrived that it stood the shock of the Revolution and survived to the nineteenth century as the fundamental law of Connecticut.

Internal difficulties growing out of conflicting ideals of Church and State had scarcely achieved the dispersion of the New England settlements before external dangers began to draw them together. As early as 1637, and again in 1639, the Connecticut settlements, threatened by the Dutch and the Indians, applied to Massachusetts Bay for support against the common danger. The Dutch and the Indians were less dangerous to Massachusetts than to Connecticut, but the possibility of royal interference touched her more nearly. In 1634 Laud had obtained the appointment of a commission to inquire into her affairs, and in 1642 the "ill news we have had out of England concerning the breach between King and Parliament" gave further apprehension with respect to the colony's chartered liberties. Accordingly, the third proposal of Connecticut in 1642 met with a favorable response, and in the following year the New England Confederation was founded. Rhode Island was without the pale, but Massachusetts, Connecticut, Plymouth, and New Haven entered into a "firm and perpetual league of friendship and amity for offense and defense, mutual advice and succor, both for preserving and propagating the truth and liberties of the Gospel, and for their own mutual safety and welfare." The affairs of the league were to be administered by a board of two commissioners from each colony. Massachusetts, with a greater population than the other three combined, agreed to bear her proper burden in men and money, and presumed at times to exercise a corresponding influence. The smaller colonies were naturally more willing to accept her money than disposed to submit to her dictation; but in spite of disputes, the Confederation was maintained for forty years, an effective influence in its day, and the first of many compromises which led in the end to that more perfect union which still endures.

IV

Neither revolution in England nor the stress of conflicting ideals in the colony turned the first generation of Massachusetts Bay leaders from the straight course which they had laid. Magistrates and clergy went steadily forward, emerging from Nonconformity into practical Separatism, as resistant to Parliamentary as to royal control, as cool toward Cromwell as toward Charles. During the quarter-century of their domination, Massachusetts maintained a virtual independence of the mother country and the effective leadership of Now England. Towards the middle of the century the theocratic principle might have seemed more firmly established than ever before. The relative tranquillity which followed the banishment of Anne Hutchinson appeared to be a clear justification of the action of the general court on that occasion. It was therefore without hesitation that the authorities acted when Anne Austin and Mary Fisher, two Quaker missionaries from Barbados, arrived at Boston in 1656. The women were reshipped to Barbados; and a law was straightway enacted which decreed the flogging and imprisonment of any of the "cursed sect of haeritics commonly called Quakers" who might come within the colony's jurisdiction.

In the seventeenth century, it was agreed that, next to the Münster Anabaptists, the Quakers were of all dissenting sects the most pestilent and blasphemous. They used no force in propagating their beliefs or in defending their lives. They were believers in equality, and refused to doff their hats to any man, respecting neither magistrate nor priest. They were believers in liberty; no man to be restrained in matters of opinion; but every man to go or come, to speak or remain silent, as God's commands, by direct inner revelation, might be laid upon him. And it appeared that God had laid his command upon many to go among the unregenerate bearing testimony, and with sharp-tongued reproach and reviling to prick as with thorns the seared conscience of a perverse and stiff-necked generation. Persecution they welcomed as the martyr's portion, the sure evidence of well-doing. "Where they are most of all suffered to declare themselves, there they least of all desire to come." And so, impelled by the force of the divine spirit, they came among the reserved and seemly Puritans of Boston, with scandalous impropriety of action bringing the staid Sunday sermon or Thursday lecture to irremediable confusion, with voluble harangue and wealth of stinging epithet pouring scorn upon the self-selected leaders of the chosen people.

The harassed magistrates wished only to be rid of them. But unlike Williams and Anne Hutchinson, the Quakers came back as often as they were banished; and as often as they returned, their conduct became more outrageous, and, the penalties inflicted more severe. Yet oppression bore its proper fruit. Persecution engendered sympathy; sympathy ripened into conviction; and the more heretics were confined in the prisons, the more heresy flourished in the streets. The popularity of Anne Hutchinson's teachings had demonstrated how eagerly the average man turned from the literalism of the Puritan clergy in response to the appeal of one who spoke "from the mere motion of the spirit." Quakerism was above all a spiritual gospel addressed to the emotions. Its humane and liberal teachings, obscured but not concealed by the extravagance of speech and conduct in its first apostles, stood out in striking contrast to the repressive policy of the Puritan government as well as to the cold, gray intellectualism of the Puritan religion. The Quakers were a political danger as well as a public nuisance; for whether few or many were likely to profess the Quaker faith, among covenanted and uncovenanted alike their teachings fell on the fruitful soil of discontent. The magistrates were well aware at last that a crisis was impending; and they went steadily forward, with circumspection and not without apprehension, indeed, but without flinching, to meet the final test. In 1659 and 1660, according to law established and known, five Quakers were condemned to death, and four were hanged on Boston Common.

The event was a significant one in early Massachusetts history, for it revealed, in respect to theory and practice alike, the insecure foundation upon which the Church-State rested. In respect to theory, the Quakers were a perplexing problem precisely because they remorselessly pressed the basic principles of Protestantism to their logical conclusion. The doctrine of the inner light, like Anne Hutchinson's notion of personal illumination, was implicit in the premises of Luther, who had grounded the great protest on the conception of a covenant of grace, and had laid it down, as the primary thesis, that "good works do not make the good man, but the good man does good works." Luther's revolt had, indeed, raised a vital social question: Are belief and conduct in matters religious to be determined by the social will registered in decrees of Church or State, or by the individual will following the promptings of reason and conscience? For most dissenters in the sixteenth and seventeenth centuries there was a logical difficulty in assenting to the first proposition and a practical objection to assenting to the second: it was logically difficult to deny the authority of Rome, which the practice and traditions of centuries had recognized as voicing the will of Christendom, without denying the validity of any external authority whatever; but it was practically impossible to appeal unreservedly to the authority of the individual reason and conscience without running into free thought and allowing religion to dissolve in an infinite variety of opinion. Generally speaking, most Protestant sects appealed from the outer to the inner authority in order to establish their beliefs, and then from the inner to the outer authority in order to maintain them. Luther himself, having denied the right of the Church to compel his conscience, straightway maintained that it was not for *Herr Omnes* to determine matters of religion, and fell back on the State as the defender of his faith against the dangers of dissent. But it is indeed true that "the business of dissenters is to dissent"; and the Massachusetts magistrates found that the very arguments they had used to deny the authority of Laud were now employed to deny their own. This was the logical opening in the Puritan armor, that the Protestant Church-State or State-Church was but a masked and attenuated Catholicism destined to be destroyed by the very principles upon which it had been originally established.

If in respect to theory the hanging of the Quakers was a confession, in the realm of practical politics it was but a Pyrrhic victory. The authority of magistrate and clergy, strained to the breaking point, never quite recovered its old security. The capital law was itself passed by a bare majority, and the successive executions carried popular opposition to the verge of insurrection. Nor did the executions achieve the desired end. The last sentence was never carried into effect, and for years the Quakers continued to molest the colony, pushing their extravagances sometimes to the farthest limit. To fall to mere flogging after having inflicted the death penalty was a fatal anti-climax which marks a turning-point in Massachusetts history—the beginning of the end of Winthrop's Bible Commonwealth.

The end was doubtless hastened by the Stuart Restoration and the recall of the charter; but the theocratic ideal, carrying the germ of its own decay, was predestined to failure. For the founders of the Bible Commonwealth it was an axiom that Church and State were but two sides of the same shield; a matter of course that the "body of the commons" must be "preserved of honest and good men"; a reasonable hope that all good men would be found within the churches. And the circumstances of the migration seemed, indeed, a miraculous preparation for this easy solution of human government; for persecution was taken to be but "a strange contrivance of God" to gather "a chosen company of men"—the sifted wheat for planting an ideal commonwealth. Yet of the first settlers more than half refused to take the covenant, thus renouncing the privileges of the ideal commonwealth without obtaining relief from its burdens. A most disconcerting circumstance this at the beginning, and of ill omen for the future! Doubtless some strange perversity of the natural man, some inscrutable judgment of God for the discipline of his people, must have kept so many outside the fold.

But in truth not all who came to Plymouth or Massachusetts were of the sifted wheat. Under the stress of persecution and the stimulus of migration, the mass of the first settlers doubtless caught something of the spiritual exaltation which inspired the leaders. But it was not for the many to live on that high level of purposeful resolution and enduring courage. It is a significant fact that of those who came over with Winthrop and Dudley two hundred returned in the ships that brought them out; and of those who remained who shall say how many met the stern realities of the New World with a sinking sense of disillusionment, finding the material conditions of life harder and the spiritual peace less satisfying than they had imagined? And many there were who had never been touched by the Puritan ideal. "Men being to come over into a wilderness," says the kindly Bradford, "in which much labour and servise was to be done about building and planting, such as wanted help in that respecte, when they could not have such as they would, were glad to take such as they could, and so, many untoward servants, sundry of them proved, were thus brought over, both men and women kind; who, when their terms were expired, became families of themselves, which gave increase hereunto. Another and maine reason hereof was, that men, finding so many godly disposed persons willing to come into these parts, some began to make a trade of it, to transport passengers and their goods, and hired ships for that end; and then, to make up their freight and advance their profite, cared not who the persons were, so they had money to pay them. And also ther were sente by their freinds some under hope that they would be made better; others that they might be eased of such burthens, and they kept from shame at home that would necessarily follow their dissolute courses. And by this means the country became pestered with many unworthy persons, who, being come over, crept into one place or other."

Such unworthy persons doubtless swelled the mass of uncovenanted. Yet the historian is apt to think that for many, honest and good men enough, the cold inner temple of the ideal commonwealth must have proved more forbidding than its wind-swept outer courts. To enter its portals was an ordeal which the average man will not readily undergo, involving, as an initial procedure, a confession of faults and a profession of faith, a public revelation of inner spiritual condition, an exposure of soul to the searching and curious inspection of the sanctified. And the covenant itself was found to be no warmed and cloistered retreat, secure from the rude impact and impertinent gaze of the world. Quite the contrary! To enter the covenant was to renounce all private spiritual possessions, to give one's intimate convictions into the keeping of others, to subscribe to a very communism of the emotional life. This un-Roman Church was after all but a public confessional, in which every brother was a confessor, and life itself a penance for constructive sin. The soul that is constantly exposed grows callous or diseased; and the New England covenant provided a regimen well suited to repel the normal mind or induce in its patients a fatal spiritual anæmia.

And with every decade the house of the covenant became at once more difficult to enter and less comfortable to abide in. The Puritan was not necessarily a sad or solemn person. Yet the light heart and the merry mind were not the salient characteristics even of the cheerful Winthrop or the genial Cotton; while the conditions of life in the wilderness—the unrelieved round of exacting labor, the ever present danger from the lurking Indians, the long cold winters with their certain harvest of death from diseases which could be ascribed only to the will of God and met with resignation instead of skill, the succession of funerals as depressing as they were public and pervading—were well calculated to deepen the somber cast of the Puritan temper and accentuate the critical and introspective tendency of his mind. Inspection of one's own and one's neighbor's conduct was, indeed, always a Puritan duty; shut within the restricted horizon of a New England village, it became a necessity and almost a pleasure. When few stirring events diverted thought from the petty and the personal, when pent-up emotion found little outlet in the graces or amusements of social intercourse, observation and introspection fastened upon the minutiæ of life and every eccentricity of speech and conduct was weighed and assessed. Close espionage on conduct was matched by the careful scrutiny accorded every novel opinion. When the weekly sermon was the universal topic of conversation, the refinements of belief were more discussed than essentials; often discussed, they were often questioned—by strict Separatists like Roger Williams; by cavilers at infant baptism like that "anciently religious woman," the Lady Deborah Moodie; by fervid emotionalists, such as Anne Hutchinson or the Quaker missionaries: and every discussion of the creed left it more precisely defined, more narrow, and more official. Under the stress of conflicting opinion and the attrition of acrid debate, the covenant of grace steadily hardened into a covenant of barren works, in which an air of sanctimony became an easy substitute for the sense of sanctification, and the tithe of mint and cummin was allowed to overbalance the weightier matters of the law.

While the covenant became more inelastic, and its rule of life more strictly defined, the call of the world became more insidious and alluring. As the colony became established beyond the fear of failure, and life fell from an artificial and self-conscious venture to be but a natural experience, as wealth increased and opportunities for relaxation and idle amusement multiplied, the elemental instincts of human nature, stronger than decrees of state, would not be denied. During the third decade after the founding, the Christmas festival found its way into the colony, and "dancing in ordinarys upon the marriage of some person" gave occasion for scandal. Extravagance in "apparill both of men and women" became the subject of repeated legislation: "we cannot but to our grief take notice," so runs the law of 1651, "that intolerable excesse and bravery have crept in uppon us, and especially amongst people of mean condition, to the dishonor of God, the scandall of our profession, the coruption of estates, and altogether unsuitable to our povertie." Non-attendance at church did not become a problem for the magistrates until 1646, but the fine then imposed proved ineffective; and year by year the desecration of the Sabbath became more marked and more difficult of correction. Many and sundry abuses were committed "by several persons on the Lord's day, not only by children playing in the streets and other places, but by youthes, maydes, and other persons, both strangers and others, uncivilly walkinge in the streets and fields, travelling from towne to towne, going on shipboard, frequentinge common howses and other places to drinke, sport, and otherwise to misspend that precious time."

"Maydes and youthes!" The words are significant, for by 1653 the first generation of native-born New Englanders had indeed come upon the scene to vex the Puritan fathers. How different from that of the first settlers must have been the outlook of those who had never been in England. They had never been oppressed by bishop or king; had never felt the insidious temptation of a cathedral church, or witnessed the mockery of the mass, or been repelled by a surpliced priesthood desecrating God's house with incense and music; had never seen a maypole with its accompaniment of licentious revelry, or witnessed the debauching effects of a holiday festival. They had solemnly sat in unwarmed churches; they had been present at elections; had seen men standing in the pillory or women whipped through the streets; they had diverted themselves at weddings or the husking-bee, or by walking in the woods, or by drinking in a tavern. But no frivolous and superstitious world of Anti-Christ compassed them about to point the moral of the harsh Puritan tale. Their Puritanism was induced by precept and example rather than by the compelling impact of a corrupt society.

Yet no conventionalized Puritanism, no mere living on the dead level of habitual virtues could satisfy the leaders of the great migration. The founding of Massachusetts was preëminently a self-conscious movement, the work of able and resolute men who brought an unquenchable moral enthusiasm to the support of a clearly defined purpose. They had counted the cost and made their choice; and every instinct of proud and self-contained men disposed them to minimize the difficulties which they encountered in the New World and to exaggerate those which they had overcome in the Old. Having staked their judgment on the wisdom of the venture, they were bound to be justified in the event. To admit that life on the physical and moral frontier was less than they had imagined would be a humiliating confession of failure; and worse than a confession of failure; for God had appointed this refuge for them, and not to abide in it in all contentment would be to cavil at his purpose, to question his decree. With the instinct of true pioneers they therefore idealized the barren wilderness, pronouncing its air most healing, its soil most fertile; and with unfailing optimism proving, by the very sufferings they endured, how practicable, how spacious and attractive was the habitation which they had set themselves to fashion.

Thus it was that the very influences which relaxed the hold of the Puritan ideal upon the mass of the people served only to strengthen its hold upon their leaders. With resolution stiffened by every obstacle, magistrates and clergy pressed on to the appointed task, never doubting that they were called upon to justify the ways of God to man. Drawing their inspiration from Geneva and the ancient Hebrew code, they assumed, with a courage as sublime as it proved futile, to foster moral and spiritual excellence by decrees of state. Indifference or opposition only called them to a stricter rule; for every physical disaster, every denial of the creed or departure from the straight line of life, was thought to be God's judgment upon them for some want of faith or failure in the law. And in later years the chastisements of the Lord were many:—the desolating King Philip's War; persistent interference with their chartered Liberties; dissensions in the Boston Church and quarrels of magistrates and clergy; the rise of "an anti-ministerial spirit" and the growth of worldliness and lax living among the people. "What are the reasons that have provoked the Lord to bring his judgments upon New England?" Such was the primary question which the Synod of 1679 was called upon to answer. "Declension from the primitive foundation work, innovation in doctrine and worship"—this, according to a committee of the deputies, was the true cause. "A spirit of division, persecuting and oppressing of God's ministers and precious saints," said Mr. Flint of Dorchester, "is the sin that is unseen." And not a few maintained that all their troubles were but well-merited punishments for having dealt too leniently with the Quakers.

And yet, in the year 1679, such explanations as these were falling to the level of the conventional for many of the magistrates and even for some of the clergy. After forty years few of the original leaders were still alive. Winthrop died in 1649, Cotton in 1652, Thomas Dudley in 1653, John Wilson in 1667, Richard Mather in 1669. The days of persecution and exile influenced the thinking of the second generation, indeed, not so much as an experience, but rather as a tradition or a tale that is told. Liberal influences, which were to oust the Mathers from control of Harvard College, were already gaining ground in Cambridge, while Boston had become the center of powerful material interests which were to prove incompatible with the rigid ideals of the founders. "The merchants seem to be rich men," writes Mr. Harris in 1675, "and their houses as handsomely furnished as most in London." In 1680 more than one hundred ships traded at the Bay, carrying fish, provisions, and lumber to southern Europe, to the Madeiras, and to the English sugar colonies in the West Indies. Many men who rose to prominence in the third quarter of the century were more concerned for the temporal than for the spiritual commonwealth; and when material interests thus came into competition with the interests of religion, not a few were prepared to compromise with the world, and so a secular and moderate spirit crept in to corrupt the counsels of government.

The rise of the moderate party and the divergence between clergy and magistrate is therefore a notable feature of the last years of Massachusetts history under the charter. In 1679, after the death of Leverett, Bradstreet was elected governor. He was the leader of the party of conciliation, one of many who, renouncing the rigid and uncompromising policy of the clergy, were ready to coöperate with Randolph in the hope of securing the essential interests of the colony by a timely submission to the English Government. And it is significant of the growing influence of the property interests that the moderates were stronger in the upper than in the lower chamber. In 1682 the governor and a majority of the assistants, "upon a serious consideration of his Majesty's intimation that his purpose is only to regulate our charter, in such a manner as shall be for his service and the good of this his colony," announced themselves willing to surrender the bulwark of the Puritan liberties. But the House of Deputies voted to "adhere to their former bills," preferring with the clergy rather to "die by the hand of others, than by their own."

The event reveals the opposition of the material and the ideal interests which was a prime cause in the defeat of the great Puritan experiment. The assistants were "men of the best estates," says Randolph, while the deputies were "mostly an inferior sort of planters." Randolph was a prejudiced observer; but it is undoubtedly true that the upper chamber spoke for the shipbuilders and traders of Boston. Forty years earlier, when Laud was preparing to annul the charter, both magistrates and clergy made ready for forcible resistance. It was no longer possible. Massachusetts had ceased to be a wilderness community cut off from contact with the outside world. Her rapidly growing trade depended upon English markets. The base of the fisheries was shifting northward, and a French company at Nova Scotia was already seizing New England ships. Without English protection trade would be ruined and the colony itself fall a prey to

France. Forcible resistance was therefore not to be thought of. The material interests of Massachusetts bound her to the home Government, and practical men were apt to think that even the spiritual City of God would suffer less under Anglican than under Catholic control.

The recall of the charter but opened free passage to the latent forces that were already beginning to transform the life and thought of New England. The theocratic ideal had so far lost its hold that the event to which the clergy and a remnant of the magistrates looked forward as to a cosmic catastrophe was accepted with resignation or indifference by the mass of the people. Neither disaster nor serious disturbance accompanied the inauguration of the new régime. The extension of the suffrage to the freeholders removed more discontent than it created. A government controlled by property interests approved itself as well as one directed by religious ideas. The colony was no more distracted by the introduction of the Anglican service than by the erection of the second Boston Church; and even the passing of Harvard College, that citadel and fortress of the old theocracy, into the hands of Boston and Cambridge liberals, was far less a tragedy to Massachusetts than it was to the Mathers.

The life of Cotton Mather was, indeed, a kind of tragedy, for he was the most distinguished of those who grew to manhood under the old order only to witness its fall and live in degenerate days. Not less able than his father, but how much less influential! In early years his voice was a commanding one, but he was destined to see his popularity wane and to live most of his long life in comparative isolation and neglect in the very community where Increase Mather had been a high priest indeed. In such men as Cotton Mather the old spirit lived on, sharply accentuated by defeat; and transformed, in such men as Jonathan Edwards, by dint of morbid introspection and brooding on the sins of a perverse generation, into a kind of disease, or spiritual neurasthenia. Such men could but look back with poignant regret to the golden age that was past. Of that golden age, Cotton Mather himself, "smitten with a just fear of encroaching and ill-bodied degeneracies," sat down to write the history, recording in the *Magnalia* "the great things done for us by our God," in the hope that he might thereby do something "to prevent the loss of the primitive principles and the primitive practices."

But he had imagined a vain thing. For even as the century drew to its close, the old Bay colony was already drifting from its back-water moorings, out into the main current of the world's thought. None could know to what uncharted seas of political and religious radicalism they were bearing on. None could foresee the time when Calvin's Institutes would give way to the Suffolk Resolutions, when Adams would speak in place of Endicott, or the later day when Emerson would preach a new antinomianism more desolating than any known to Winthrop or Bradford.

BIBLIOGRAPHICAL NOTE

This period is fully treated in Channing's *History of the United States*, I, chaps, VIII-XIV; and in Tyler's *England in America*, chaps. V-VII, IX-XIX. See also Fiske's *Old Virginia and Her Neighbours*, I, chaps. VII-XI, XIV; and

Eggleston's *Beginners of a Nation* and *The Transit of Civilization from England to America*. The constitutional aspects of the colonial settlements are exhaustively treated in Osgood's *The American Colonies in the 17th Century*. For the economic and social history of the colonies, see Bruce's *Social Life in Virginia* and *The Economic History of Virginia in the 17th Century*, and Weeden's *Economic History of New England*. Contemporary pamphlets relating to the colonies are to be found in Force's *Tracts and Other Papers*, 4 vols. Washington, 1838. To understand the motives and ideals of the Separatists and Puritans one must read their own accounts. Of these, the most charming is Bradford's *History of Plymouth Plantation*. This, as well as Governor Winthrop's *Journal*, is printed in Jameson's *Original Narratives of Early American History*. Johnson's *Wonder Working Providence*, in the same collection, is a history from the point of view of a loyal Puritan of average education and intelligence. Morton's *New English Canaan* (1632) and *The Simple Cobler of Aggawam* (1647) are printed in Force's *Tracts and Other Papers*, vols. II, III. A hostile account of the Puritan experiment is in Samuel Gorton's *Letter to Nathaniel Morton*, in Force's *Tracts*, etc., vol. IV. About three quarters of a century after the founding of Massachusetts, Cotton Mather wrote his *Magnalia Christi Americana, or the Ecclesiastical History of New England*, 2 vols. Hartford, 1855. In Bk. I he gives an account of the founding from the point of view of one who felt that New England was then departing from the "primitive principles."

CHAPTER IV

ENGLAND AND HER COLONIES IN THE SEVENTEENTH AND EIGHTEENTH CENTURIES

Your trade is the mother and nurse of your seamen; your seamen are the life of your fleet; your fleet is the security of your trade, and both together are the wealth, strength, and glory of Britain.

Lord Haversham.

I

The decay of the old Puritanism in Massachusetts, so distressing to Cotton Mather, was but a faint reflection of the change which had come over England since the return of Charles II to Whitehall. With the fall of the Puritan régime moral earnestness and high emotional tension, regarded as contrary to nature and reason, gave way to a rationalizing habit of mind, to seriousness tempered with well-bred common sense or spiced with a pinch of cynical indifference. Religion fell to be a conventional conformity. Theologians, wanting vital faith in God, were content to balance the probabilities of his existence. Amusement became the avocation of a leisure class, and the average man was intent like Samuel Pepys to put money in his purse, in order to indulge himself "a little the more in pleasure, knowing that this is the proper age to do it." From Milton and the Earl of Clarendon to William Pitt, England was no country of lost causes and impossible enthusiasms. It was a pragmatic age, in which the scientific discoveries of Newton are the highest intellectual achievement, and the conclusion of Pope that "everything that is is best" gives the quality of poetic insight.

In this ago the direction of English affairs fell to men well suited to the national temper. The first Charles suffered martyrdom for his faith; the second, determined never again to go on his travels, set the standard of public morality by selling himself to France, and with a smile professing the belief that honor in man and virtue in woman were but devices to raise the price of capitulation. And so he often found it; for he was himself served by men who, having renounced their Puritan principles for place and power, were prepared to forswear the Stuarts in order to follow the rising star of William of Orange. William was an able statesman, indeed, but his interest was in the grand alliance; he "borrowed England on his way to Versailles," and governed it in the interest of the Dutch Coalition. Queen Anne and the first Georges reigned but did not govern; and in the early eighteenth century power fell to men of supple intelligence and complacent conviction—to Marlborough and little Sidney Godolphin, to Harley and St. John and Sunderland, and at last to Robert Walpole, the very personification of the shrewd curiosity, the easy-going morals, the material ambitions of his generation.

Little wonder if in such an age colonies were regarded as providentially designed to promote the trade's increase. The recall of the Massachusetts charter was but one of many circumstances which reveal the rise in England of renewed interest in the plantations. Faith in colonial ventures had never, indeed, quite disappeared, nor had the early Stuarts ever been wholly indifferent to their American possessions. But the fate of the Virginia Company had cooled the ardor of moneyed men, and the Civil War, focusing attention for a generation upon fundamental questions of morals and politics, absorbed the energies of government and nation. With the establishment of the Protectorate imperial interests again claimed attention. Cromwell, calling the merchants to counsel, inaugurated a vigorous policy of maritime and colonial expansion. The Dutch war and the conquest of Jamaica recalled to men's minds the triumphs of Elizabeth; and those who gathered round Charles II—bankrupt nobles, pushing merchants, and able statesmen—turned to the business of trade and colonies with an enthusiasm unknown since the days of Gilbert and Raleigh.

Yet it was an enthusiasm well tempered to practical ends, purged of resplendent visions and vague idealisms. The plantations, regarded as incidents in the life of commerce, were thought to be important when they were found to be prosperous. In 1661 the king was assured that his American possessions were "beginning to grow into Commodities of great value and Esteeme, and though some of them continue in tobacco yet upon the Returne hither it smells well, and paies more Custome to his Majestie than the East Indies four times ouer." It was a statement of which the new king was not likely to miss the significance. Determined to preserve the prerogative without offending the nation, Charles was never indifferent to the material welfare of England; the expansion of trade would increase his own revenue, while the vigilance which preserves liberty he thought likely to be relaxed among a prosperous and well-fed people. To commercial and colonial expansion the merry monarch therefore gave his best attention. If he yawned over dull reports in council, he listened to them with ready intelligence, and was prepared to encourage every reasonable project for the extension of the empire.

For new colonial ventures opportunity was not lacking. Widely separated settlements along the American coast were cut in twain by New Netherland and flanked on either side by the possessions of France and Spain. To forestall rivals in occupying all the territory claimed by England, and to exploit intelligently its commercial resources, seemed at once a public duty and a private opportunity. And no region was thought more important, either in a commercial or a military way, than the Cape Fear and Charles River valleys. So at least reasoned the Earl of Clarendon, Ashley Cooper, and Sir John Colleton; to them, associated with five others, was accordingly issued in 1663, and again in 1665, a proprietary grant to the Carolinas. The patentees, upon whom the charter conferred the usual right to establish and govern colonies, expected that the surplus population of Barbados and the Bahamas, where capital and slavery were driving out white laborers and small farmers, would readily migrate to the Charles River, and there engage in the cultivation of commodities—such as silk, currants, raisins, wax, almonds, olives, and oil—which, being raised neither in England nor in any English plantation, would serve to redress the balance of trade and doubtless net a handsome profit to those with faith to venture the first costs of settlement. With the English market assured, a thriving trade and a prosperous colony seemed the certain result.

In these expectations the patentees were disappointed. Dissenters already settled in the region of Albemarle Sound were little disposed to submit to restrictions which they had left Virginia to avoid. In 1665 and 1666 some discontented Barbadians, making an essay to settle on the coast farther south, found the country less inviting than they had been led to expect, and returned to Barbados as the lesser evil. The terms on which the proprietors granted land, liberal enough but frequently changed; restrictions laid on trade almost before there was anything to exchange; the doctrinaire Fundamental Constitutions which John Locke, fresh from the perusal of Harrington, wrote out in the quiet of his study for governing little frontier communities the like of which he had never seen,—all had little effect but to irritate those who were already on the ground and discourage others from going there. In 1667, there were no inhabitants in Carolina south of Albemarle Sound; in 1672 scarcely more than four hundred. Not silk and almonds but provisions were raised; for it was necessary "to provide in the first place for the belly" before endeavoring to redress the balance of England's commerce. As late as 1675 the proprietors complained that an expenditure of £10,000 had returned them nothing but the "charge of 5 or 600 people who expect to live on us." An exaggeration, doubtless; but in truth the Carolinas never profited the proprietors anything, never drew off much of the surplus population of Barbados, nor supplied England with olives or capers. North Carolina raised tobacco, which was carried by New England traders to Virginia or the Northern colonies. The inhabitants of the Southern province, reinforced by French Huguenots and English dissenters, exported provisions to the West Indies. Yet South Carolina, disappointing to the proprietors, was destined in the next century, when rice became its staple product, to serve in an almost ideal way the purpose for which it had been founded.

The Carolina charter had scarcely been issued before the Dutch were ousted from the valley of the Hudson. It was an old grievance that the Hollanders, under many obligations to England, should have presumed to occupy territory already granted by James I to the Plymouth Company. And now, wedged in between the New England and the Southern colonies, holding the first harbor on the continent and well situated to share with France in exploiting the fur trade, the grievance had become intolerable. But the offense of all was the complacence with which the merchants of New Amsterdam ignored the English Trade Acts. Reconciled at last to the strange perversity of Virginia in raising tobacco, the English Government had made the best of a bad bargain by laying a prohibition upon its cultivation in England; yet with this result: an English industry had been suppressed by law only that the Dutch, who still contested England's right to share in the spice and slave trade, might carry Virginia tobacco to European ports, smuggle European commodities into the English settlements, and so diminish the profits of British merchants and annually deprive the royal exchequer of £10,000 of customs revenue. When the Dutch war was imminent in 1664, an English fleet, therefore, took possession of Now Amsterdam in order to secure to England the commercial value of the tobacco colonies. Before the conquest was effected the king conferred upon his brother, the Duke of York, a proprietary feudal grant of all the territory lying between the Connecticut and Delaware Rivers.

At the time of the conquest the colony of New Netherland was occupied by Dutch farmers and traders on western Long Island and on both sides of the Hudson as far north as the Mohawk River; central Long Island was inhabited in part by New Englanders; the eastern end entirely so. To establish English authority in the province, harmonizing at once the interests of the Catholic Duke of York, the Dutch Protestants, and the New England Puritans, was a difficult task, but it was accomplished with much skill by Colonel Nicolls, who was the first English governor. Religious toleration was granted; land titles were confirmed; and a body of laws, known as the Duke's Laws, based upon Dutch custom and New England statutes, was prepared by the governor and with some murmuring accepted by the inhabitants. In 1683 Governor Dongan, yielding to popular demand, established a legislative body consisting of the governor's council and a house of eighteen deputies elected by the freeholders, and the freemen of the corporations of Albany and New York. With the accession of James as King of England, the province temporarily lost its popular assembly; in 1688 it was annexed to New England under the jurisdiction of Andros; and after the Revolution it was distracted for many years by political quarrels growing out of the Leisler Rebellion. Yet none of these events interfered with the economic development of the colony. In 1674 the population was about 7000. Natural increase, together with immigrants from England and New England, Huguenot exiles from France, and refugees which the armies of Louis XIV drove out of the Palatinate, swelled the number to about 25,000 in 1700. Dutch merchants at Albany did a thriving business in furs; and in 1695 New York City, with a population of 5000, was already the center of an active trade, mainly West Indian, by no means wholly legal, in provisions and sugar.

The conquest of New Amsterdam was scarcely completed before the Duke of York, by "lease and re-lease," and for the sum of ten shillings, conveyed to his friends, Lord Berkeley and Sir George Carteret, the territory between the Hudson and the Delaware Rivers, afterwards known as New Jersey. Dutch settlers already occupied the west shore of New York Harbor; and there were Swedes as well as Dutch on the lower Delaware. Favorable concessions offered by the proprietors soon attracted New Englanders from Long Island and Connecticut, who located in the region of Monmouth and Middletown. The proprietors nevertheless found more vexation than profit in their venture; and in 1673 Lord Berkeley sold his rights to two Friends, John Fenwick and Edward Byllinge, who were intent upon founding a refuge for the Quakers in America. Many Quakers soon settled in West Jersey along the Delaware, and upon the death of Carteret the proprietary rights to East Jersey were purchased by William Penn and other Friends who had succeeded to the rights of Fenwick and Byllinge. A mixed population and conflicting claims made the history of the first Quaker colony a turbulent one. In 1688 both Jerseys were annexed to New York; and in 1702, the proprietors having surrendered all their rights, the two colonies became the single royal province of New Jersey.

Of those who were interested in securing a refuge for the Quakers, the most active was William Penn, who had suffered ridicule and persecution for his faith, and who now desired a clearer field than the Jerseys offered for his political and religious experiments. In 1681 he therefore procured from the king a proprietary grant of the territory lying west of the Delaware from "twelve miles north of New Castle Town unto the three and fortieth degree of Northern Latitude." The land within these vague limits was thought to be "wholly Indian," and the purposes of Penn did not run counter to the colonial policy of the Government. Optimism or ignorance disposed the Lords of Trade to believe that Pennsylvania could as readily as the Carolinas be devoted to the cultivation of "oyle, dates, figgs, almons, raisins, and currans." To the political hobbies of Penn the Government was indifferent, while the intractable Quakers were classed with jailbirds and political offenders as people who were more useful to England in the plantations than at home. The proprietor's "Account of the Province of Pennsylvania," translated into Dutch, German, and French, promising religious and political liberty, and offering land on easy terms to rich and poor alike, attracted good colonists in large numbers. Within ten years there were 10,000 people, mostly Quakers, in Pennsylvania and the Delaware counties. Political wrangling, somewhat difficult to understand and scarcely worth unraveling, distracted the colony of brotherly love for many years; but from the beginning the province prospered. The settlers were as thrifty as New England Puritans, and they had better soil and a more hospitable climate. Provisions were soon raised for export; and in 1700, according to Robert

Quarry, the Quakers of Pennsylvania had "improved tillage to that degree that they have made bread, flower, and Beer a drugg in all the markets of the West Indies."

II

As early as 1656 London merchants were inquiring "whether it would not be a prudentiall thing to draw all the Islands, Colonies, and Dominions of America under one and the same management here." Enterprising capitalists who had ventured their money in Jamaica or Barbados were content to leave the honor and profit of founding new colonies to idealists like Penn and Shaftesbury; but they eagerly welcomed the restored monarch after the unsettled conditions of 1659, and were prepared, even before he landed, to tell him "how the forraigne plantations may be made most useful to the Trade and Navigation of these Kingdomes." Of all the busy promoters whose private interests were, by some strange whim of Providence, in such happy accord with the nation's welfare and the theories of economists, none was more conspicuous than Martin Noel. He was a man of varied activities: a stockholder in the East India Company; a farmer of the inland post office and of the excise; a banker who made loans, and issued bills of exchange and letters of credit. His many ships traded in the West Indies, in New England and Virginia, and in the Mediterranean. During the wars of the Protectorate he was himself a commissioner of prize goods, issued letters of marque, and judged the prizes taken by his own vessels. A center of great interest was his place at the Old Jewry; the resort of ship captains, merchants, investors, contractors, officials of the Government. The capital for financing one of the Jamaica expeditions was raised there by Noel, who was rewarded by a grant of twenty thousand acres of sugar land after the conquest of the island. He had been intimate with Cromwell, and after the return of Charles won the reputation of being, in all affairs of trade and plantations, "the mainstay of the Government." It was through Martin Noel, and men of his kind, that the old colonial system began to be shaped to serve the ends of the moneyed and mercantile interests of England.

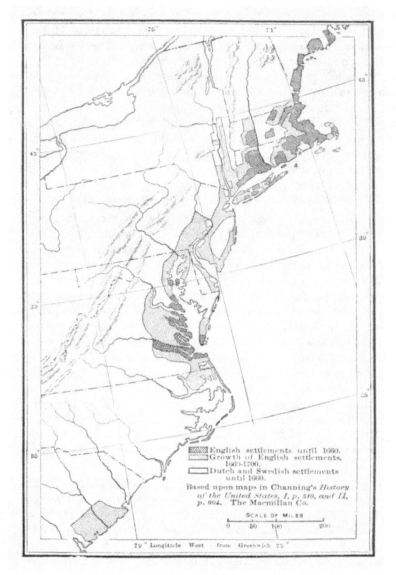

Areas settled by 1660, and between 1660 and 1700

Enterprising men like Noel were prosperous enough, but their extended vision enabled them to complain intelligently of the decay of trade. In the year 1660 exports made not more than a fourth part of the eight and a half millions of England's foreign commerce. Money was scarce, interest high, rents and prices low. No one doubted that the effective remedy for these ills lay in establishing a "favorable balance of trade." But in the path of this achievement stood the old rivals of England—Holland, Spain, and France. Imports from France overbalanced exports thither in the proportion of 2.6 to 1.6. Spain still worked the rich silver veins of the Andes, and the conquest of Jamaica had opened

English eyes to the high value of her West Indian possessions. Above all, the thrifty Dutch, intrenched in the East Indies and on the west coast of Africa, supplied Europe with the major part of Oriental products and denied England's right to share with them the honor and profit of importing slaves into Spanish America. To restore the balance of the French trade, and to contest with Holland and Spain for the lucrative commerce of the East and the West Indies was the underlying economic motive of the wars and diplomacy, as well as of the colonial policy of the Restoration period; it was for this that the Royal African and Hudson Bay Companies were organized; for this the Dutch and French wars were waged; for this regulations were enacted for trade and plantations. And to contemporaries the wisdom of such measures was evident in the result: at the close of the century, although imports remained approximately the same as in 1660, exports had reached the unprecedented figure of seven millions sterling.

In achieving this result, the plantations were expected to play an important part; and no one doubted that they had done so. During the decade after the Restoration, the commerce between England and her American possessions was about one tenth of her total foreign trade; in 1700 it was about one seventh. Imports from the colonies rose from £500,000 to more than £1,000,000, and exports to the colonies from £105,910 to £750,000. But the mere increase of trade was no perfect index of the importance of the plantations; for the colonial trade built up the merchant marine far more, in proportion to its volume, than any other. The American voyages were long; plantation commodities bulked large in proportion to their value; and whereas much of the commerce between England and Europe was carried in foreign ships, colonial trade was confined to British vessels. If, therefore, the merchant marine more than doubled during the Restoration, that happy result was thought to be largely due to the colonies. "The Plantacion trade is one of the greatest nurseries of the Shipping and Seamen of this Kingdome, and one of the greatest branches of its trade," said the customs commissioners in 1678; "the Plantacions, New Castle trade, and the fisheries, make 3/4 of all the seamen in ye Nation."

The colonies which enlisted the enthusiasm of the commissioners were the plantations proper. There were men, such as Charles Davenant, who thought New England might have its uses; but the high value of Maryland and Virginia, of Barbados and Jamaica, was obvious to all. Maryland and Virginia, it is true, were not quite ideal colonies, since it was found necessary, in their interest, to prohibit the raising of tobacco in England. But the sugar islands were without reproach. England was not now, as in the time of James I, thought to be overpopulated; and Barbados and Jamaica found favor, not only because their products were neither raised nor made in England, but because they could be exploited by slave labor. It was pointed out that happily "by taking off one useless person, for such generally go abroad [to the islands], we add Twenty Blacks to the Labour and Manufactures of the Nation." Negroes procured in Africa at slight cost might, indeed, be counted as commodities of export, while the island colonies cultivated precisely those commodities which England would otherwise have imported from foreign countries. And the statistics of the custom-house confirmed the theory of the pamphleteer; in 1697, seven eighths of all colonial commerce was with the tobacco and sugar plantations, and Jamaica alone offered a greater market than all the Northern and Middle colonies combined.

It was thus the West Indies which statesmen had chiefly in mind when they set about regulating trade and navigation to the end that "we may in every part be more sellers than buyers, and thereby the Coyne and present stocke of money be preserved and increased." Three acts of Parliament, embodying the ideas of London merchants interested in the tobacco and sugar plantations, formulated the principles of England's commercial code. The famous Navigation Act of 1660 confined colonial carrying trade wholly, and the foreign carrying trade mainly, to English and colonial shipping, and provided that certain colonial products—sugar, tobacco, cotton-wool, indigo, ginger, dyeing-woods; the so-called "enumerated" commodities—could be shipped only to England or to an English colony. In 1663 the Staple Act prohibited the importation into the colonies of any commodities raised or made in Europe,—with the exception of salt, of horses and provisions from Scotland and Ireland, of wine from the Madeiras and the Azores, and of commodities not allowed to be imported into England,—unless they were first landed in England. In order not to discriminate against English in favor of colonial consumers of colonial products, a third act was passed in 1673 providing that enumerated commodities, which paid a duty when shipped directly to England, should pay a duty when shipped from one colony to another. In 1705 rice, molasses, and naval stores were added to the list of enumerated commodities, and in 1733 prohibitive duties, never enforced, were laid upon rum, molasses, and sugar imported from foreign islands into the continental colonies. The purpose of these laws, and of the supplementary acts, of which more than half a hundred were passed between 1689 and 1765, was to foster the industries of the empire at the expense of foreign countries, and to develop colonial industry along lines that did not bring it into competition with English agriculture or manufactures.

Information gathered by the Privy Council committees, which the Stuarts appointed to coördinate the work of managing trade and the plantations, soon demonstrated that it was easier to make laws than it was to enforce them. Until the end of the century, illicit trade, inseparably connected with piracy, became increasingly flagrant in nearly every colony. West Indian buccaneers, lineal descendants of the Elizabethan "sea dogues," nesting at Jamaica under English sanction until after the peace with Spain in 1670, resorted to Charleston, New York, Providence, or Boston, and under licenses granted by royal governors joined hands with the colonial free-trader or East Indian "interlopers" to make the acts of trade a byword and a reproach. New England and Dutch merchants, "regarding neither the acts of trade nor the law of nature," carried provisions to Canada during the French wars. Tobacco was taken to Holland and Scotland, or smuggled from Maryland through Pennsylvania into the Northern colonies. Bolted flour and provisions were exchanged by New York traders in the Spanish islands for molasses and rum. European commodities and the spices and fabrics of the Orient, secured at trifling cost from pirates or "interlopers" in exchange for rum or Spanish pieces of eight, were carried in small boats up the innumerable estuaries that indent the coast from New England to Virginia. Indolent governors were often ignorant of the law; dishonest ones, willing for money down to wink at its violation; and even those, like Bellomont, who were honest and energetic, found themselves without the necessary machinery for its effective enforcement.

If the violation of the Trade Acts called loudly for a more direct supervision of the colonies, the growing menace of Canada enforced the same lesson. Under the imbecile Charles II, Spain was no longer, as in Elizabethan times, the first danger. Colbert's attention to colonial affairs, as well as Louis XIV's European ambitions, soon obscured the commercial rivalry of England and Holland, while the accession of William of Orange to the throne of the Stuarts, by pledging England to twenty years of war against the House of Bourbon, revealed the startling fact that it was New France rather than New Spain which threatened the security of British America. English settlements had not yet passed the Alleghany foothills before French missionaries and explorers had penetrated by the chain of lakes to the heart of the continent. Jean Nicolet as early as 1640, Radisson and Grosseilliers in 1660, were canoeing down the Wisconsin River toward the Mississippi; and in 1671, the year before Count Frontenac landed at Quebec to begin the regeneration of Canada, Saint-Lusson, with impressive ceremony in the presence of fourteen native tribes at Sault Ste. Marie, took possession of the great Northwest in the name of the Grand Monarch.

It was no mere spirit of adventure, or dream of limitless empire, that dispersed the French settlements over so wide an area. As Virginia was founded on tobacco, so was Canada on furs; and unless the Indians on the northern lakes could be induced to bring their furs down the St. Lawrence, Quebec might add luster to the crown of Louis, but it could not greatly increase the commercial strength of France. A firm alliance with the northern tribes was therefore the first object. It was for this that military posts were established on the waterways of the interior. And every stockaded fort was at once a trading camp and a mission house: merchants lured the Indian with brandy and firearms; civil officials and men at arms impressed him with the authority of the great king; Jesuit priests, strangely compounding true devotion and unscrupulous intrigue, learned the native languages, and with the magic of the crucifix and the *Te Deum* converted the spirit-fearing savages into loyal children of the Bishop of Rome. Canada, with its center at Quebec, and its outposts at Michilimackinac and Sault Ste. Marie, was little more than "a musket, a rosary, and a pack of beaver skins": not so much a colony, indeed, as a mesh of interlacing interests cunningly designed to convert fur into gold. And so long as the tribes of the northern lakes annually brought their rich freightage of mink and beaver to Fort Frontenac or Montreal, to be exchanged there for arms and brandy, beads, hatchets, bracelets, and gay-colored fabrics, gold was not lacking—for the pockets of clever merchant and corrupt official, if not always for the royal treasury of France.

"The colonies of foreign nations so long settled on the sea board," wrote the Intendant Talon in 1671, "are trembling with fright in view of what your Majesty has accomplished here in the last seven years." In fact, the thrifty and unadventurous farmers along the Atlantic were as yet only too indifferent to the importance of Canada; still less did they foresee the New France of which La Salle was at that moment dreaming. After a dozen years of heart-breaking discouragements, that somber idealist finally reached the Gulf of Mexico by way of the Mississippi. It was on the 9th of April, 1682, at the mouth of the Father of Waters, that he proclaimed the sovereignty of Louis XIV over "this country of Louisiana, from the mouth of the river St. Louis, otherwise called the Ohio, as also along the river Colbert, or Mississippi, and the rivers that discharge thereinto, from its source as far as its mouth at the sea." To make sure the title thus announced to the silent wilderness, a pillar bearing the arms of France was erected, and a lead plate buried in the sand. The inscription would scarcely have frightened away even a stray Englishman, had he chanced to see it; but when, in December of the same year, La Salle built his wooden fort on the rock of St. Louis, there began to emerge from the world of dreams to the world of realities the vision of a greater New France, held together by a chain of forts on all the inland waterways from the mouth of the St. Lawrence to the mouth of the Mississippi, and exploiting, through friendly alliance with the native tribes, the rich fur trade of the continent.

It was during the last decade of the Stuart régime, when the efficient committee known as the Lords of Trade had charge of colonial affairs, that the English Government first set seriously about the task of checking the growing power of France and of suppressing illicit trade. To aid the governors in enforcing the navigation laws, collectors and comptrollers of the customs had been established in nearly every colony by 1678; in 1688 William Dyre, responsible to the English customs commissioners, was appointed surveyor-general and placed at the head of the American service; and it was mainly on the ground of illegal trade that Massachusetts was made a crown colony in 1684. The doughty Colonel Dongan, who came out as Governor of New York in 1683, was one of the first to see the importance of Canada; and after 1685 he was supported by James in the attempt to divert the fur trade from Montreal to Albany by bringing the Iroquois Indians under English control. The scheme, which involved nothing less than the ruin of Canada, was by no means a visionary one. The Five Nations, lying south of the chain of lakes, could profit but little by the fur trade while it remained in French hands. But let Albany replace Montreal as the chief market, and they would become the indispensable middle carriers between the northern tribes and the English. And the northern tribes were themselves not ill-disposed to such a change. Undoubtedly the French had better manners than the English; undoubtedly French fire-water was of excellent flavor. But the traders whom Dongan sent to Michilimackinac proved beyond cavil that English goods were cheap; and so long as a beaver skin was the price of a debauch on French brandy, whereas a mink skin was sufficient to attain the same exaltation by means of English rum, the French control of the fur trade rested on a precarious basis. The chief obstacle to Dongan's scheme was the division of executive authority in the colonies, the apathy of colonial assemblies, and the lack of an adequate military force to protect the Iroquois from the enmity of the French. It was precisely to change these conditions, and to avoid the very evils which soon came to pass, that James II, who had at least the merit of an intelligent interest in the colonies, placed all New England under the single jurisdiction of Andros in 1686, and, in 1688, united New York and the Jerseys to New England.

The Revolution which drove James from the throne discredited his measures, but the twenty years of war with France which the Revolution brought in its train proved the wisdom of his policy. When Indian massacres inspired at Quebec made a desolate waste of the New England frontier, while Boston and New York merchants filled their pockets by supplying the enemy with munitions of war, the inadequacy of the colonial system for defense, as well as all the worst evils of illicit trade, stood clearly revealed. Until 1715, the Board of Trade, which William appointed in 1696, maintained the traditions, if it did not exhibit all the efficiency, of the old committee of the Lords of Trade. The Navigation Act of 1696, providing for nearly thirty officials at an annual cost of £1605, for the first time systematically extended the English customs service to the colonies. In the following year seven admiralty courts, subject to the Lords of the Admiralty, were erected in the continental colonies to try cases arising out of the violation of the Trade Acts, while special courts for dealing with piracy were established in 1700. But the customs and admiralty services, although directly responsible to the English Government, could never be fully effective unless they were vigorously supported by the colonial Governments. It was in order to make the enforcement of the commercial code more effective, as well as to secure better coöperation among the colonial Governments for military defense, that the Board of Trade repeatedly advised the recall of all the charters as a measure necessary above all others. The advice of the Board was followed only in part. The union of New England and New York was abandoned. Massachusetts received a new charter; Connecticut and Rhode Island retained their old ones; Penn's charter, annulled in 1692, was restored in 1694. But under the charter granted to Massachusetts in 1691 the governor was appointed by the Crown; New Jersey was made a royal province in 1702; and Maryland in 1691, although it was given back to the Baltimores in 1715. When the Peace of Utrecht was signed in 1713, the system devised by the Board of Trade for controlling the colonies thus lacked little of being completely established. The English customs and admiralty services had been fully extended to America; and while control of legislation was left mainly in the hands of assemblies elected in each colony, executive authority was entrusted to Crown officials in every colony except Pennsylvania, where the governor was appointed by the proprietor, and Rhode Island and Connecticut, where he was still elected by the people.

III

It is only by courtesy that these measures for confining the trade of the empire may be called a colonial system; and it would have been well if England, profiting by the experience of the French wars, had set seriously about the task of fashioning a method of government adapted to the political as well as the commercial needs of her New World possessions. But it was not to be. With the accession of George I, enthusiasm for plantation ventures declined; interest in the colonies, undiminished, indeed, was more than ever concentrated upon their commercial possibilities; and the constructive policy of the Stuarts gave way, in the phrase of Burke, to one of "salutary neglect." The neglect was, indeed, by no means complete. Information was assiduously gathered; many new laws were passed; the number of officials greatly increased, and governors more carefully instructed; colonial statutes, more consistently inspected, were more often annulled. Yet it is true that for three decades after the Peace of Utrecht no attempt was made to transform the commercial code into a colonial system. And even the commercial code was administered in "a gentlemanlike and easy-going fashion: little was embitered and nothing solved."

Of many circumstances which contributed to this result, the effect of the Revolution on English politics was fundamental. Kings who ruled by grace of a statute, instead of by divine right, inevitably lost administrative as well as legislative authority. Colonial policy was therefore no longer determined, as in Stuart times, by the king in council, but by the ministers; by ministers who might listen to the Board of Trade, but could not take advice unless it squared with the wishes of the Parliament that made them. When, in 1715, Secretary Stanhope appointed George Vaughan, an owner of sawmills in New Hampshire, to be lieutenant-governor of that province, the Board of Trade protested; and quoted, in support of its protest, the remarks of Bellomont about Mr. Partridge. "To set a carpenter to preserve woods," said Bellomont, "is like setting a wolf to guard sheep; I say, to preserve woods, for I take it to be the chiefest part of the business of a Lt. Governor of that province to preserve the woods for the king's use." The protest was ignored; and for thirty years, while the Board of Trade fell almost to the level of a joke, the colonies were managed by a Secretary of State who was likely to be less interested in preserving the woods for the king's use than in advancing the interests of the Whig oligarchy which governed England.

It could not well have been otherwise. The Whig oligarchy, having driven the Stuarts from the throne, was bound to identify the welfare of the empire with the maintenance of the House of Hanover. Convinced that so long as there was peace and plenty in the land Jacobite exiles would wait in vain for the day when the body of James II, lying unburied in the church of St. Jacques, might be restored to English soil, ministers labored to make the nation loyal by making it comfortable. It was therefore necessary to guard with jealousy the material interests of the inarticulate Tory squire, who still harbored a sullen loyalty to the Stuarts, as well as of the merchants and moneyed men whose fortunes were bound up with the Revolution settlement. And year by year the Parliamentary influence of the latter increased. Members of the South Sea and East India Companies had seats in the House of Commons; and the West India Islands, where, it was estimated in 1775, property to the value of £14,000,000 was "owned by persons who live in England," were in very truth represented there. William Beckford, who entered Parliament in 1747, possessed of a great fortune acquired in Jamaica sugar plantations, and soon to become all-powerful in "the City," was only the most famous of those who effectively voiced the demands of colonial landlords and London merchants. "Such men used in times past to come hat in hand," said Newcastle; "now the second word is, 'you shall hear of it in

73

another place.'" In fact, although ministers bowed to the king and spoke of His Majesty's Government, they knew well that the fortunes of the kingdom were in the hands of the big property interests that buttressed an unstable throne.

And these masters of England, never interested in the colonies apart from their commercial value, were less so than ever during this Indian summer of prosperous content. Rising prices made the era of, the first Georges a golden age of agriculture; while the effect of the French wars was to "exalt beyond measure the maritime and commercial supremacy of England." The Treaty of Meuthen facilitated the importation of cloth into Portugal and the flow of Brazilian bullion to London. Levantine trade began to open to England after the conquest of Gibraltar and Minorca. English merchants acquired special privileges at Cadiz by the Treaty of Utrecht; and the *Assiento* gave to the South Sea Company a monopoly of importing slaves into New Spain, and enabled it to secure, "by the ingenuity of British merchants," the greater part of the general commerce of the Spanish colonies. In 1710, the number of vessels clearing from English ports was 3550; it was 6614 in 1714; and during the same period the shipping of London increased from 806 to 1550. In 1758, imports from the continental colonies into England stood at £648,683, and from the West Indies at £1,834,036. "The colonies," said the elder Horace Walpole, "are the source of all our riches"; for it was the colonies, and above all the West Indies,—that subterranean channel by which the silks and teas from Vera Cruz, and Peruvian gold from Puerto Bello, found their way into England,—which alone "preserve the balance of trade in our favour."

If, as sometimes happened, powerful Parliamentary interests complained of conditions in the colonies, the Government was ready to comply with their demands. During the Walpole régime, the private smuggler in Spanish commerce, whether Englishman or New Englander, was suppressed in order that the South Sea Company might enjoy a monopoly of that profitable business. When Jamaica planters, unable to sell their sugar in Europe or Massachusetts in competition with the French islands, clamored for relief, the famous Molasses Act of 1733 was passed, laying prohibitive duties upon the importation of sugar, molasses, and rum into the continental colonies. And in 1750, at the behest of the woolen and iron interests, rapidly growing industries in New England and Pennsylvania were restricted in order that the English landowner and English woolen and iron manufacturers might find in America the markets which they were losing in Europe. But in general neither the landed nor the industrial interests pressed the Government to meddle with the plantations; and when no one complained, ministers of the temper of Walpole or Newcastle were not disposed to concern themselves with the reform of the colonial system, or to inquire too curiously into the honesty or the efficiency with which it was administered. According to their philosophy, it mattered little whether the Governor of Virginia was an able man, or whether he resided in London or Jamestown; what mattered was that Newcastle should succeed, by a judicious distribution of offices, in maintaining a Parliamentary majority for the party which guarded the liberties of England. It mattered little whether the admiralty courts fell under the control of the merchants and landowners who dominated colonial assemblies; what mattered was that the colonial merchant and landowner should be prosperous and maintain a safe credit balance with English merchants. And therefore let the governors be punctiliously instructed to perform their duties strictly; but let those be recalled who irritated the best people in the colonies by too officiously endeavoring to carry out their instructions. So long as the colonial planter was content and the Tory squire could not complain of high taxes or low rents, so long as merchants of standing in London or New York found business good, so long as the English manufacturer had ready markets and the trading companies distributed high dividends, it seemed folly indeed to attempt, with meticulous precision, to enforce the Trade Acts at every unregarded point, to construct ideal governments for communities that were every year richer than the last, or to provide at great expense for an adequate military defense against Canada when peace with France was the settled policy of England.

Unhappily for this policy of *quieta non movere*, peace with France came to an end after thirty years. And if since the Peace of Utrecht the English colonies had grown rich and populous, the French had strengthened their hold on all the strategic points of the interior from Quebec to New Orleans. The province of Louisiana, founded in 1699 by D'Iberville to forestall the English in occupying the mouth of the Mississippi, contained a population of more than ten thousand white settlers in 1745. The governor maintained friendly relations with the Choctaw Indians, and endeavored to alienate the Cherokees and the Creeks from the English alliance, and so to divert the rich peltry trade of the Southwest from Fort Moore and Charleston to New Orleans. Attached to Louisiana for administrative purposes were the small but thriving French settlements on the Mississippi, between the Illinois and the Ohio Rivers, centering about Forts Chartres, Cahokia, and Kaskaskia. Between Louisiana and Canada all the connecting waterways, save alone the upper Ohio, were guarded by military establishments and trading posts—on Green Bay, on the Wabash and Miami Rivers, at the southern end of Lake Michigan, at Detroit and Niagara. By discovery and occupation, the French claimed all the inland country; denied the right of Englishmen to settle or trade there; were prepared to defend it by force, and, in case of war, to release upon the unguarded English frontier from Maine to Virginia those savage tribes, whom legend credits with many noble virtues, but whom the colonists by bitter experience well knew to be cruel and treacherous and bestial beyond conception.

The possession of this hinterland was now, toward the middle of the century, become the vital issue; for the claims of France could not stay the populous English colonies from pushing their frontier across the mountains, or prevent skillful English traders from undermining the loyalty of her Indian allies. There were settlements in the southern up-country as far west as Fort Moore on the Savannah, as far as Camden and Charlottesburg, and beyond Hillsborough. The outpost of Virginia was at Wills Creek, within striking distance of the Ohio; the valleys of the Blue Ridge were filling with Scotch-Irish and Pennsylvania Dutch; while German and Dutch farmers of New York occupied both sides of the Mohawk nearly to its source. Oswego, long since established on Lake

Ontario, was abundantly justifying the ambitious scheme inaugurated sixty years earlier by Governor Dongan; for official corruption at Montreal had not made French goods cheaper since the days of Frontenac, and the northern Indians yearly resorted to Oswego to trade with the English. And every year unlicensed traders, such as Christopher Gist and William Trent, not to mention many "more abandoned wretches," hired men on the Pennsylvania or Virginia frontier and with goods on pack-horses crossed the Alleghanies to traffic among the western Indians. In 1749, Céloron de Bienville, sent by the Governor of Canada to take possession of the Ohio Valley, found English traders at Logstown and Scioto, and in nearly every village as far west as the Miami. This was the very year that John Hanbury, a London merchant, and some Virginia gentlemen, among whom were Lawrence and Augustine Washington, petitioned the Board of Trade for a grant of five hundred thousand acres of land on the upper Ohio. And the petition was granted, in order that the country might be more rapidly settled, and "to cultivate the friendship and carry on a more extensive commerce with the native Indians, and as a step towards checking the encroachments of the French."

Those who went into the back country received little assistance from Government, either English or colonial, in extending the frontier, and but little in defending it. Tide-water rice or tobacco planters, peaceful and gain-loving Quakers at Philadelphia, New York or Boston merchants trading in the West Indies, all untouched by Indian massacre and absorbed in local politics, begrudged money spent to protect a half-alien people, often without their jurisdiction. The English Government, for its part, had long observed the comfortable maxim that if her navy policed the sea, the colonists were bound to provide their own defense in time of peace. Money for Indian presents was regularly sent; garrisons maintained in Nova Scotia and in the West Indies; assistance sometimes given for forts on the exposed New York or Carolina frontier. But the expense was slight indeed: in 1783 the total amount appropriated for defending the continental colonies, exclusive of Nova Scotia and not counting money for Indian presents, was £10,000; in 1743, it was £25,000. And the war which opened in 1743 demonstrated that a government which neglected defense in time of peace could scarcely provide it in time of war. The New England frontier was once more devastated by pillage and massacre; and Philip Schuyler, to the high disgust of his Iroquois allies, was forced to abandon and burn Fort Saratoga for lack of supplies to maintain it. Yet New England farmers made possible the capture of Louisburg, and the colonies together raised nearly eight thousand troops to coöperate, in the conquest of Canada, with the fleet and army which the Duke of Newcastle promised but never sent. Massachusetts was, indeed, generously repaid for the heavy expense which she incurred; but two hundred and seventeen chests of Spanish dollars and one hundred barrels of copper coin, sufficient to restore her credit, were scarce full return for the restoration of Louisburg to France after the war was over.

With how much ease, during the six years that followed the Peace of Aix-la-Chapelle, might the English and colonial Governments have prevented the worst horrors of the French and Indian War! Deprived of her Indian allies, Canada would scarce have been a danger; and at no time were the Indians better disposed toward the English. "All I can say," Céloron de Bienville announced when he returned from the Ohio in 1750, "is that all the nations of these countries are very ill-disposed toward the French, and devoted to the English." And in the next year Père Piquet complained that Oswego "not only spoils our trade, but puts the English into communication with a vast number of our Indians far and near. It is true that they like French brandy better than English rum; but they prefer English goods to ours, and can buy for two beaver skins at Oswego a better silver bracelet than we sell at Niagara for ten." Strongly garrisoned forts at Albany, at Oswego, and on the Ohio would have transformed this friendly disposition into a firm alliance. But there was little loyalty in the red man's heart for an unmilitary people; and cheap goods, however they might win the Indian in time of peace, made but a silken cord to hold him in time of war. "We would have taken Crown Point, but you prevented us," said Chief Hendrick at the conference hastily summoned at Albany to prepare for defense on the eve of war. "Instead you burned your own fort at Saratoga and ran away from it. You have no fortifications, no, not even in this city. The French are men; they are fortifying everywhere. But you are all like women, bare and open, without fortifications." Not one representative of seven colonies had authority to reassure him. Sir William Johnson did, indeed, negotiate a treaty of alliance with the Iroquois and the western Indians; and the Virginia assembly, yielding at last to Governor Dinwiddie's insistent demands, appropriated some money for maintaining the wooden fort, well named Fort Necessity, which Colonel Washington had built on the Ohio. But it was too late. The French built a better fort at Duquesne; and they had scarcely defeated the Virginia colonel and destroyed his fort before the English traders were driven from the Indian villages, and no English flag was to be seen west of the mountains. It was the western tribes that brought Braddock's expedition to a disastrous end. While the Quakers at Philadelphia denounced the iniquity of war, these quondam allies of England ravaged the frontiers of Pennsylvania and Virginia, and the northern tribes that had gladly come to Oswego to trade in 1754, assisted Montcalm to capture and destroy it in 1756.

Reverses in America were but part of the multiplied disasters which befell English arms at the opening of the Seven Years' War. At the close of the year 1756, with Hanover threatened and Minorca taken, with the Bourbon arms victorious in India and the Bourbon fleet unchecked upon the sea, with a million and a half of colonists seemingly helpless before eighty thousand French in America, it was clear at last that ministers who employed organized corruption to buttress the throne, who rarely read the American dispatches, and were not quite sure where Nova Scotia was, had endangered that very peace and material prosperity with which they had been so long and so exclusively occupied. In this crisis many plans were forthcoming, at Albany and in London, for colonial union and imperial defense; plans doubtless excellent in themselves, but impracticable under the circumstances. They were therefore laid aside until the war should be over. A plan of attack, not of defense, was now the prime necessity. In face of this necessity, the Whig oligarchy, abdicated its high function of "muddling through" the business of government, while "an afflicted despairing nation turned to a private gentleman of slender fortune, wanting the parade of birth and title, as the only saviour of England." "I know," said William Pitt, "that I can save England, and that nobody else can."

A most galling boast for both your houses of Pelham and Yorke, but a true one. Within three years the nation was raised from the depths of despair to the high level of its great leader's assured and arrogant confidence. It was not by colonial systems that Pitt brought victory, but by organizing efficiency in place of corruption and by inspiring many men to heroic effort. Wisdom born of sympathy and common sense soon accomplished in America what neither the bullying of Loudoun nor the New Englander's hatred of the French could effect. In 1756 no more than five thousand troops were raised in all New England and New York. Governor Pownall was haggling as usual with his assembly over a levy of two thousand men, when there arrived in Boston Pitt's order that henceforth colonial officers should take rank with regulars, according to the date of their commissions. The simple order was worth more than many plans of union. The very next morning, when the dispatch was read out, the Old Bay assembly voted the entire seven thousand men originally asked of the Northern colonies; and during the year 1758 nearly twenty-five thousand provincial troops were raised for the war. With this support, the English army and fleet, for the first time ably led and efficiently directed, soon destroyed the power of France in Canada: Louisburg was once more captured; Crown Point and Niagara were taken; Oswego was rebuilt; while the French, deserted by their savage allies as soon as the English won victories, destroyed their own fort at Duquesne; and at last the intrepid General Wolfe, fortunately aided by a strange combination of accidents, scaled the Heights of Quebec and defeated the army of Montcalm on the Plains of Abraham.

When the war was over and Canada no longer the menace it had been, men without imagination, turning again to the schemes which had been laid aside in 1756, began to devise measures for a closer supervision of the "plantations," and for raising "a revenue in Your Majesty's dominions in America for defraying the expenses of defending, protecting, and securing the same." They were not aware that since the recall of the Massachusetts charter the colonies had become something more than plantations, or that there was arising on the continent of America a people whose interests were national rather than imperial, and whose ideals of well-being transcended the dead level of material ambitions.

BIBLIOGRAPHICAL NOTE

For the settlement of the Southern and Middle colonies in this period, see Channing *History of the United States*, II, chaps. II, IV; Andrews, *Colonial Self-Government*, chaps. VI-VII, IX, XI. The best discussion of the reasons for a revival of interest in the colonies during the Restoration, and of the establishment and practical application of a system of colonial administration and control, is Beer's *The Old Colonial System*, Part I, 2 vols. See particularly, I, chaps, I-IV. For this subject, see also, Channing, II, chaps. I, VIII; Andrews, *Colonial Self-Government*, chaps. I-II; Andrews, *British Committees, Commissions, and Councils of Trade and Plantations* (Johns Hopkins Studies,

1908); and Andrews, *The Colonial Period*, chap. V. For the relations between England and her colonies in the first half of the eighteenth century, see Dickerson, *American Colonial Government* (Cleveland, 1912); Andrews, *The Colonial Period*, chaps. VI, VII; Greene, *Provincial America*, chaps. II-IV, XI; and Beer, *British Colonial Policy*, chap. I. The importance of the West Indies in determining the policy of Walpole is brought out by Temperley, *American Historical Association Reports*, 1911, vol. I, p. 231. For the rise of New France and the conflict of France and England in America, see Fiske, *New France and New England*, chaps, I-II, IV, VIII-X; Thwaites, *France in America*, chaps. I, IV, VI, VIII; Channing, II, chaps. V, XVIII-XIX. The most fascinating as well as the fullest treatment of this subject is contained in the works of Francis Parkman. His *Count Frontenac and New France under Louis XIV; Half Century of Conflict*, 2 vols., and *Montcalm and Wolfe*, 2 vols., make a fairly continuous history of the subject from 1672 to 1763.

CHAPTER V

THE AMERICAN PEOPLE IN THE EIGHTEENTH CENTURY

America is formed for happiness but not for empire,
Richard Burnaby.

At length one mentioned me, with the observation that I was merely an honest man, and of no sect at all, which prevailed with them to chuse me.
Benjamin Franklin.

I

All accounts agree in celebrating the marvelous growth of the continental colonies in the eighteenth century. When the Massachusetts charter was recalled they were in fact British "plantations"; weak and scattered coast settlements, hemmed in by hostile Indians, separated from each other by long stretches of wilderness; without the inclination or the opportunity for intercourse, they struggled in isolation, often for bare existence. At the time of the passage of the Stamp Act they were wealthy and stable communities, whose thrifty and venturesome people had long since joined colony to colony all along the coast, and were already pushing across the mountains to occupy the great interior valleys. And with rapid material development there had come a confident and aggressive spirit, a proud and intractable temper, a certain self-righteous sense of separation from the Old World and its traditions. The very rivalries between colony and colony were the result of close contact and daily intercourse, their very jealousies born of interrelated interests and the recognition of a common destiny.

In 1689 not more than 80,000 people lived in New England, a trifle more in the Southern, and half as many in the Middle colonies. Seventy years later, when all New France could not boast more than 80,000 people of European birth or descent, New England alone had a population of 473,000, the Middle Colonies about 405,000, and the plantations south, of Delaware 417,000, not including

300,000 negro slaves. Within three quarters of a century the people of the continental colonies had increased nearly eightfold—from 200,000 in 1689, to 1,500,000 in 1760. And material prosperity had kept pace with the increase in population; so that there was some truth, even if some exaggeration, in the statement of Peter Kalm that "the English colonies in this part of the world have increased so much in their numbers of inhabitants, and in their riches, that they almost vie with Old England."

Of this rapid growth the colonists were well aware. They took to themselves full credit, as their descendants have done ever since, for having transformed a wilderness into a land of peace and plenty. With Richard Burnaby they could quite agree that such a town as Philadelphia, planted scarce eighty years, must be the "object of every one's wonder and admiration." It was this sense of unparalleled achievement that gave courageous conviction to the steady assertion of colonial rights. And the form of government in the provinces was well suited to secure for the colonists that independence which they claimed as a birthright, and the practical achievement of which is the cardinal political fact of the century. For it was no part of British policy to burden the English exchequer with the maintenance of the colonial establishments. The normal province was thought to be one in which legislation was entrusted mainly to local assemblies elected by the colonists, while executive and administrative authority rested mainly with a governor and council responsible to the king. At the opening of the eighteenth century, colonial governments mostly conformed to this model: in each colony the owners of property regularly elected an assembly which levied taxes and made laws; in each colony, except in Rhode Island and Connecticut, the governor, and usually the council as well, were appointed by the Crown.

With authority thus divided, conflict was sure to arise. In theory, the interests of colony and Crown may have been identical; in fact the assemblies looked at the affairs of the colony from the point of view of immediate local needs, while the governor was bound by his instructions to regard his province as but one of many whose special interests must be subordinated to the welfare of the whole empire. Of the assemblies' many advantages in this perennial conflict, control of the purse was the chief. "The governor," says a contemporary, "has two masters; one who gives him his commission, and one who gives him his pay." It required no little courage, and was likely to prove useless in the end, to ignore the latter master in obedience to the former. Placemen were little inclined to irritate those who paid them and were on the spot to watch their every move; while even the ablest governors often found themselves deserted by the Crown whose interests they attempted to defend. Before the middle of the century ministers were generally indifferent to the constitutional tendencies in the colonies; repeated recommendations of the Board of Trade for an independent civil list went unheeded, and governors, such as Spotswood, who stirred up trouble by endeavoring to carry out their instructions, were likely to be replaced by others whose adroit concessions to the assemblies created the illusion of a successful administration.

The concrete disputes in which the persistent opposition of governor and assembly found expression were many—quit-rents in Maryland, control of the judges in New York, taxation of proprietor's estates in Pennsylvania, and everywhere questions growing out of the problem of defense and the demand for paper money. Instructed in English precedent, the assemblies knew well how to condition the grant of salary or necessary revenue upon the governor's surrender to their demands. But more insidious and far-reaching in its constitutional effects was the practice by which the governor's executive and administrative functions were restricted. Money bills, even when unconnected with special riders, were often made minutely specific, both in respect to the purposes for which the money was to be used, and in respect to the officials by whom it was to be expended. Even salaries in the army were sometimes granted by individual appropriation. In many colonies, and notably in New York, it was by the constant and excessive use of specific appropriations that the governors were reduced to the level of executive figureheads—mere agents of the colonial assembly rather than representatives of the Crown exercising wise and effective administrative discretion. This process was especially rapid during the French wars, when the assemblies were enabled to exact tremendous concessions in return for indispensable aid against the common enemy. "The New York Assembly," said Peter Kalm about 1750, "may be looked upon as a Parliament or Diet in miniature. Everything relating to the good of the province is here debated." In 1763 he might have said the same, not of New York alone, but of Massachusetts and Pennsylvania, Maryland, and Virginia. And the governors of these provinces could have told him, as they repeatedly told the Board of Trade, that not only was everything debated there, but there everything was finally decided.

The assemblies, which had thus so largely taken to themselves the functions of government, claimed to declare the rights and defend the interests of the people. But in fact they represented their colonies very much as Parliament represented England. In every colony a property test restricted the number of those who had a voice in the elections; while political methods and the traditions of society united to place effective control in the hands of the eminent few. No secret ballot or Australian system guarded the independence of the voter. It was not an age in which every individual was supposed to count for one and none for more than one. The rigid maintenance of class distinctions, even in New England, where students in Harvard College were seated according to social rank and John Adams was but fourteenth in a class of twenty-four, made it presumptuous for the ordinary man to dispute the opinion of his betters or contest their right to leadership: to look up to his superiors and take his cue from them was regarded as the sufficient exercise of political liberty. The times were thought to be out of joint when effective control of colonial politics rested not with a few men who, through wealth or social standing, through official position, through well-considered marriage connections, had built up the rival or consolidated "interests" which played, each on its little stage, the part of Bedford or Pelham or Yorke in Old England.

The foundation of this miniature aristocracy was wealth; wealth acquired in the South mainly from the great plantations, in the North mainly from commerce. In South Carolina the unhealthful swamp lands, driving the planters

81

to the coast during most of the year, made Charleston one of the first commercial centers of America. Three hundred and sixty vessels cleared from that port in 1764. Manigault and Mazyck, Laurens and Rutledge, were therefore merchants of note as well as planters, exporting provisions to the West Indies, the staples rice and indigo to England or to the Continent south of Finisterre, and bringing back slaves and English manufactures. In Virginia and Maryland, where there were no cities of importance, the planters turned all their profits into slaves and land. The second William Byrd, inheriting 26,000 acres, left to his son 179,000 acres of the best land in Virginia, and the right to represent his county in the assembly. All the great planters, Ludlow and Carter, Randolph, Fairfax and Blair, lived on their estates, and from their private wharves exported the tobacco which English commission merchants sold in London, and for which they sent in return such English commodities of all kinds as the planter might order. The great estates along the Hudson, owned by men like Van Rensselaer, a descendant of the old Dutch patroon, or Phillipse and Courtland and Livingston, who had profited by the lavish grants of early English governors, rivaled in extent the plantations of Virginia; and like the planters of South Carolina their owners were often engaged in commerce, and were connected, through business or marriage, with the wealthy merchant families of New York City—the Van Dams, Crugers, Waltons, and Ludlows.

Elsewhere in America there were not, as in these provinces, great estates ranging from two hundred thousand to more than a million acres. But the thrifty Quakers of eastern Pennsylvania, engaging in less extensive enterprises, were less often in debt than the planters of the South, and no less shrewd at a bargain than the Dutch merchants of New York. Possessed of the best land in the province, or engaged at Philadelphia in the export of provisions to the West Indies, they built up many respectable estates among them, and by effective organization the leaders of the sect controlled the colony for many decades in the interest of a Quaker-merchant aristocracy inhabiting the three eastern counties of the province. And even in New England material interests were transforming the structure of society. Slave-owning planters of Newport now dominated the little colony which Roger Williams had established as an experiment in democracy and soul liberty. Boston shared with New York and Philadelphia the export of provisions with which the farms of the Middle and Northern colonies supplied the West Indies. It was the chief center of the New England fisheries. Shipbuilding was there, as at Newport, a great industry; and there, as at Newport, rum was extensively distilled from molasses procured in the sugar islands. The vessels of Boston and Newport merchants, loaded with rum and fish and tropical products, traded in many European ports, in the Azores, or on the African coast, returning with wine and slaves and every kind of English manufacture. In this material atmosphere the old Puritan spirit was being strangely subdued to the stuff it worked in. Wealth and shrewdness were more effective than orthodoxy in achieving social and political eminence. A few names familiar to the seventeenth century are still to be met with in high places—Sewall, Dudley, Quincy, Hutchinson; but in the middle of the eighteenth century the names of repute in the Old Bay colony are mostly new—

Oliver, Bowdoin, Boylston, Cooper, Phillips, Cushing, Thatcher; names rescued from obscurity by men who had won distinction in the pulpit or at the bar, or by men who had made money in trade, and whose descendants, marrying with the old clerical or official families, had pushed their way, in the second or third generation, into the social and political aristocracy of the province.

Such were the "men of considerable estates" in whose hands the English Government was generally well content to leave the control of colonial politics; and as they were the men who profited most by the connection with England, they were the men whose outlook upon the world was least provincial and most European. Planters and merchants of the South, exporting their staples directly to England, were in constant communication with their London agents. Business or politics had taken many of them more than once across the ocean. Not a few had been sent in their youth to be educated in England; and had resided there for some years, forming acquaintance with prominent English families, listening to debates in the Commons or to arguments in the courts of law, diverting themselves in theaters and coffee-houses, acquiring the latest modes and mannerisms, moulding themselves upon some favorite model of a city magnate or country gentleman. In the Northern colonies, trade relations with England were less direct. Business rarely called the merchant to Europe; and Yale or Harvard was regarded as a satisfactory substitute for Oxford or Cambridge. Yet the merchants of Boston and New York had their agents in many European ports; kept informed of conditions of trade and shipping throughout the world; and eagerly scanned the foreign gazettes which recounted the political and social happenings of Old England. In North and South, the well-to-do, as they were able, built and furnished their houses upon English models, and were not content with modes of dress which were known, twelve months late, not to be the fashion abroad. Especially fortunate were those whose wealth was dignified by distinction of birth, the walls of whose houses were hung with oil portraits of eminent ancestors.

And the genuine colonial aristocrat, such as Colonel Byrd or Governor Thomas Hutchinson, was proud to have it thought that his mind as well as his house was furnished after the best English fashion. Even more than others, those who were condemned to be provincials of the province consciously endeavored, to avoid provincialism of the spirit; to be mistaken in London for an English gentleman of parts was a much-sought compensation for being, at Williamsburg or Boston, no more than the first gentleman of America. In the middle of the eighteenth century, eccentricity was not yet a mark of genius; and the "best people in the colonies" learned from English authors what high intellectual merit there was in being close to the center. "Your authors know but little of the fame they have on this side of the ocean," Franklin assured William Strahan when he wrote to order six sets of a new edition of Pope's works. The four thousand volumes at Westover, or the books in Governor Hutchinson's Boston house, would have given any cultivated Englishman a reputation for good taste and discriminating judgment. Colonel Byrd could as readily as Voltaire detect in the fantastic beliefs of an American savage "the three great articles of Natural Religion." We find the youthful Adams, who read Bolingbroke for his style and laboriously copied out Berkeley and Tillotson, entering the lists of "moderns" to defend the advantages of eighteenth-century Boston against those of Rome in the age of Tully, renouncing, with the assurance of Locke, and with some of his phrases, the outworn fallacy of innate ideas, and naïvely confiding to his journal, after the manner of Diderot, that a man born blind would have never a notion of color. Franklin was only the most distinguished of those who read with pleasure the Queen Anne poets and essayists, who learned in Tillotson that theology might be compatible with reason and common sense, or in Shaftesbury that an enlightened free-thinker might still be a gentleman and a man of virtue. Among the cultivated and the well-bred it was no more than good form to open the mind to all the tolerant liberalisms of the age; and no one in the colonies lost caste who endeavored, in the manner if not in the substance of his thinking, to achieve the polished urbanity of those Englishmen who made a point of being scholars without a touch of pedantry, and men of virtue without the taint of prejudice.

Yet few of these emancipated citizens of the world had permitted the dissolvent philosophy of the century to enter the very pith and fiber of their mental quality. For the rich and the well-born it was rather an imported fashion, an attractive drapery laid over the surface of minds that were conventional down to the ground, the modish mental recreation of men who lived by custom and guided their steps in the well-worn paths of precedent. In America, as in England, as in France, itself, the formulæ of radicalism were well pronounced by many whose hearts grew faint at the first rude contact with the thing itself. And of all the phrases of that age, the ones best suited to the temper and purposes of the colonial aristocracies, and understood by them with reservations the most characteristically English, were those employed by Locke to justify the natural right of Englishmen to become free while remaining unequal. The colonials of substantial estates, long occupied in their assemblies in resisting the governor's authority, thought of themselves often enough as but rehearsing the traditional conflict between Crown and Parliament. Like their prototypes they identified the rights of property with natural right, and translated political liberty in terms of prescriptive privilege. The rights of man and the rights of Englishmen were thus thought to be synonymous terms: a happy confusion by which it was possible for them to defend liberty against the encroachments of their equals in England, without sharing it with their inferiors in the colonies.

II

"My ancestors," says Devereaux Jarrett, who was born on a small plantation in New Kent County, Virginia, about 1733, "had the character of honesty and industry, by which they lived in credit among their neighbors, free from real want, and above the frowns of the world. This was also the habit in which my parents were. They always had plenty of plain food and raiment, suitable to their humble station. We made no use of tea or coffee; meat, bread, and milk was the ordinary food of all my acquaintance. I suppose the richer sort might make use of those and other luxuries, but to such people we had no access. We were accustomed to look upon what were called *gentle folks* as beings of a superior order. For my part, I was quite shy of them, and kept off at a humble distance. A periwig in those days, was a distinguishing badge of gentle folk. Such ideas of the difference between gentle and simple, were, I believe, universal among all my rank and age."

The distinction between gentle and simple was doubtless less absolute than the disillusioned Jarrett represents it to have been. Even in the South there were many gradations of wealth, and it was no uncommon thing for a man to rise, as Jarrett did himself, from mean birth to a considerable eminence. Yet in none of the colonies was the distinction altogether unreal. The mass of the voters,— small freehold farmers in the country and "freemen" in some of the towns,— holding themselves superior to the unfranchised, yet not claiming equality with the favored few; the tenant farmer or small shopkeeper, deferring to the freeholder and the freeman, but aware that fortune had placed him above the artisan and day laborer; the artisan and the day laborer, proud that none could call them "servant":—these were the simple folk who in all the colonies made the great majority of free citizens. Chiefly occupied with earning daily bread by the labor of their hands, many were content to escape the debtor's prison, the best well satisfied with a modest competence. They heard of countries beyond sea, but their outlook was bounded by the parish. The provincialism of their minds was not dispelled by communion with the classics of all ages, and no cheap magazine or popular novel came to dull the edge of native shrewdness or curiosity. They read not at all, or they read the Bible, the *Paradise Lost* or the *Pilgrim's Progress*, or some chance book of sermons or of theology, or book of English ballads. Periwigs and gold braid were not for them, nor was it any part of their ambition to enter the charmed circle of polite society, to associate on terms of equality with the "best people" in the colony.

Yet with whatever semblance the older settlements might take on the character of European civilization, America was bound to be the land of opportunity so long as there was abundance of free land to entice the ambitious and the dispossessed. Early in the century, as good land became scarce in the older towns of New England, and proprietors began to deny the commons to the landless, venturesome and discontented men, accepting the challenge of a savage-infested wilderness, moved northward along the rivers into Maine and New Hampshire, or beyond the original Connecticut settlements into the valley of the Housatonic. Here land was less often than formerly disposed of to groups of proprietors intent to maintain the traditions of town and church; acquired by the older towns or by land agents, it was more often sold to companies or to individuals for the profit it would bring. The famous New Hampshire grants, one hundred and thirty townships in the present State of Vermont, fell mainly to speculators who sold to the highest bidder, covenanted and uncovenanted alike, among the throng of home-seekers who pushed into this western country in the seventh decade of the century. Long before the Revolution opened, there thus existed in New England a fringe of pioneer settlements—such as Vassalboro and Durham on the Androscoggin and the Kennebec, Concord and Hinsdale on the Merrimac and the Connecticut, Pittsfield and Great Barrington on the Housatonic—which formed a newer New England, less lettered and scriptural than the old, where class distinctions were little known, where contact with the Indian and the wilderness had added a secular ruthlessness and ingenuity to the harsh Puritan temper, and where the individual, freed from an effective "village moral police," learned in the rough school of nature a new kind of conformity unknown to the ancient Hebrew code.

In the Middle and Southern colonies, even more than in New England, expansion of population into the interior was a notable feature of the eighteenth century. In 1700 the estate of William Byrd at the James River Falls was on the Indian frontier; North Carolina was unoccupied south of Albemarle Sound or west of the Nottaway River; there were few settlers in South Carolina north of the Santee, or south or west of it except the Charleston planters who had appropriated all the land within sixty miles of the coast and within twenty of every navigable river. Sixty years later the unoccupied coast regions were settled, and the surplus population of Virginia and Maryland, excluded from the tide-water by the engrossers of great estates, or oppressed by its restricted social conditions, had occupied the cheap lands of eastern North Carolina, or, following the James and the Rappahannock, had settled in the up-country between the "Fall Line" and the Blue Ridge. Cattle-raisers, learning from Indian traders of the fertile interior, followed the trails with their "cowpens," which in turn gave place to permanent farms. In this back country, the great plantation was not often found, and slavery played little part. There were few superiors where farms were comparatively small, and where most men worked with their hands and consumed provisions raised by their own labor. Of those who came from the older settlements to occupy the up-country, many were "such as have been transported hither as servants, and being out of their time ... settle themselves where land is to be taken up that will produce the necessities of life with little labor." William Byrd described with engaging wit the ne'er-do-wells who maintained a precarious existence below the Dividing Line; and Governor Spotswood deplored the shiftless servants who lived on the Virginia frontier. Yet we may suppose that freedom often transformed the idle bondsman into an industrious freeholder. Nor were all the settlers of the Virginia back country emancipated servants. In 1732 Peter Jefferson patented a thousand acres at the foot of the Blue Ridge Mountains. It was in this frontier community above the Fall Line that Patrick Henry and Thomas Jefferson were born; here they grew to manhood; here they were inspired with those ideals of society so inimical alike to the imperial designs of the British Government and to the complacent pretensions of the slave-owning aristocracies of the tide-water.

Yet the first distinctive American frontier was not created alone by the movement of population westward from the older settlements; like every successive frontier in our history, it became the mecca of emigrants from British and continental lands. Before 1700, exiled Huguenots and refugees from the Palatinate began to seek the New World; and during the eighteenth century men of non-English stock poured by the thousands into the up-country of Pennsylvania and of the South. In 1700 the foreign population in the colonies was slight; in 1775 it is estimated that 225,000 Germans and 385,000 Scotch-Irish, together nearly one fifth of the entire population, lived within the provinces that won independence. Persecution and the ravages of war, taxes that were heavy at any time and intolerable in time of famine, were among the causes that disposed many thousands of Protestant families from Ulster, and from the thickly populated districts of Switzerland and the Rhine country, to seek new homes in a land of better promise. To cross the ocean was no slight undertaking for unlettered and home-keeping people. But since the founding of Pennsylvania knowledge of America had spread among the peasants of Germany, and there was no lack of "Neulanders"—the emigrant agents of that day—who described the New World in glowing terms, and stood ready for a consideration to carry any who wished to be transported to its shores. And the way was facilitated by the English and colonial Governments: to forestall the French in settling the interior, secure the trade of the Indians in time of peace, and erect a barrier against them in time of war, foreigners were accorded naturalization, land was offered on easy terms, and toleration granted to all Protestant sects.

Foreigners were not attracted to New England, where the Puritans scrutinized all newcomers with a jealous eye; while New York was avoided on account of the unhappy experience of Governor Hunter's Palatines and the refusal of the great landowners along the Hudson to grant freehold title. Most of the Germans, seeking homes in the best advertised and most German of all the colonies, landed at the port of Philadelphia. Germantown had been founded by Francis Daniel Pastorius in 1683, but it was not until forty years later, after the devastating wars of the Spanish Succession, that his countrymen occupied in force the neighboring counties of Lancaster, Montgomery, and Bucks, pushed up into Lehigh and Northampton, and across the Susquehanna into Cumberland and Adams. Much to their surprise, doubtless, for it was scarcely the business of the emigrant agent to inform them, they learned that land in this German mecca sold for from £10 to £15 per hundred acres, and bore a quit-rent of one halfpenny. Many occupied the land as squatters, and it is estimated that 400,000 acres were settled without title between 1732 and 1740. But the newcomers or their children soon learned of better opportunities to the south, where Maryland land sold for from £2 to £5 per hundred acres, and the up-country forestallers, such as Carter and Beverley, under-sold the Pennsylvania land office in order to attract settlers. As early as 1726 the stream of German migration began, therefore, to move along the mountain slopes to the south and west. During the middle decades of the century, they occupied in increasing numbers the Piedmont of Virginia, crept southward along the west side of the Blue Ridge in the Shenandoah Valley, and out into the up-country of the Carolinas west of the great Pine Barrens.

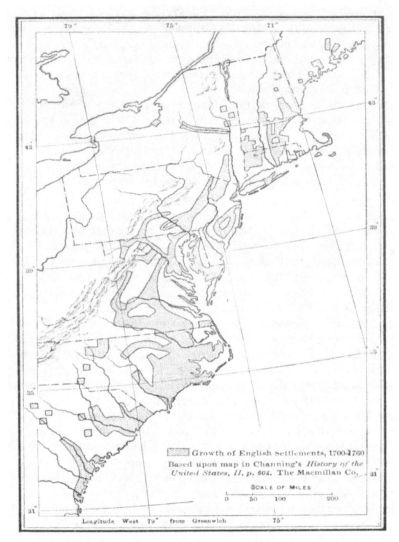

Growth of English Settlements, 1700-1760

At the same time as the Germans, and in even greater numbers, came the Scotch and Scotch-Irish, mostly disappointed settlers in Ulster who found land titles insecure there and the promise of religious liberty unfulfilled. A few, not easily discouraged, came to the Berkshires and the New Hampshire hills; more occupied the Mohawk and Cherry Valleys of New York; the great majority, like the Germans, settled in Pennsylvania and the up-country of the South. In Pennsylvania, they went for the most part beyond the German frontier, occupying the country from Lancaster to Bedford, the Juniata Valley and the Redstone country, and in the decades before the Revolution, attracted by free lands west of the Alleghanies, as far as Pittsburg on the upper Ohio. Like the Germans they pushed south into the Piedmont of Virginia, and along the

88

Alleghany slope of the Shenandoah, and into the Southern up-country as far as the Savannah River. Sometimes mixing with the Germans, the main body of the Scotch-Irish was everywhere farther west. Too martial to fear the Indians, and too aggressive to live at peace with them, they were the true borderers of the century, the frontier of the frontier, forming, from Londonderry in New England to the Savannah, an outer bulwark, behind which the older settlements, and even the peace-loving Germans themselves, rested in some measure of security.

The German or Scotch-Irish immigrant was doubtless grateful to the Government which offered him a refuge; but in the breast of neither was there any sentimental loyalty to King George, or much sympathy with the traditions of English society. Whether Mennonite or Moravian, German Lutheran or Scotch Presbyterian, they were men whose manner of life disposed them to an instinctive belief in equality of condition, whose religion confirmed them in a democratic habit of mind. That every man should labor as he was able; that no man should live by another's toil or waste in luxurious living the hard-earned fruits of industry; that all should live upright lives, eschewing the vanities of the world, and worshiping God, neither with images nor vestments nor Romish ritual, but in spirit and in truth:—these were the ideals which the foreign Protestants brought as a heritage from Wittenberg and Geneva to their new home in America. And if we may accept the impressions of an English observer, life in the Shenandoah Valley was in happy accord, in the middle of the century, with the arcadian simplicity of these ideals. "I could not but reflect with pleasure on the situation of these people," says Richard Burnaby. "Far from the bustle of the world, they live in the most delightful climate, and the richest soil imaginable; they are everywhere surrounded with the most beautiful prospects and sylvan scenes; ... they ... live in perfect liberty; they are ignorant of want, and acquainted with but few vices. Their inexperience of the elegancies of life precludes any regret that they possess not the means of enjoying them; but they possess what many persons would give half their dominions for, health, content, and tranquillity of mind."

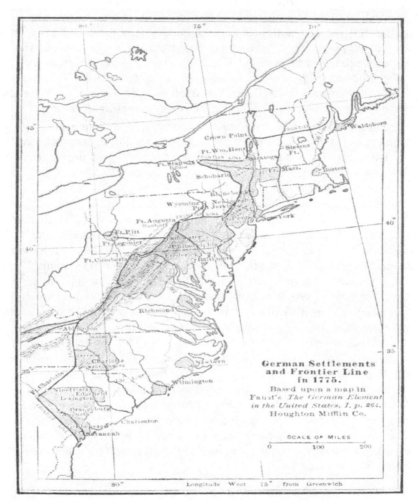

Area of German Settlements and Frontier Line in 1775

The description does not lack truth, but perhaps it somewhat smacks of fashionable eighteenth-century philosophy. And assuredly no region on the frontier was more favored than the famous Shenandoah Valley. Little question that conditions were less idyllic in other places. Missionaries who preached the Great Awakening in western Pennsylvania and in the Southern back country were often enough appalled by evidence of ignorance and low morals. And on the far outer frontier at White Woman's Creek, Mary Harris, still recalling after forty years' exile that "they used to be very religious in New England," told Christopher Gist in 1751 that "she wondered how white men could be so wicked as she had seen them in these woods." Neither the lyric phrase of Burnaby nor the harsh verdict of Mary Harris fitly describes those interior communities that stretched from Maine to Georgia. But there, as elsewhere, doubtless, the practice of men's lives, even among the frontier Puritans of New England, or the German

90

Protestants and Scotch Presbyterians of the Middle and Southern colonies, often fell short of their best ideals. Leaving the sheltered existence of long-settled communities, set down on a dangerous Indian frontier or at best in a virgin country, where customary restraints were relaxed, where churches were few and schools often unknown, where action more readily followed hard on desire and men's will made all the majesty of the law, the aggressive primary instincts had freer play, and society could not but take on a strain of the primitive. Even more than the original colonists, these dwellers on the second frontier caught something of the wild freedom of the wilderness, something of the ruthlessness of nature, something also of its self-sufficiency, something of its somber and emotional influence.

Between this primitive agricultural democracy of the interior and the commercial and landed aristocracy of the coast, separated geographically and differing widely in interests and ideals, conflict was inevitable. When, in 1780, Thomas Jefferson said that "19,000 men below the Falls give law to more than 30,000 living in other parts of the state," he was proclaiming that opposition between the older and the newer America which found expression in provincial politics from the middle of the eighteenth century, which made a part of the Revolution, and which in every period since has been so decisive a feature of our history. In the eighteenth century the frontier was the home of a primitive radicalism. Where offenses were elemental and easily detected, legal technicalities and the chicanery of courts seemed but devices for the support of idle lawyers; where debtors were most numerous and specie most scarce, few could understand why paper money would not prove a panacea for poverty; where every man earned his own bread and where submission to the inevitable was the only kind of conformity that was deemed essential, slavery and a state church were thought to be but the bulwark of class privilege and the tyranny of kings. After the French wars the interior communities of the Middle and Southern colonies, finding themselves unfairly represented in the assemblies, were first made aware that their interests were little likely to be seriously regarded either by the king's ministers or the merchants and landlords who shaped legislation at Williamsburg, Philadelphia, or New York. For defending the border in the desolating war that drove the French out of America, it now seemed that they were to be rewarded by land laws made for the rich, an administration of justice burdensome for sparsely settled communities, a money system that penalized them for being debtors, or taxes levied for the support of a church which they never entered. And so, before the Revolution opened, the Western imagination had conjured up the specter of a corrupt and effete "East": land of money-changers and self-styled aristocrats and a pliant clergy, the haunt of lawyers and hangers-on, proper dwelling-place of "servants" and the beaten slave: a land of cities, scorning the provincial West, and bent on exploiting its laborious and upright people. And who could doubt that men who bought their clothes in London would readily crook the knee to kings? Who could question that special privilege in the colonies was fostered by the laws of trade, or that aristocracy in America was the reward of submission to England?

III

91

The appearance before the Revolution of class and sectional conflict within the colonies was no more incompatible then than it has been since with a growing sense of solidarity against the outside world. And in developing this sense of Americanism, this national consciousness, the frontier was itself an important influence. Physiographically separated from the coast region, untouched by its social traditions, often hostile to its political activities, the people of the back country had but little of that pride of colony which made the Bostonian critical of the New Yorker, or gave to the true Virginian a feeling of superiority to the "zealots" of New, England. To the Scotch-Irish or German dweller in the Shenandoah Valley it mattered little whether he lived north or south of an imaginary and disputed line that divided Maryland from Pennsylvania. Political subjection to Virginia could not remove the Blue Ridge Mountains which isolated him far more effectively from Williamsburg than from Baltimore, or the racial and religious prejudice that disposed him to give more credit to ministers trained at Princeton than to clergymen ordained by the Bishop of London. In the back country, lines of communication ran north and south, and men moved up and down the valleys from Pennsylvania to Georgia, whether in search of homes or in pursuit of trade or to spread the gospel, scarcely conscious of the political boundaries which they crossed, and in crossing helped to obliterate.

If the physiography of the back country cut across provincial boundaries, the mingling of diverse races, in an environment which constrained men to act along similar lines while leaving them free to think much as they liked, could not but wear away the sharp edges of warring creeds and divergent customs. The many Protestant sects, differing widely in externals, were not far apart in fundamentals; and as in leaving their European homes the chief causes of difference disappeared, so life in America brought all the similarities into strong relief. In this new country, where schools were few and great universities inaccessible, the Presbyterian ideal of an educated clergy could not be always maintained, while sects which in Europe had professed to despise learning came to regard it more highly in a land where the effects of ignorance were more apparent than the evils of pedantry. No man could afford to be fastidious in any minor point of religious practice when a good day's journey would no more than bring him to the nearest church. Mr. Samuel Davies, one of the early presidents of Princeton, and for some years a missionary on the Virginia frontier, said that people in the up-country came twenty, thirty, and even forty miles to hear him preach. In a letter to Mr. Bellamy, of Bethlehem, he describes his labors, and asks for ministers to help him, from "New England or elsewhere." So true is it, as Colonel Byrd had observed in North Carolina, that "people uninstructed in any religion are ready to embrace the first that offers."

Yet in many a community, on the frontier and in every part of the Middle colonies, the mingling of races compelled men, however well instructed, to ignore the minor points of their proper creeds. The Moravian missionary Schnell, preaching at South Branch, Virginia, to an audience of English, Germans, and Dutch, quite satisfied them all by discoursing from the text, "If any man thirst, let him come to me and drink." Although his principles forbade him to baptize the children which were brought to him, they "liked Brother

Schnell very much," and desired him to remain with them. And communities there were where men had forgotten the very names almost of Protestant sects. Some people in Hanover County, assembling on Sundays to read a book of Whitefield's sermons which by some chance had come their way, and being desired by the county court to declare what religion they were of, found themselves at a loss for a name, "as we knew but little of any denomination of Protestants, except Quakers." But at length, "recollecting that Luther was a noted reformer, and that his books had been of special service to us, we declared ourselves Lutherans; and thus we continued until Providence sent us the Rev. Mr. William Robinson." Aided by Luther and edified by Whitefield, they were quite content to be further instructed and "corrected" by Mr. Robinson, Presbyterian though he was, "being informed that his method of preaching was awakening."

And, indeed, toward the middle of the century, the "awakening" preacher was everywhere welcome. In America, as in England itself, a strange lethargy had fallen on the churches in that interlude between the Puritan régime and the Revolution. Dead literalism had crept into the pulpits, and conventional conformity too often did duty for conviction among the people. It was a condition which could not endure in communities where religion was still the chief intellectual and emotional refuge from the daily routine of commonplace duties. Thus it happened that both in the older settlements, where for the unlettered the dull round of life was rarely broken either by real or fictitious adventure, and in those newer regions where primitive conditions brought the primal passions readily to the surface, the burning words of the revivalist met with ready and unprecedented response. Let him but preach "vital" religion, and none questioned too closely into his formal beliefs, or inquired of what nationality or province he might be. For the preachers of "vital" religion— whether the Moravian Schnell or the Methodist Whitefield, whether the Puritan Jonathan Edwards, profoundest theologian of his generation, or the Presbyterian enthusiasts, such as Gilbert Tennant and Mr. Davies, who went out from the little Log College to carry the gospel to the mixed population of the Middle and Southern colonies—all alike appealed to those instinctive emotions which make men kin and from which every religion springs. In forming the new spirit of Americanism, few events were more important than the Great Awakening. During that sudden up-surging of religious emotionalism, which for a decade rolled like a tidal wave over the colonies, provincial boundaries and the distinctions of race and creed were in some measure forgotten in a new sense of common nature and human brotherhood.

True it is that the Great Awakening was accompanied by no lack of acid jealousies and unchristian recrimination. In almost every sect "New Light" separated from "Old Light," "New Side" from "Old Side," in most unfraternal division. Gilbert Tennant, imitating Whitefield and out-heroding Herod, exhausted ecclesiastical billingsgate in quest of terms to characterize those clergymen—Congregational or Presbyterian or Anglican; those "letter-learned Pharisees," those "moral negroes," those "plastered hypocrites"—who stood out in stiff-necked opposition to revivalist methods of inculcating vital religion.

Schism divided the Presbyterians for more than a decade; many congregations in eastern Connecticut, renouncing the Say brook Platform and the Half-Way Covenant, "separated" from the Association; and in Massachusetts the quarrel between revivalists and anti-revivalists only accentuated the breach between new and old Calvinists. And true it is that the flood tide was followed by the ebb: the tremendous emotional upheaval, which began with the Northampton sermons of Jonathan Edwards in 1734, seemed to cease after 1744 as suddenly as it came. For more than a year scarcely one person was converted in all Boston, said Thomas Prince in 1754. Jonathan Edwards waited in vain from 1744 to 1748 for a single applicant for admission to the Northampton Church. And the great Whitefield himself, returning to America in 1744, 1754, and 1764, although always gladly heard by thousands, found that the old magic had unaccountably lost its wonder-working power.

Yet division is sometimes the prelude to more effective union. It was precisely in sowing dissension within the sects that the Great Awakening broke down barriers between the sects; and by separating men in the same locality it united men in different localities. The graduates of Log College, a very seminary of revivalism, disowned by Philadelphia Presbyterians, found encouragement among New Englanders of East Jersey and New York Presbyterians who had been educated at New Haven. In 1746, men from three colonies, whom the Great Awakening had brought in to closer relations, founded the College of New Jersey, afterwards located at Princeton. Although destined to become the intellectual citadel of a new Presbyterianism, two of its first three presidents were born in New England, two were graduates of Yale College, and one was a Congregationalist, while Samuel Blair, an alumnus of the new institution, was not thought unworthy to be minister of the Old South Church of Boston. These are but isolated instances of the leveling of religious barriers between Protestant sects in the Northern colonies. In the decades following the Great Awakening New England religious solidarity was already a thing of the past. While cultivated and tolerant liberals of Boston, dallying with Arminian and Arian delusions that were but the prelude to Unitarianism, departed from the old Calvinism in one direction, Jonathan Edwards and his disciples were formulating the "New England Theology" which enabled the clergy of Connecticut and western Massachusetts to approach within hailing distance of Scotch Presbyterianism. Ministers of "Consociated" churches scrupled not, indeed, to call themselves Presbyterians. From 1766 to 1775, representatives from the Connecticut Association, and from the Synods of New York and Philadelphia, snuffing on every tainted breeze the danger of a prospective Anglican Episcopate, met annually in joint convention; and a few years later it was without reproach that the Connecticut Congregationalists could refer to the plan for a still more intimate fellowship as "a Scheme for the Union of the Presbyterians of America."

The fear of Anglicanism may remind us that the leveling of religious barriers was in part brought about by the movement toward political union. And in generating this new sense of solidarity, whether in respect to religion or politics, better facilities for intercourse and communication were not without importance.

It is difficult for us, living in an age when a man may breakfast in Philadelphia and dine the same day in Boston, to remember that Franklin was "about a fortnight" making the same distance in 1724. Yet a quarter of a century later, when the means of travel were not much more expeditious even if they were more certain, men journeyed continuously up and down the road that led from Boston to New York and Philadelphia, and from Philadelphia out into the back country and along the Shenandoah Valley. So much so, that the inhabitants of the little town of New Brunswick, says Peter Kalm, "get a considerable profit from the travellers who every hour pass through on the high road." Communication by correspondence, immensely facilitated after the establishment of the "General Post Office" by Parliament in 1710, served often to create cordial relations between men living in different colonies; men who perhaps had never seen each other, and who might have been, as the good John Adams sometimes was, disillusioned by personal contact. Newspapers, long since established in Philadelphia and Charleston, as well as in New York and Boston, regularly carrying the latest intelligence from every colony into every other, wore away provincial prejudice and strengthened intercolonial solidarity by revealing the common character of governmental organization and of political issues from Massachusetts to South Carolina. The assembly at Williamsburg or at Philadelphia, guarding local privileges against the encroachments of prerogative, was made aware that in fundamentals the conflict was American rather than merely provincial, and proclaimed its rights more stubbornly and with far greater confidence for knowing that assemblies in New York and Boston were enlisted in the common cause.

In strengthening this sense of political solidarity, the last French wars were of great importance. Aroused as never before to a realization of the common danger, colonial Governments coöperated, imperfectly, indeed, but on a scale and with a unanimity hitherto unknown, in an undertaking which none could doubt was of momentous import to America and to the world. Never before were so many men from different colonies brought into personal contact with one another; never before had so many Americans of all classes heard the speech and observed the manners of Britons. It was an experience not to be forgotten. The Puritan recruit from Massachusetts might write home lamenting the scandalous irreligion that prevailed among the levies from other colonies; but the irritating condescension of British regulars made him aware that he had after all more in common with the most unregenerate American than with any Englishman. The provincial, subtly conscious of his limitations when brought into contact with more traveled and cosmopolitan men, endures less readily than any other to be reminded of his inferiority. Who shall estimate the effect upon the proud and self-contained Washington of intercourse with supercilious British officers during the Braddock expedition? In how many unrecorded instances did a similar experience produce a similar effect? No bitterness endures like that of the provincial despised because of his provincialism. He has no recourse but to make a virtue of his defects, and prove himself superior by condemning qualities which he may once have envied. And Americans were the more confirmed in this attitude by the multiplied proofs of the Englishman's real inferiority for the business in hand. Who were these men from oversea to instruct natives in the art of frontier warfare?—men who proclaimed their ignorance of the woods by standing grouped and red-coated in the open to be shot down by Indians whom they could not see! From the experience of the last French war there emerged something of that sublime self-confidence which stamps the true American. And in that war was generated a sense of spiritual separation from England never quite felt before—something of the contempt of the frontiersman for the tenderfoot who comes from the sheltered existence of cities to instruct him in the refinements of life.

After the Peace of Paris provincial politics takes on, indeed, a certain militant and perfervid character hitherto unknown, and not wholly due to the restrictive measures of the Grenville Ministry. It was as if the colonists, newly stirred by a naïve, primitive egoism, still harboring the memory of unmerited slights, of services unappreciated oven if paid for, had carried over into secular activities some fanatical strain from the Great Awakening, something of the intensity of deep-seated moral convictions. And in no unreal sense this was so. The mantle of Samuel Davies fell upon Patrick Henry. The flood tide of religious emotionalism ebbed but to flow in other channels? and men who had been so profoundly stirred by the revivalist were the more readily moved by the appeal of the revolutionary orator.

In diverting the current of quickened religious feeling into political channels, the influence of Princeton College was a memorable one. Founded by Presbyterians less interested in creeds than in vital religion, and barring no person on "account of any speculative principles," the new institution furnished an education that was "liberal" in the political as well as in the intellectual sense of the term. From this center emanated a new leaven. Here young men came from all the Middle and Southern country to receive the stamp of a new Presbyterianism compounded of vital religion and the latter-day spirit of Geneva. In this era, by such men as John Madison, Oliver Ellsworth, and Luther Martin, were founded the two famous societies, *Cliosophic* and *American Whig*, where the lively discussions were doubtless more often concerned with history and politics than with the abstract points of theology or religion. It was in 1768 that John Witherspoon, the very personification of the new influence, became president of the college. A Scotchman educated at Edinburgh, he became at once an ardent defender of the colonial cause, as "high a Son of Liberty as any man in America," destined to be better known as a signer of the Declaration of Independence than as a Presbyterian minister of the gospel. During twenty years previous to the Revolution, many men went out from Princeton to become powerful moulders of public opinion. Few were counted as theologians of note; few were set down as British Loyalists. But they were proud to be known as Americans and patriots: ministers who from obscure pulpits proclaimed the blessings of political liberty; laymen who professed politics with the fervor of religious conviction.

And the Puritan spirit, in like manner deserting the worn-out body of old theologies, was reincarnated in secular forms, to become once more the animating force of New England civic life. The fall of the Puritan theocracy was

96

followed, half a century later, by the rise of the Puritan democracy. As the old intimacy between State and Church disappeared, the churches turned to the people for that support which was no longer accorded by government. Thus there came into general use the famous Half-Way Covenant, a wide-open back door through which all men of blameless lives and orthodox beliefs might press into the churches, a kind of ecclesiastical manhood suffrage undermining the aristocracy of the fully regenerate. As a partial remedy for the evils arising out of this democratization of religion and church government, a closer union of the churches under ministerial supervision was advocated, and finally adopted in Connecticut under the name of "Consociation." But the scheme was defeated in Massachusetts; and it is significant that the men who defeated it, no friends, many of them, of the Half-Way Covenant, appealed to that very democratic principle of which the Half-Way Covenant was a practical application. It was a son of Cotton Mather who warned the people of the churches never blindly to "resign themselves to the direction of their ministers; but consider themselves, as men, as Christians, as Protestants, obliged to act and judge for themselves in all the weighty concernments of Religion." To resign themselves to their ministers was thought, indeed, to be but the first step backward toward Anglican oppression and Papal tyranny.

A far more profound opponent of ecclesiastical aristocracy was the Reverend John Wise, of Ipswich. He belongs to that illustrious minority which stood out against the witchcraft delusion. Fined and imprisoned upon one occasion for leading his town to refuse the collection of taxes not imposed by a representative assembly, he was a proper man to declare that "power is originally in the people." As men are "all naturally free and equal," civil government "is the effect of human free-compacts and not of divine instigation." And "if Christ has settled any form of power in his Church he has done it for the benefit of every member. Then he must needs be presumed to have made choice of that government as should least expose the people to hazard, either from fraud, or arbitrary measures of particular men. And it is as plain as daylight, there is no species of government like a democracy to attain this end." So argued the Ipswich preacher in 1717. Fifty years later, his *Vindication of the Government of the New England Churches*, too radical for his own day, was seen to be the very thing needed; in 1772, when "consociation" had broken down even in Connecticut, when Anglicanism was associated in men's minds with royal oppression, and when political and religious liberty seemed destined to stand or fall together, then the work of John Wise was reprinted and two editions were exhausted within the year.

Accompanying the endeavor to find a common theoretical basis for Church and State was the disposition to apply a common test to public and private conduct. Rousseau voiced one of the strongest convictions of his age when he said that "those who would treat politics and morality apart will never understand anything about either one or the other." With the decay of creeds, true religion was thought by many to be inseparable from civic virtue, while political philosophy, preaching the regeneration of an "artificial" society by returning to the simple life of nature, was often conceived with an emotional

97

fervor which raised civic duties to the level of religious rites. In America, long before Rousseau startled the world with his paradoxes, men who could not agree on creeds or forms of government found common ground in thinking that the test of true religion was that it made good citizens, the test of rightly ordered society that it made good men. In the early letters of John Adams we may note how one man's mind was won to this new ideal. "There is a story about town," he writes to Charles Cushing, "that I am an Arminian." Time was when such a rumor would have been too serious to be reported, without comment, in the postscript of a long letter. In 1756, even this young candidate for the ministry felt that such issues were becoming remote and unreal. He but voiced the growing discontent when he asked, "where do we find a precept in the gospel requiring ecclesiastical synods, councils, creeds, oaths, subscriptions, and whole cart-loads of other trumpery that we find religion encumbered with in these days?" Independent thinking, fortified by the authority of Locke and Sidney, Bacon and Tillotson, and the author of Cato's Letters, enabled him to announce, in the very spirit and all but the very words of Diderot and Rousseau, of whom he had never heard, that "the design of Christianity was not to make good riddle-solvers or good mystery-mongers, but good men, good magistrates, and good subjects." And so he renounced the ministry in favor of "that science by which mankind raise themselves from the forlorn, helpless state, in which nature leaves them, to the full enjoyment of all the inestimable blessings of social union."

It is but an evidence of the force of this new ideal that Benjamin Franklin, in whose life and writings it finds best expression, became the most influential American of his time and won in two continents the veneration that men accord to saints and prophets. At the age of sixteen some books against Deism came his way; but "the arguments of the Deists, which were quoted to be refuted, appeared to me to be stronger than the refutations; [and] I soon became a thorough Deist." Yet experience straightway led this original pragmatist to the conclusion that, although a materialistic philosophy of life "might be true, it was not very useful." Without faith in religions, yet unable to do without religion, he set down the list of virtues which he thought might be of benefit to himself and at the same time of service to his fellows; qualities which all the sects might unite in proclaiming good, and which any man might easily acquire by a little persistence in self-discipline. Aiming to become himself "completely virtuous," he dreamed of some day formulating the universal principles of the "Art of Virtue," and of uniting all good men throughout the world in a society for promoting the practice of it. And what was this Art of Virtue but a socialized religion divested of doctrine and ritual? "I think vital religion has always suffered when orthodoxy is more regarded than virtue; and the Scriptures assure me that at the last day we shall not be examined what we *thought*, but what we *did*; and our recommendation will be that we did good to our fellow creatures." The evangelist Whitefield, when Franklin once promised to do him a personal service, assured the philosopher that if he made that kind offer for Christ's sake he should not miss a reward. It was in the spirit of the new age speaking to the old that the sage replied: "Don't let me be mistaken; it was not for Christ's sake, but for yours."

Franklin spoke indeed for the new age and the New World. He was the first American: the very personification of that native sense of destiny and high mission in the world, and of that good-natured tolerance for the half-spent peoples of Europe, which is the American spirit; a living and vocal product, as it were, of all the material and spiritual forces that were transforming the people of the British plantations into a new nation. All racial and religious antagonisms, all sectional and intercolonial jealousies, all class prejudice, were in some manner comprehended and reconciled in Franklin. He was as old as the century and touched it at every point. What an inclusive experience was that of this self-made provincial who as a printer's boy heard Increase Mather preach in Boston and in his old age stood with Voltaire in Paris to be proclaimed the incomparable benefactor of mankind! Provincial! But was this man provincial? Or was that, indeed, a province which produced such men? Was that country rightly dependent and inferior where law and custom were most in accord with the philosopher's ideal society? In that transvaluation of old values effected by the intellectual revolution of the century, it was the fortune of America to emerge as a kind of concrete example of the imagined State of Nature. In contrast with Europe, so "artificial," so oppressed with defenseless tyrannies and useless inequalities, so encumbered with decayed superstitions and the débris of worn-out institutions, how superior was this new land of promise where the citizen was a free man, where the necessities of life were the sure reward of industry, where manners were simple, where vice was less prevalent than virtue and native incapacity the only effective barrier to ambition! In those years when British statesmen were endeavoring to reduce the "plantations" to a stricter obedience, some quickening influence from this ideal of Old World philosophers came to reinforce the determination of Americans to be masters of their own destiny.

BIBLIOGRAPHICAL NOTE

For the constitutional and political tendencies in this period, see Charming, *History of the United States*, II, chaps, X-XII; Greene, *Provincial America*, chaps, V, XII; Andrews, *The Colonial Period*, chap. VII. Economic, social, and intellectual characteristics are well described in Channing, II, chaps, XV-XVII; Greene, chaps, XVI-XVIII; Andrews, *The Colonial Period*, chaps, III, IV. The best account of religious changes in the eighteenth century is in Walker, *History of Congregationalism in America*. See also, Fiske, *New France and New England*, chap. VI. Of special importance for the influence of Princeton College and for the religious conditions in the up-country are *The Life of Devereaux Jarrett* (Baltimore, 1806); and Alexander, *Biographical Sketches of the Founder and the Alumni of Log College* (Princeton, 1845). The expansion of population into the interior and the coming of the Germans and Scotch-Irish are well described in Channing, II, chap, XIV; and Greene, chap. XIV. For a full treatment of the German migration see Faust, *The German Element in the United States* (2 vols. 1909); for the Scotch-Irish see Hanna, *The Scotch-Irish* (2 vols. 1902). The best account of the characteristics of frontier society in this period is in Turner, *The Old West*, in *Proceedings of the Wisconsin Historical Society*, 1908, p. 184. Of considerable importance for understanding colonial society in this period are the observations of foreign travelers, notably Kalm and Burnaby whose narratives are printed in Pinkerton, *Voyages* (London, 1808-14), vol. XIII. For understanding the temper and ideals of America in the eighteenth century, no writings are of equal importance with those of John Adams and Benjamin Franklin, especially the *Diary* of the former (*Works of John Adams*, 10 vols. Boston, 1856) and the *Autobiography* of the latter, in his collected works and separately printed in many editions. See Bigelow edition. *The Life of Benjamin Franklin written by Himself.*

CHAPTER VI

THE WINNING OF INDEPENDENCE

If they accept protection, do they not stipulate obedience?
Samuel Johnson.
The decree has gone forth, and cannot now be recalled, that a more equal liberty than has prevailed in other parts of the earth, must be established in America.
John Adams.

I

As Chateaubriand said of the Revolution in France, that it was complete before it began, so may it be said that America was free before it won independence. The strict letter of the law counts for less in times of emotional stress than the strong sense of prescriptive right, and formal allegiance is in no way incompatible with a deep-seated feeling that submission must be voluntary to be honorable. Before the outbreak of the French war such a feeling was common throughout the colonies. The state of mind which conditioned the formal argument for colonial rights and drove the colonists into revolution is revealed in a sentence which Franklin wrote in 1755: "British subjects, by removing to America, cultivating a wilderness, extending the domain, and increasing the wealth, commerce, and power of the mother country, at the hazard of their lives and fortunes, ought not, and in fact do not thereby lose their native rights." It was as much as to say that Americans were in fact free because they ought to be free, and that they ought to be free because they had made for themselves a new country.

The issue between England and America is therefore not be resolved by computing the burden of a penny tax, or by exposing the sordid motives of British merchants and Boston smugglers, still less by coming "armed at all points with law cases and acts of Parliament, with the statute-book doubled down in dog's ears" to defend either the cause of liberty or authority. The issue, shot through and through, as all great issues are, by innumerable sordid motives and personal enmities and private ambitions, was yet one between differing ideals of justice and welfare; one of those issues which, touching the emotional springs of conduct, are never composed by an appeal to reason, which formal argument the most correct, or the most skilled dialectic, serve only to render

100

more irreconcilable. "In Britain," said Bernard in 1765, "the American governments are considered as corporations empowered to make by-laws, existing only during the pleasure of Parliament. In America they claim to be perfect states, no otherwise dependent upon Great Britain than by having the same king." Few Englishmen could imagine an empire of free states; few Americans could understand a nation bound against its will.

The policy which history associates with the name of Grenville did not originate with him, nor yet with his royal master, George III. It was the unhappy experience of the Austrian Succession War that enforced upon the English Government the necessity of a stricter attention to the colonies. Ministers who then set themselves to read the American dispatches were amazed to find the governors everywhere without adequate support against the assemblies, the assemblies everywhere indifferent to imperial interests. After the Peace of Aix-la-Chapelle plantation affairs were accordingly placed under the direction of the able Halifax; and in 1752 the governors were instructed to transmit all correspondence "to His Majesty by one of His Majesty's principal Secretaries of State." To remedy an untoward situation many schemes were broached, on the eve of the Seven Years' War, designed to bring the colonies "to a sense of their duty to the king, to awaken them to take care of their lives and fortunes." The need of the hour was a union of the colonies for military defense; and in 1754, on the initiative of the English Government, representatives from seven colonies adopted a scheme drafted by Franklin and known as the Albany Plan of Union. It was ominous for the success of all such attempts in the future that a plan which was thought by the ministers too weak to be effective was thought by the colonial assemblies too strong to be safe. In any case, with hostilities already begun, the issue could not be pressed to a conclusion when, as the Board of Trade asserted, "a good understanding between your Majesty's governors and the people is so absolutely necessary." Under the stress of war, all ministerial projects for a stricter control of the colonies were accordingly laid aside until the restoration of peace.

The war itself only proved once more how defective was England's colonial administration. Three years of devastating Indian warfare again demonstrated the necessity of an adequate defense of the frontier, and a stricter control of Indian trade. A customs service which collected annually £2000 of revenue and cost £7000 to maintain, manned by officials who sold flags of truce to traders carrying ammunition and supplies to the enemy, was seen to be but an expensive luxury in time of peace and a military weakness in time of war. The assistance which Pitt, and Pitt alone, could induce the colonists to render, however adequate, was purchased at the price of concessions which deprived the governors of all but nominal influence, while placing in the assemblies the effective powers of government. And the results achieved by the Peace of Paris but confirmed the conclusions which followed from the experience of the war. The territory then acquired by England was imperial in extent; and the acquisition of it had in six years raised the annual cost of her military and naval establishment from £70,000 to £350,000. This far-flung and diversified empire had to be organized in order to be governed, and defended in order to be maintained. In view of the unprecedented responsibilities thus thrust upon the little island kingdom, it seemed that the oldest and most prosperous, the most English and best disposed of England's colonies might well be asked to submit to reasonable restraints in the interests of the empire, and in their own defense to furnish a moderate assistance.

Before the war was over assiduous royal governors were offering counsel as to the "regulation of the North American governments." If there is to be a new establishment "upon a true English constitutional bottom," wrote Bernard in 1761, "it must be upon a new plan," for "there is no system in North America fit to be made a module of." High officials in England were not lacking who agreed with the Massachusetts governor. The Peace of Paris was scarcely signed before Charles Townshend, First Lord of Trade in Bute's Ministry, proposed that the authority of Parliament should be invoked to remodel the colonial Governments upon a uniform plan, to pass stringent laws for enforcing the Trade Acts, and by taxation to raise a revenue in America for paying the salaries of royal officials and for the maintenance of such British troops as might be stationed there for the defense of the colonies. Townshend's proposals would doubtless have been formulated into law had it not been for the fall of Bute's Ministry in April; but the measures which were finally carried by Grenville, if they left the colonial charters untouched, were no less comprehensive, in respect to the purely imperial matters of trade and defense, than those initiated by his brilliant predecessor.

Adequate and well-administered laws for advancing the trade and securing the defense of the empire were, indeed, the primary objects of Grenville's colonial legislation. Grenville, who was the fingers rather than the soul of good government, could not endure the lax administration of the customs service which in the course of years had given the colonies, as it were, a vested interest in non-enforcement. He accordingly set himself to correct the faults which Walpole had condoned in the interest of the Hanoverian succession, and which Newcastle had utilized in the service of the Whig faction. Commissioners of the customs, long regarding their offices as sinecures and habitually residing in England, were ordered to repair at once to their posts in America. Additional revenue officers were appointed with more rigid rules for the discharge of their duties. Governors were once more instructed to give adequate support in the enforcement of the Trade Acts. The employment of general writs, or "writs of assistance," was authorized to facilitate the search for goods illegally entered; and ships of war were stationed on the American coast to aid in the suppression of smuggling.

More careful administrative supervision was but the prelude to additional legislation. Throughout the eighteenth century, the trade of the Northern and Middle colonies with the French and Spanish West Indies had been one of the most extensive branches of colonial commerce. To divert this traffic to the British sugar islands, Walpole had carried the Molasses Act in 1733. But the Molasses Act, though many times renewed and now in 1763 once more about to expire, had never been enforced, and had never, therefore, either benefited the British sugar planters or brought any revenue into the treasury. It was to secure one or both of these advantages that Grenville procured from Parliament the passage in 1764 of the law known as the Sugar Act; a law which reduced the duty upon foreign molasses imported into the continental colonies from 6*d.* to 3*d.*, and imposed new duties upon coffee, pimento, white sugar, and indigo from the Spanish and French West Indies, and upon wine from the Madeiras and the Azores. Even such men as Bernard, Hutchinson, and Colden believed that the new duties would destroy a trade which they asserted was indispensable to the Northern colonies and highly beneficial to the commerce of the empire. But the sugar planters, powerfully represented in Parliament, demanded protection, while to Grenville's mind the systematic violation of a law was rather an argument against its repeal than an evidence of its impracticability. The measure, therefore, became a law; and for its better enforcement the jurisdiction of the admiralty courts was extended, and naval officers were empowered to act as collectors of the customs.

Less noticed at the time, but scarcely less important in its effects upon trade and industry, was the law passed by Parliament in the same year for regulating colonial currency. With the rapid development of commerce in the eighteenth century, and on account of the steady flow of specie to London, the colonies had commonly resorted to the use of paper money as a legal tender in the payment of local debts. Such men as Franklin and Colden defended the practice on the ground of necessity, and it was undoubtedly true that without the issue of new bills of credit the colonies could not have given the military assistance required of them for the conquest of Canada. But it was equally true that in most colonies, except Massachusetts where the issues had been retired in 1749, and New York where their par value had been consistently maintained, the evils of depreciated currency had long existed and still went unremedied. Debtors profited at the expense of creditors, while colonial assemblies often took advantage of the situation to pass laws enabling the American trader to avoid meeting his just obligations to English merchants. In response to the loud complaints of the latter, and without adequately discriminating between the uses and the abuses of a colonial paper currency, Parliament passed the act "to prevent paper bills of credit hereafter issued in any of his Majesty's colonies, from being declared to be a legal tender in payment of money, and to prevent the legal tender of such bills as are now subsisting, from being prolonged beyond the periods limited for calling in and sinking the same."

Meanwhile, the Ministry of Grenville had already turned to the problem of defense, so inseparably connected with the question of Indian relations and Western settlement. The English Government had long recognized the necessity of securing the friendship of the Indians; and to this end it had fostered the settlement of the interior. Indian traders, employing methods none too scrupulous, had been encouraged to ply their traffic beyond the mountains. Many thousands of acres of land had been granted, to individuals and to companies of promoters, in the belief that "nothing can more effectively tend to defeat the dangerous designs of the French," or better enable the English "to cultivate a friendship and carry on a more extensive commerce with the Indians inhabiting those parts." It was a policy which all Americans could understand.

To those colonists who had fought with Washington to beat back the tide of Indian massacre, to those who had witnessed the destruction of Fort Duquesne, the conquest of Canada had no meaning unless it opened the great West to free settlement. And during the latter years of the war, thousands of families in all the old provinces were prepared, as Franklin said, "to swarm," while many hundreds had crossed the mountains and were already seated in the upper valleys of the Ohio.

Yet before the war began, the Board of Trade perceived that the policy originally advocated required serious modification. It was obvious enough that if titles to land were granted, not only by the English Government, but also by different colonies claiming jurisdiction over the same territory, endless conflict and litigation would be the sure result. And it soon appeared that the actual occupation of the interior was after all far more likely to provoke the hostility than to win the allegiance of the Western tribes. Overreached and defrauded in nearly every bargain, the Indian hated the trader whose lure he could not resist, and with the coming of the surveyor and the settler was well aware that the pretended friendship of the English was but a thin mask to conceal the greed of men who had no other desire than to rob him of his land. During the latter years of the war, after the conquest of Canada placed the allies of France under the heavy hand of Amherst and opened the way to actual settlement, it became clear that an ominous spirit of unrest was spreading throughout all the Northwest. It was precisely to guard against the danger of an Indian uprising, which in fact came to pass in the formidable conspiracy of Pontiac, that the Board of Trade formulated as early as 1761 the policy which found expression in the famous Proclamation of October 7, 1763. The Proclamation announced the intention of the English Government to take exclusive control of Indian relations and Western settlement. "For the present," all territory west of the Alleghanies, from the new provinces of Florida on the south to Canada on the north, was to be "reserved to the Indians." Governors were forbidden to grant land there. Those who had already settled within reserved territory were required to remove forthwith; and every Indian trader was bound to give security for observing such rules as the Imperial Government might establish. It was the intention of the ministers, although unfortunately not so expressed in the Proclamation, to open the reserved lands to settlement as soon as Indian titles could be justly extinguished. In accordance with this intention, the Government negotiated the Treaty of Fort Stanwix in 1768, by which the Six Nations ceded to the Crown their rights to lands south of the Ohio; and both before and after that event it was seriously concerned with projects for new colonies in the interior. The most famous of these projects was that of the Vandalia Colony, for which a royal grant was about to be executed in 1775 when the promoters were requested to "wait ... until hostilities ... between Great Britain and the United Colonies should cease."

Undoubtedly the Proclamation of 1763 was primarily a measure of defense; but even if strictly enforced, which was found to be quite impossible in fact, it could not alone have secured unbroken peace on the frontier. Primitive in his instincts and treacherous in his nature, the Indian harbored in his vengeful heart the rankling memory of too many grievances, was too easily swayed by his ancient but now humiliated French allies, to be held in check without a show of force to back the most just and wisely administered policy. The English Government would doubtless have been content to leave the management of defense in the hands of the colonists had they shown a disposition to undertake it in a systematic manner. After the Albany Plan was rejected by the assemblies, the Board of Trade recommended a scheme by which commissioners, appointed in each colony by the assembly and approved by the governor, should determine the military establishment necessary in time of peace, and apportion the expense for maintaining it among the several provinces on the basis of wealth and population. Shirley and Franklin were heartily in favor of such a plan. But there is no reason to think that a single assembly could have been got to agree to it, or to any measure of a like nature. "Everybody cries, a union is absolutely necessary," said Franklin in amused disgust, "but when it comes to the manner and form of the union, their weak noddles are perfectly distracted." The colonies being thus unwilling to coöperate in the management of their own defense, the Board of Trade could see no alternative but an "interposition of the authority of Parliament." This alternative the Government therefore adopted; and the permanent establishment of British troops in America to overawe the Indians and maintain the conquest of Canada, already proposed by Townshend, was now determined upon by Grenville. It was the opinion of Grenville, as well as of most men in England and of many in America, that the colonies might rightly be expected to contribute something to the support of such troops. The Mutiny Act, requiring the assemblies to furnish certain utensils and provisions to soldiers in barracks, was now first extended to the colonies; and for raising in America a portion of the general maintenance fund, the ministry, with some reluctance on the part of Grenville, proposed a stamp tax as the most equitable and the easiest to be levied and collected. "I am, however, not set upon this tax," said Grenville. "If the Americans dislike it, and prefer any other method of raising the money themselves, I shall be content." It was soon apparent that the Americans did dislike it; and in February, 1765, Franklin, speaking for the colonial agents then in England, urged that the money be raised in "the old constitutional way," by requisitions upon the several assemblies. "Can you agree on the proportions each colony should raise?" inquired the minister. Franklin admitted that it was impossible; and Grenville, more concerned with what was equitable than with what was politic, pressed forward with his measure to require the use of stamped paper for nearly all legal documents and customs papers, for appointments to offices carrying a salary of £20 except military and judicial offices, for grants of franchises, for licenses to sell liquor, for packages containing playing-cards and dice, for all pamphlets, advertisements, hand-bills, calendars, almanacs, and newspapers. The revenue which might be raised by this law, estimated at £60,000, was to be paid into the exchequer, and to be expended solely for supporting the British troops in America.

At the time there were few men either in England or in the colonies who imagined that the Stamp Act would release forces that were destined to disrupt the empire. It was scarcely debated in the House of Commons. "There has been nothing of note in Parliament," wrote Horace Walpole, "but one slight day on the American taxes." And even in America few men supposed that it would not be executed, however much they might dislike it. It was impossible to prevent the passage of the act, Franklin assured his friends. "We might as well have hindered the sun's setting. That we could not do. But since 't is down, my friend, ... let us make as good a night as we can. We may still light candles." It was not candles alone that were lighted, but a conflagration; a conflagration which soon spread from the New World to the Old and burned away, as with a renovating flame, so much that was both good and bad in that amiable eighteenth-century society.

II

If the experience of the last French war convinced the English Government that a stricter control of the colonies was necessary, the conquest of Canada convinced the colonists that they could defend themselves, and at the same time removed the only danger which had ever made them feel the need of English protection. As early as 1711, Le Ronde Denys warned the New Englanders that the expulsion of the French from North America would leave England free to suppress colonial liberties, while another French writer predicted that it would rather enable, the colonies to "unite, shake off the yoke of the English monarchy, and erect themselves into a democracy." The prediction was often repeated. Between 1730 and 1763, many men, among them Montesquieu, Peter Kalm, and Turgot, asserted that colonial dependence upon England would not long outlast the French occupation of Canada. The opposition to Grenville's colonial legislation, which gathered force with every additional measure, seemed now about to confirm these predictions.

No single law of these early years would have caused its proper part of the resistance which all of them in fact brought about. A measure of oppression could be attributed to each of them, but the pressure of any one was not felt by all classes or all colonies alike. The Proclamation of 1763 was an offense chiefly to speculators in land, and to those border communities that had fought to open free passage to the West only to find the fertile Ohio valleys "reserved to the Indians"—the very tribes which had brought death and desolation to the frontier. The Sugar Act was a greater grievance to the New England distiller of rum and the exporters of fish and lumber than it was to the rice and tobacco planters of the South. New York merchants were seriously affected by the Currency Act, which scarcely touched Massachusetts, and which, in Virginia, meant money in the pockets of creditors, but bore hardly on debtors and the speculators who bought silver at Williamsburg in depreciated paper in order to sell it at par in Philadelphia. The famous Stamp Act itself chiefly concerned the printers, lawyers, officeholders, the users of the custom-house, and the litigious class that employed the courts to enforce or resist the payment of debt.

Only when regarded as a whole was the policy of Grenville seen to spell disaster. Each new law seemed carefully designed to increase the burdens imposed by every other. The Sugar Act, for example, taken by itself, was perhaps the most grievous of all. The British sugar islands, to which it virtually restricted the West Indian trade of the Northern colonies, offered no sufficient market for their lumber and provisions, nor could they, like the Spanish islands, furnish the silver needed by continental merchants to settle London balances on account of imported English commodities. Exports to the West Indies and imports from England must, therefore, be reduced; the one event would cripple essential colonial industries such as the fisheries and the distilling of rum, while the other would force the colonists to devote themselves to those very domestic manufactures which it was the policy of the English Government to discourage. These disadvantages, which attached to the Sugar Act itself, were accentuated by almost every other cardinal measure of Grenville's colonial policy. With the chief source of colonial specie cut off, the Stamp Act increased the demand for it by £60,000; when the need for paper money as a legal tender was more than ever felt, its further use was shortly to be forbidden altogether; when the diminished demand for labor, occasioned by restrictions upon the West Indian trade, was likely to stimulate migration into the interior, the West was closed to settlement. And the close of the French war, which had raised the debt of the colonies to an unprecedented figure, was the moment selected for restricting trade, remodeling the monetary system, and imposing upon the colonies taxes for protection against a danger which no longer threatened. Little wonder that to the colonial mind the measures of Grenville carried all the force of an argument from design: any part, separated from the whole, might signify nothing; the perfect correlation of the completed scheme was evidence enough that somewhere a malignant purpose was at work bent upon the destruction of English liberties.

Members of the House of Commons who yawned while voting the new laws were amazed at the commotion they raised in America. In all the colonies scarcely a man was to be found to defend any of them. Those afterwards known as loyalists, with Hutchinson, Colden, Dulaney, and Galloway as their most distinguished representatives, were of one accord with the Lees, with Patrick Henry, with Dickinson, and the Adamses, in asserting that the Stamp Act and the Sugar Act were inexpedient and unjust. Hutchinson urged the repeal of both measures. Colden assured the Board of Trade that the Currency Act, so far as New York was concerned, was uncalled for and very prejudicial to colonial industry and the manufactures of England. The three-penny duty on molasses, said Samuel Adams, will make useless one third of the fish now caught, and so remittances to Spain, Portugal, and other countries, "through which money circulates into England for the purchase of her goods of all kinds," must cease. "Unless we are allowed a paper currency," Daniel Coxe wrote to Reed, "they need not send tax gatherers, for they can gather nothing—never was money so very scarce as now." Governor Bernard expressed the belief that if the proposed measures were executed "there will soon be an end to the specie currency of Massachusetts." Undoubtedly the general opinion of America was voiced by the Stamp Act Congress when it affirmed that the payment of the new duties would prove, "from the scarcity of specie, ... absolutely impracticable," and render the colonists "unable to purchase the manufactures of Great Britain."

But the colonists did not ground their case upon expediency alone, or rest content with argument and protest. And the bad eminence of the Stamp Act was due to the fact that it alone, of all the measures of Grenville, enabled the defenders of colonial rights to shift the issue in debate and bring deeds to the support of words. Last of all the cardinal measures to be enacted, the Stamp Act attracted to itself the multiplied resentments accumulated by two years of hostile legislation. It alone could with plausible arguments be declared illegal as well as unjust, and it was the one of all most open to easy and conspicuous nullification in fact. The Proclamation of 1763 was, indeed, nullified almost as effectively, but with no accompaniment of harangue, or of burning effigies, or crowds of angry men laying violent hands upon the law's officials. If the Stamp Act seemed the one intolerable grievance, round which the decisive conflict raged, it was because it raised the issue of fundamental rights, and because it could be of no effect without its material symbols—concrete and visible bundles of stamped papers which could be seen and handled as soon as they were landed, and the very appearance of which was a challenge to action.

While all Americans agreed that the Stamp Act, like the Sugar Act, was unjust, or at least inexpedient, not all affirmed that it was illegal. Hutchinson was one of many who protested against the law, but admitted that Parliament had not exceeded its authority in passing it. But the colonial assemblies, and a host of busy pamphleteers who set themselves to expose the pernicious act, agreed with Samuel Adams and Patrick Henry, with the conciliatory John Dickinson, and the learned Dulaney, that the colonists, possessing all the rights of native-born Englishmen, could not legally be deprived of that fundamental right of all, the right of being taxed only by representatives of their own choosing. Duties laid to regulate trade, from which a revenue was sometimes derived, were either declared not to be taxes, or else were distinguished, as "external" taxes which Parliament was competent to impose, from "internal" taxes which Parliament could impose only upon those who were represented in that body. And the colonies were not represented in Parliament; no, not even in that "virtual" sense which might be affirmed in the case of many unfranchised English cities, such as Manchester and Liverpool; from which it followed that the Stamp Act, unquestionably an internal tax, was a manifest violation of colonial rights.

The ablest arguments against the Stamp Act were those set forth by John Dickinson, of Philadelphia, and Daniel Dulaney, of Maryland: the ablest and the best tempered. Unfortunately, the conciliatory note was all but lost in the chorus of angry protest and bitter denunciation that was designed to spur the Americans on to reckless action rather than to induce the ministers to withdraw an unwise measure. Clever lawyers seeking political advantage, such as John Morin Scott; zealots who knew not the meaning of compromise, such as Patrick Henry and Samuel Adams; preachers of the gospel, such as Jonathan Mayhew, who took this occasion to denounce the doctrine of passive resistance, and with over-subtle logic identified the defense of civil liberty with the cause of religion and morality;—such men as these, with intention or all unwittingly raised public opinion to that high tension from which spring insurrection and the irresponsible action of mobs. Everywhere stamp distributors, voluntarily or to the accompaniment of threats, resigned their offices. Stamped papers were no sooner landed than they were seized and destroyed, or returned to England, or transmitted for safe-keeping to the custody of local officials pledged not to deliver them. Often inspired and sometimes led by citizens of repute who were "not averse to a little rioting," the mobs were recruited from the quays and the grogshops, and once in action were difficult to control. In true mob fashion they testified to their patriotism by parading the streets at night, "breaking a few glass windows," and destroying the property of men, such as Hutchinson and Colden, whose unseemly wealth or lukewarm opinions were an offense to stalwart defenders of liberty.

The November riots disposed of the stamps but not of the Stamp Act. Business had to go on as usual without stamps or cease altogether. Either course would make the law of no effect; but the latter course would be a strictly constitutional method of resistance, while the former would involve a violation of law. Many preferred the constitutional method. Let the courts adjourn, they said, and offices remain vacant; let print-shops close, and ships lie in harbor: English merchants will soon enough feel the pressure of slack business and force ministers to another line of conduct. A good plan enough for the man of independent fortune, for the judge whose income was assured, or the thrifty merchant who, signing a non-importation agreement, had laid in a stock of goods to be sold at high prices. But the wage-earner, the small shopkeeper who was soon sold out, the printer who lived on his weekly margin of profit, the rising lawyer whose income rose or fell with his fees: such men were of another mind. The inactivity of the courts "will make a large chasm in my affairs, if it should not reduce me to distress," John Adams confides to his *Diary* in December; and adds naïvely that he was just on the point of winning a reputation and a competence "when this execrable project was set on foot for my ruin as well as that of my country." Men who saw their incomes dwindle were easily disposed to think that the cessation of business was an admission of the legitimacy of the law, a kind of betrayal of the cause. And it was to counteract the influence of lukewarm conservatives, men who were content to "turn and shift, to luff up, and bear away," that those who regarded themselves as the only true patriots, uniting in an association of the Sons of Liberty, set about the task of "putting business in motion again in the usual channels without stamps."

The object of the Sons of Liberty was in part, but only in part, attained. Newspapers were printed as usual, and certainly there was no lack of pamphlets. Retailers did not hesitate to sell playing-cards or dice, nor were the grogshops closed for want of stamped licenses. Yet the courts of law were nearly everywhere closed for a time, and if the clamor of creditors and the influence of lawyers forced them to open in most places, in New York and Massachusetts, at least, they did little business or none at all so long as the Stamp Act remained on the statute-book. But it was in connection with commercial activities that the plan of the conservatives was most effective. Non-importation agreements, generally signed by the merchants, were the more readily kept because the customs officials were inclined to refuse any but stamped clearance papers, while the war vessels in the harbors intercepted ships that attempted to sail without them. As the conservatives had predicted, the effect was soon felt in England. Thousands of artisans in Manchester and Leeds were thrown out of employment. Glasgow, more dependent than other cities upon the American market, loudly complained that its ruin was impending; and the merchants of London, Bristol, and many other towns, asserting that American importers were indebted to them several million pounds sterling, which they were willing but unable to pay, petitioned Parliament to take immediate action for their relief.

And, indeed, to ignore the situation in America was now impossible. The law had to be withdrawn or made effective by force of arms. When the matter came up in Parliament in January, 1766, Grenville, as leader of the opposition, still claimed that the Stamp Act was a reasonable measure, and one that must be maintained, more than ever now that the colonists had insolently denied its legality, and with violence amounting to insurrection prevented its enforcement. But the Rockingham Whigs, whose traditions, even if somewhat obscured, marked them out as the defenders of English liberties, were pledged to the repeal of the unfortunate law. Lord Camden, in defense of the colonial contention, staked his legal reputation on the assertion that Parliament had no right to tax America. Pitt was of the same opinion. Following closely the argument in Dulaney's pamphlet, which he held up as a masterly performance, the Great Commoner declared that "taxation is no part of the governing or legislating power." He was told that America had resisted. "I rejoice that America has resisted," he cried in words that sounded a trumpet call throughout the colonies. "Three millions of people, so dead to all the feelings of liberty as voluntarily to submit to be slaves, would have been fit instruments to make slaves of all the rest.... America, if she fell, would fall like the strong man with his arms around the pillars of the constitution." More convincing than the eloquence of Pitt was the evidence offered by the merchants' petitions, and by the shrewd and weighty replies of Franklin in his famous examination in the House of Commons, to show that the policy of Grenville, legal or not, was an economic blunder. The Stamp Act was accordingly repealed, March 18, 1766; and a few weeks later, as a further concession, the Sugar Act was modified by reducing the duty on molasses from $3d.$ to $1d.$, and some new laws were passed intended to remove the obstacles which made it difficult for the Northern and Middle colonies to trade directly with England. Yet the ministers had no intention of yielding on the main point: the theoretical right of Parliament to bind the colonies in all matters whatever was formally asserted in the Declaratory Act; while the reënactment of the Mutiny Law indicated that the practical policy of establishing British troops in America for defense was to be continued.

III

The repeal of the Stamp Act was the occasion for general rejoicing in America. Loyal addresses were voted to the king, and statues erected to commemorate the virtues and achievements of Pitt. Imperfectly aware of the conditions in England that had contributed to the happy event, it was taken by the colonists to mean that their theory of the constitution had been accepted. The Declaratory Act was thought to be no more than a formal concession to the dignity of government; and although the Mutiny Act was causing trouble in New York, and merchants were petitioning for a further modification of the Trade Laws, most men looked forward to the speedy reëstablishment of the old-time cordial relations between the two countries. The Sons of Liberty no longer assembled; rioting ceased; the noise of incessant debate was stilled. "The repeal of the Stamp Act," John Adams wrote in November, 1766, "has hushed into silence almost every popular clamor, and composed every wave of popular disorder into a smooth and peaceful calm."

And no doubt most Englishmen would willingly have let the question rest. But an unwise king, stubbornly bent on having his way; precise administrators of the Grenville type, concerned for the loss of a farthing due; egoists like Wedderburne, profoundly ignorant of colonial affairs, convulsed and readily convinced by the light sarcasms with which Soame Jenyns disposed of the pretensions of "our American colonies": such men waited only the opportune moment for retrieving a humiliating defeat. That moment came with the mischance that clouded the mind of Pitt and withdrew him from the direction of a government of all the factions. The responsibility relinquished by the Great Commoner was assumed by Charles Townshend, Chancellor of the Exchequer, a man well fitted to foster the spirit of discord which then reigned, to the king's great content, in that "mosaic" ministry. In January, 1767, without the knowledge of the Cabinet, this "director of the revels" pledged himself in the House of Commons to find "a mode by which a revenue may be drawn from America without offense." Since the Americans admit that external taxes are legal, he said, let us lay an external tax. Backed by the king, he accordingly procured from Parliament, in May of the same year, an act laying duties on glass, red and white lead, paper, and tea. The revenue to be derived from the law, estimated at £40,000, was to be applied to the payment of the salaries of royal governors and of judges in colonial courts. A second act established a board of commissioners to be stationed in America for the better enforcement of the Trade Acts; while a third, known as the Restraining Act, suspended the New York Assembly until it should have made provision for the troops according to the terms of the Mutiny Act.

The Townshend Acts revived the old controversy, not quite in the old manner. Mobs were less in evidence than in 1765, although riots occasioned by business depression disturbed the peace of New York in the winter of 1770, and the presence of the troops in Boston, the very sight of which was an offense to that civic community, resulted in the famous "massacre" of the same year. Yet the duties were collected without much difficulty; and although the income derived from them amounted to almost nothing, the commissioners reorganized the customs service so successfully that an annual revenue of £30,000 was obtained at a cost of £13,000 to collect. Forcible resistance was, indeed, less practicable in dealing with the Townshend Acts than in the case of the Stamp Act; but it was also true that men of character and substance, many of whom in 1765 had not been "averse to a little rioting," now realized that mobs and the popular mass meeting undermined at once the security of property rights and their own long-established supremacy in colonial politics. Desiring to protect their privileges against encroachment from the English Government without sharing them with the unfranchised populace, they were therefore more concerned than before to employ only constitutional and peaceful methods of obtaining redress. To this end they resorted to non-importation agreements, to petition and protest, so well according with English tradition, and to the reasoned argument, of which the most notable in this period was that series of *Farmer's Letters* which made the name of John Dickinson familiar in Europe and a household word throughout the colonies.

If in point of action the defenders of colonial rights were inclined to greater moderation, in point of constitutional theory they were now constrained to take a more radical stand. When Franklin, in his examination before the House of Commons in 1766, was pressed by Townshend to say whether Americans might not as readily object to external as to internal taxes, he shrewdly replied: "Many arguments have lately been used here to show them that there is no difference;— at present they do not reason so; but in time they may possibly be convinced by these arguments." That time was now at hand. As early as 1766, Richard Bland, of Virginia, had declared that the colonies, like Hanover, were bound to England only through the Crown. This might be over-bold; but the old argument was inadequate to meet the present dangers, inasmuch as the Townshend Acts, the establishment of troops in Boston and New York, and the attempt to force Massachusetts to rescind her resolutions of protest, all seemed more designed to restrict the legislative independence of the colonies than to assert the right of Parliamentary taxation. Franklin himself, to whom it scarcely occurred in 1765 that the legality of the Stamp Act might be denied, could not now master the Massachusetts principle of "subordination," or understand what that distinction was which Dickinson labored to draw between the right of taxing the colonies and the right of regulating their trade. "The more I have thought and read on the subject," he wrote in 1768, "the more I find ... that no middle doctrine can well be maintained, I mean not clearly with intelligible arguments. Something might be made of either of the extremes: that Parliament has a power to make all laws for us, or that it has a power to make no laws for us; and I think the arguments for the latter more numerous and weighty than those for the former." Before the Townshend duties were repealed, the colonists were entirely familiar with the doctrine of complete legislative independence; and the popular cry of "no representation no taxation" began to be replaced by the far more radical cry of "no representation no legislation."

In support of argument and protest, the colonists once more resorted to the practice of non-importation. The earliest agreement was signed by Boston merchants in October, 1767. But a far more rigid association, not to import with trifling exceptions any goods from England or Holland, was formed in New York in August, 1768, and agreed to by the merchants in most colonies. Better observed in New York than elsewhere, it was so far maintained as to reduce the English importations into the Middle and Northern colonies from £1,333,000 in 1768 to £480,000 in 1769. In inducing the Ministry of Lord North to repeal the duties the association played its part; but from the point of view of the conservatives it was not without its disadvantages. The importation of goods from Holland was forbidden in order to catch the smuggler; but the smuggler ignored the agreement as readily as he signed it. Yet for a time the association was no burden to the fair trader, who in anticipation had doubled his orders, or sold "old, moth-eaten goods" at high prices. The merchants were "great patriots," Chandler told John Adams, "while their old rags lasted; but as soon as they were sold at enormous prices, they were for importing." And in truth the fair trader's monopoly could not outlast his stock, whereas the smuggler's business improved the longer the association endured. In the spring of 1770, the New York merchants, with their shelves empty, complaining that Boston was more active in "resolving what it ought to do than in doing what it had resolved," declared that the association no longer served "any other purpose than tying the hands of honest men, to let rogues, smugglers, and men of no character plunder their country." Supported by a majority of the inhabitants of the city, and undeterred by the angry protests of the Sons of Liberty, they accordingly agreed to "a general importation of goods from Great Britain, except teas and other articles which are or may be taxed." Boston and Philadelphia soon followed the lead of New York, and before the year was out the policy of absolute non-importation had broken down.

The adoption of the modified non-importation policy was the more readily approved by conservative patriots everywhere inasmuch as the English Government had already made concessions on its part. It was on March 5, the very day of the Boston massacre, that Lord North, characterizing the law as "preposterous," moved the repeal of all the Townshend duties, saving, for principle's sake, that on tea alone. For the second time a crisis seemed safely passed, and cordial relations seemed once more restored. British officers concerned in the massacre, defended by the patriots John Adams and Josiah Quincy, were honorably acquitted in a Massachusetts court. The New York Assembly, recently permitted to issue bills of credit to the extent of £120,000, made annual provision for the troops, and friendly relations between soldiers and citizens were again resumed. Imports from England at once rose to an unprecedented figure. Tea was procured from Holland; the 3d. duty well-nigh forgotten. In England most men regarded the ten years' quarrel as finally composed. For three years the colonies were barely once mentioned in Parliament, and a page or two of the *Annual Register* was thought sufficient space to chronicle the doings of America. America also seemed content. During these uneventful years the high enthusiasm for liberty burned low, even in Massachusetts. "How easily the people change," laments John Adams, "and give up their friends and their interests." And Samuel Adams himself, implacable patriot, working as tirelessly as ever, but deserted by Hancock and Otis and half his quondam supporters, had so far lost his commanding influence as to inspire the sympathy of his friends and the tolerant pity of his enemies.

It was hardly for the purpose of restoring the prestige of Samuel Adams, though nothing could have been better designed to that end, that Lord North, rising in the House of Commons on April 17, 1773, offered a resolution permitting the East India Company to export teas stored in its English warehouses free of all duties save the 3d. tax in America. Many years later the Whig pamphleteer Almon asserted that the measure was inspired by the king's desire to "try the question with America." The statement is unsupported by contemporary evidence. Lord North said that the measure was intended solely in the interest of the Company, which had in fact but just been rescued from bankruptcy by the interposition of the Government, and the resolution was passed into law without comment and without opposition. Information obtained from reliable American merchants determined the directors to take advantage of the opportunity thus offered. They were assured that, although there was strong opposition to the 3d. tax, "mankind are in general governed by interest," and "the Company can afford their teas cheaper than the Americans can smuggle them from foreigners, which puts the success of the design beyond a doubt." Acting upon this assurance, cargoes of assorted teas amounting to 2051 chests were sent to the four ports of Boston, New York, Philadelphia, and Charleston.

But the American merchants who advised this step had fatally misjudged the situation. The approach of the tea-ships was the signal for instant and general opposition. Smugglers opposed the East India Company venture because it threatened to destroy the very lucrative Holland trade; the fair trader because it conferred a monopoly upon an English corporation, but above all because, if the Company could sell its tea, the non-importation agreement, that favorite conservative method of obtaining redress, at once effective and legal, would have proved after all a useless measure. Unless they were ready for decisive action, the long struggle against Parliamentary taxation must end in submission. Many conservatives were content to try non-consumption agreements; but it was a foregone conclusion that if the tea was once landed, it would be sold, and a great majority were in favor of destroying it or sending it back to England. The latter method was employed in New York and Philadelphia; but in Boston Governor Hutchinson refused to issue return clearance papers until the cargoes were discharged. There the radicals, with the moral support of the great body of conservative citizens, carried the day. On December 16, 1773, undisturbed by the English ships of war, men disguised as Mohawks, "no ordinary Mohawks, you may depend upon it," boarded the East India Company's vessels and emptied its tea into Boston Harbor.

Neither the Government nor the people of England were now in any mood for further concessions. The average Briton had given little thought to America since the repeal of the Stamp Act. He easily recalled that three years before the ministers had good-naturedly withdrawn the major part of the Townshend duties, and since then had rested in the confident belief that the quarrel was happily ended. The destruction of the tea seemed to him a gratuitous insult, for it passed his understanding that the Americans should resent a measure which enabled them to buy their tea cheaper than he could himself; and he was, therefore, ready to back the Government in any measures it might take for asserting the authority of Parliament over these excitable colonists whose whims had too long been seriously regarded. This task the Government, now for the first time effectively controlled by the king, was quite willing to undertake, all the more so on account of the recent burning of the Gaspée and the dishonorable publication of Hutchinson's letters. By overwhelming majorities Parliament accordingly passed the coercive acts, closing Boston Harbor to commerce until the town made compensation to the East India Company, remodeling the Massachusetts charter in such a manner as to give to the Crown more effective control of the executive and administrative functions of government, making provision for quartering troops upon the inhabitants, and providing for the trial in England of persons indicted for capital offenses committed while aiding the magistrates to suppress tumults or insurrection.

Drastic as these measures were, they were regarded in England as the necessary last resort, unless the Government, hitherto so indulgent and long-suffering, was prepared to ignore the most flagrant flouting of its laws and to renounce all effective control of the colonies. In the colonies, on the other hand, they were generally thought, even by conservative patriots, to be clear evidence of a bold and unblushing design, unapproved by the majority of Englishmen, no doubt, but harbored in secret for many years by the king's hireling ministers, to enslave America as a preliminary step in the destruction of English liberties. Firm in this belief, the colonists elected their deputies to the First Continental Congress, which was called to meet at Philadelphia on the 1st of September, 1774, in order to unite upon the most effective measures for defending their common rights.

IV

The causes which had brought the two countries to this pass lie deeper than the hostile designs of ministers, or the ambition of colonial agitators bent on revolution. It has been said that the Revolution was the result of an unfortunate misunderstanding. A misunderstanding it was, sure enough, in one sense; but if by misunderstanding is meant lack of information there is more truth in the famous epigram which has it that Grenville lost the colonies because he read the American dispatches, which none of his predecessors had done. In the decade before the Declaration of Independence every exchange of ideas drove the two countries farther apart, and personal contact alienated more often than it reconciled the two peoples. It was the years of actual residence in England that cooled Franklin's love for the mother country. "Had I never been in the American colonies," he writes in 1772, "but was to form my judgement of civil society from what I have lately seen, I should never advise a nation of savages to admit of civilization." Governor Hutchinson, one of the most aristocratic and most English of Americans, was amazed to find himself but an alien in a far country during the years of exile which gave him his first sight of English society since 1742. Cultivated man of the world as he thought himself, but Puritan still, it was with a profound sense of disillusionment that he mingled with the "best people" of England. How pathetic are those London letters of this unhappy exile who likes the people of Bristol best because they remind him of Boston select-men, whose one desire is to return home and lie buried in the land of his fathers! It is not too fanciful to think that if Hutchinson had lived earlier in England he might have died a patriot, whereas had Franklin seen as little of England as his son he might have ended his days as a Loyalist. It was "Old England" indeed that these cultivated Americans loved: the England of Magna Carta and the Petition of Right; the England of Drake, of Pym and Falkland, and of the Glorious Revolution; the little island kingdom that harbored liberty and was the builder of an empire justly governed: they thought of England in terms of her history, scarcely aware that her best traditions were more cherished in the New World than in the Old.

Rarely, indeed, would an appeal to England's best traditions have met with less cordial response among her rulers. For during the decade following the Peace of Paris the vision of liberty was half obscured by the vision of empire. Observant contemporaries noted the sudden rise of an insular egoism following the war that in Voltaire's phrase saw "England victorious in four parts of the world." Cowper was not alone in complaining "that thieves at home must hang, but he that puts into his over-gorged and bloated purse the wealth of Indian provinces, escapes"; and Horace Walpole has recorded in his incomparable letters, with a cynical and an engaging wit which reflects the spirit of the times better than his own sentiments, the corruption and prodigality, the levity and low aims of that generation. With many noble exceptions, the men who gathered round the young king, the men who "lived on their country or died for her," who too often admired if they could not always emulate the brutal degradation of a Sandwich or the matchless *abandon* of the young Charles James Fox, had singularly little in common with those American communities which the Frenchman Ségur fancied "might have been made to order out of the imagination of Rousseau or Fénelon."

Had they known them better they would have liked them less; and in fact ten years' "discussion of the points in controversy only served to put farther asunder" men who reasoned from different premises and in a different temper. Englishmen were generally content with the fact of power registered in legal precedents; but Americans, profoundly convinced that they deserved to be free, were ever concerned with its moral justification. "To what purpose is it to ring everlasting changes ... on the cases of Manchester and ... Sheffield," cried James Otis. "If these places are not represented, *they ought to be*." This *ought* is the fundamental premise of the entire colonial argument. "Shall we Proteus-like perpetually change our ground, assume every moment some new strange shape, to defend, to evade?" asks a Virginian in 1774. This was precisely what could not be avoided. For the end determined the means. If, therefore, the distinction between external and internal taxes was untenable, it convinced the American, not that Parliament had a right to tax the colonies, but only that it had no right to legislate for them. And when Englishmen grounded the legislative rights of Parliament upon the solid basis of positive law, the colonial patriot appealed with solemn fervor to natural law and the abstract rights of man. Little wonder that the more logical the American argument became the less intelligible it appeared to most Englishmen, and what seemed at last the very axioms of politics to the colonial radical struck the conservative British mind as the sophistry of men bent on revolution.

If ten years' discussion convinced American patriots that they possessed more rights than their philosophy had yet dreamed of, constant dwelling on their condition developed a sensitiveness which registered oppression where none had been felt before. What a profound influence had those liberty-pole festivals so assiduously promoted by men like Samuel Adams and Alexander MacDougall: "for they tinge the minds of the people; they impregnate them with the

116

sentiments of liberty; they render the people fond of their leaders in the cause, and averse and bitter against all opposers." In August, 1769, John Adams dined with three hundred and fifty Sons of Liberty at Dorchester, in an open field. "This," he said, noting the effect of the patriotic toasts and the inspiring popular songs, "is cultivating the sensations of freedom." For a decade these excitable Americans did, indeed, cultivate the sensations of freedom; went out periodically, as it were, to "snuff the approach of tyranny on every tainted breeze"; a practice which, becoming habitual, developed a peculiar type of mind which marked a man out from his fellows. Such a man was William Hall, Esquire, of North Carolina, at whose house Josiah Quincy stopped; "a most sensible, polite gentleman, and, although a Crown officer, a man replete with the sentiments of general liberty." How useless, indeed, were arguments drawn from positive law, or the citation of many legal precedents, to convince men *replete with sentiments of general liberty!*

And those who so assiduously cultivated the sensations of freedom could not easily deny themselves the martyr's crown. Like the Girondins in France at a later day, many American patriots, such as Josiah Quincy himself and Richard Henry Lee, have somewhat the air of loving liberty because they had read the classics. They liked to think of themselves as exhibiting "a resolution which would not have disgraced the Romans in their best days"; and seem almost to welcome persecution in order to prove that the spirit of Regulus still lived. It was no mere dispute in the practical art of politics that engaged them, but a cosmic conflict between the unconditioned good and the powers of darkness. "It is impossible that vice can so triumph over virtue," writes Lee in all soberness, "as that the slaves of Tyranny should succeed against the brave and generous asserters of Liberty and the just rights of Humanity." Even the common people, said Joseph Warren, "take an honest pride in being singled out by a tyrannous administration." Knowing that "their merits, not their crimes, make them the objects of Ministerial vengeance," they refused to pay a penny tax with the religious fervor of men doing battle for the welfare of the human race. Consider the dry common sense with which Dr. Johnson disposed of the alleged Tyranny of Great Britain: "But I say, if the rascals are so prosperous, oppression has agreed with them, or there has been no oppression"; and contrast it with the reverent spirit which pervades the writings of John Dickinson or the formal protests of the Continental Congress. Reconciliation was indeed difficult between men who could treat the matter lightly, in the manner of Soame Jenyns, and men who, with John Adams, thought themselves one company with that "mighty line of heroes and confessors and martyrs who since the beginning of history have done battle for the dignity and happiness of human nature against the leagued assailants of both."

This lyric enthusiasm for liberty, and the radical political theories which were its most formal expression, were all the more incomprehensible to the average Briton inasmuch as they were the result of a conflict of interests in America quite as much as of English legislation. "The decree has gone forth," said John Adams, "that a more equal liberty than has prevailed in other parts of the earth, must be established in America." Not for home rule alone was the Revolution fought, but for the democratization of American society as well. The quarrel with Great Britain would hardly have ended in war, had the landed and commercial interests, those little aristocracies which had hitherto controlled colonial politics, been free to conduct it in their own fashion. At every stage in the controversy, the most uncompromising opponents of Parliamentary taxation were those who felt themselves inadequately represented in colonial assemblies. Fear of British tyranny was most felt by those who had little influence in shaping colonial laws. And half the bitter denunciation of corruption in England was inspired by jealous dislike of those high-placed families in America whose ostentatious lives and condescending manners were an offense to the laborious poor, or to men of talent ambitious to rise from obscurity to influence and power.

What Heaven-sent opportunity, then, was this quarrel with Britain for all those who resented the genial complacence with which fortune's favorites, "with vanity enough to call themselves the better sort," monopolized privilege in nearly every colony! The Virginia Stamp Act Resolutions, which according to Governor Bernard of Massachusetts sounded "an alarum bell to the disaffected," would assuredly never have been passed by the Pendletons or the Blands, nor yet by Peyton Randolph, who swore with an oath that he would have given £500 for a single vote to defeat them. They were carried by the western counties under the leadership of Patrick Henry, recently elected from the back country to sit in sober home-spun garb with the modish aristocrats of the tide-water. Product of the small farmer democracy beyond the "Fall Line," uniting the implacable temper of the Calvinist with the humanitarian sentiments of the eighteenth-century *philosophe*, he joined hands with Jefferson and the Lees to form the radical party. It was this party which carried Virginia into rebellion against England. And it was this party which destroyed the domination of the little coterie of great planters by abolishing entail, disestablishing the Anglican Church, and proclaiming a state constitution founded, in theory if not altogether in fact, upon the principles of liberty and equality and the rights of man.

From the point of view of most cultivated and conservative Americans, admirable indeed were the restrained and conciliatory arguments of John Dickinson in support of the right of the colonies to be taxed only by their own representatives. But how vulnerable was his position in defending the existing government in Pennsylvania, by which the three Quaker counties, with less than half the population of the province, elected twenty-four of the thirty-six deputies in the assembly! "We apprehend," so runs a petition from the German and Scotch-Irish counties of the interior, "that as freemen and English subjects, we have an indisputable title to the same privileges and immunities with his Majesty's other subjects who reside in the counties of Philadelphia, Chester, and Bucks." German Protestants and Scotch-Irish Presbyterians, resenting Quaker domination more than they feared British tyranny, and the mechanics and artisans and small shopkeepers of Philadelphia, unwilling "to give up our liberties for the sake of a few smiles once a year," made the strength of the radical and revolutionary party in Pennsylvania. Opposed to all attempts to infringe their rights "either here or on the other side of the Atlantic," they at last gained control of the anti-British movement, and made use of it, employing the very arguments which Dickinson and his kind had used in resistance to British oppression, to overthrow the Quaker-merchant oligarchy that had so long governed the colony in its own interests.

One day in 1772 old Governor Shirley, then living in retirement, heard that the "Boston Seat" was responsible for the opposition to Hutchinson's administration. When they told him who it was that made the Boston Seat, he is said to have replied: "Mr. Cushing I knew, and Mr. Hancock I knew, but where the devil this brace of Adamses came from I know not." He might have been told that they had risen from obscurity to inject into politics the acrid and self-righteous spirit of their Puritan ancestors. It would be interesting to inquire to what issue the quarrel with England would have been conducted had it been left to Mr. Cushing and Mr. Hancock. Half the persistent opposition of the brace of Adamses to British legislation was inspired by the commanding position of a few families in Boston—the Hutchinsons and Olivers, who "will rule and overbear in all things." As a youngster John Adams had confided to his *Diary*: "I will not ... confine myself to a chamber for nothing. I'll have some boon in return, exchange: fame, fortune, or something." Laborious days had gained him little. "Thirty seven years, more than half the life of man, are run out," he complains in 1773, "and I have my own and my children's fortunes to make." Yet there was his boyhood friend, Jonathan Sewall, already attorney-general, "rewarded ... with six thousand pounds a year, for propagating as many ... slanders against his country as ever fell from the pen of a sycophant." And the Hutchinsons and Olivers! With what concentrated bitterness does the young lawyer write of these men who, he is convinced, had submitted to be ministerial tools for the aggrandizement, of their families. His bitterness is the greater, and his conscious rectitude the more obtrusive, because he also, the virtuous Adams, might have sat in that gallery. For the wily Hutchinson had offered him the lucrative post of solicitor-general—the open road to power; but he had declined it; he could not be bought by the man "whose character and conduct have been the cause for laying a foundation for perpetual discontent and uneasiness between Britain and the colonies, of perpetual struggle of one party for wealth and power at the expense of the liberties of this country, and of perpetual contention in the other party to preserve them." Not in England was the plot hatched, but in Boston itself; and much brooding on his injuries and his abnegations had brought Adams to the pass, in 1774, that he could set down the names of the three "original conspirators."

It was this opposition of interests in America that chiefly made men extremists on either side. Adams would have been less radical had Hutchinson and Jonathan Sewall been more so; and perhaps Hutchinson and Sewall might have been more loyal patriots had the brace of Adamses been less bitter ones. Most of those who in the end became Loyalists were men who had once been opposed to the ministerial policy, and many remained so to the end of their lives. But with every stage in the conflict they looked with increasing apprehension upon the growing influence of obscure leaders who proclaimed the rights of the people. The prevalence of mobs; the entrance of the unfranchised populace, by means of "body" meetings and mass meetings, into the political arena; the leveling principles and the smug self-righteousness of the patriot politicians;—all this led many a conservative to consider whether his interest were not more threatened by the insurgence of radicalism in America than by the alleged oppression of British legislation. Boston is indeed mad, Hutchinson writes in 1770. The frenzy, kept up by "two or three of the most abandoned atheist fellows in the world, united with as many precise enthusiast deacons, who head the rabble in all their meetings," was not higher "when they banished my pious great-grandmother, when they hanged the Quakers." People of "the best character and estate ... decline attending. Town Meetings where they are sure to be outvoted by men of the lowest orders." And even in Philadelphia, where, according to Joseph Reed, "there have been no mobs, the frequent appeals to the people must in time occasion a change." "We are hastening on to desperate resolutions," he assured Dartmouth, and "our most wise and sensible citizens dread the anarchy and confusion that must ensue."

They were, indeed, hastening on to desperate resolutions on that 5th of September when men from twelve colonies assembled in Carpenter's Hall to form the First Continental Congress. A body of able men, it represented the division as well as the unity that prevailed in America; for there Galloway and Isaac Low, soon to become Loyalists, sat with Patrick Henry and Samuel Adams, ready to welcome independence; of one opinion that American rights were threatened, irreconcilably opposed in their methods of defending them. John Adams, traveling by easy stages to Philadelphia, had noted with some surprise how greatly the Middle colonies feared "the levelling spirit of New England"; and he now found in the Congress many men who would hear "no expression which looked like an allusion to the last appeal"; men who were quite content to confine the action of Congress to protest and negotiation, deeming a non-intercourse measure useless if voluntary and revolutionary if maintained by force. For two weeks the advantage seemed to lie with these men; but on September 17, when the famous "Suffolk Resolutions" were laid before Congress, many conservatives, unwilling to abandon a neighboring colony however much they might regret the step it had taken, voted with the radicals of New England and Virginia to approve the act which virtually put Massachusetts in a state of rebellion. The final stand of the conservatives was made eleven days later when Galloway introduced his Plan for a British American Parliament, a serious and practicable plan according to Lord Dartmouth, "almost a perfect plan," thought John Rutledge, of South Carolina, for effecting a permanent reconciliation. But the motion, upon which "warm and long debates ensued," was finally rejected by a majority of one colony, and late in October the resolution itself, and all minutes concerning it, were expunged from the records of Congress.

After the rejection of Galloway's Plan, conservatives and radicals united to formulate the non-intercourse measures, which New England delegates thought so essential, and those famous addresses—to the King, to the Inhabitants of Great Britain, to the Inhabitants of the British Colonies—which Pitt declared to be unsurpassed for ability and moderation. Able and moderate the addresses undoubtedly were; the work of conservative deputies, designed to conciliate conservatives in America and win Whig support in England. But the important work of the First Continental Congress was embodied in the "Association," through which Congress "recommended" to the colonies the adoption of non-importation, non-consumption, and non-exportation agreements to become effective December 1, 1774, March 1 and September 10, 1775. From previous experience it was well understood that such agreements as these, far more drastic than any which had yet been tried, would prove ineffective if they remained purely voluntary associations; and what made the non-intercourse policy of the First Congress distasteful to conservative men were the measures taken to enforce it. To this end it was provided that there should be appointed in "every county, city, and town" a committee of inspection "whose business it shall be to observe the conduct of all persons touching the Association"; to publish the names of all who violated it; to inspect the customs entries; and to seize and dispose of all goods imported contrary to its provisions. Thus was a voluntary agreement not to do certain things transformed into a kind of general law to be enforced upon all alike by boycott and confiscation of property.

The Association of the First Congress created a revolutionary government and gave birth to the Loyalist as distinct from the conservative party. Radicals and conservatives had differed in respect to the theoretical basis of colonial rights and the most effective methods of securing redress. But the authority now assumed in the name of Congress raised the ultimate question of allegiance. Of the pamphleteers and preachers who now denounced the Association as a revolutionary measure, Samuel Seabury perceived the issue most clearly and stated it most effectively: "If I must be enslaved, let it be by a King at least, and not by a parcel of upstart, lawless committeemen." Whether to submit to the king or to the committee—this was, indeed, the fundamental question during those crucial months from November, 1774, to July, 1776. For extremists on either side, the question presented no difficulty; for conservatives like Hutchinson, who had long since lost all sympathy with prevailing measures of resistance, or for radicals like Samuel Adams and Patrick Henry, who pressed eagerly forward toward independence. But in 1774 the great majority of thinking men, abhorring the notion of war or separation from England, were yet convinced that strong protest, and even a kind of forcible resistance, was justified in order to maintain their just rights. These men sooner or later found themselves "between Scylla and Charybdis ": compelled to choose what was for them the lesser evil; to acknowledge the authority of Parliament in spite of laws which they regarded as oppressive and unconstitutional, or to identify themselves with the cause of Congress however ill-advised they may have thought its action. Those men who wished to take a safe middle ground, who wished neither to renounce their country nor to mark themselves as rebels, could no longer hold together, and the conservative party disappeared: perhaps one half chose sooner or later to submit to British authority; the other half, either with deliberation or yielding insensibly to the pressure of events, went with their country.

That a majority of conservatives refused to meet this issue until after the battle of Lexington, and many not until the Declaration of Independence "closed the last door of reconciliation," was largely due to the widespread belief that if the colonies took a bold, stand the English Government would once more back down. Upon the conduct of radicals and conservatives alike, this persistent belief, one of those delusions which often change the course of history, exercised, indeed, a decisive influence. Even as high a Son of Liberty as Richard Henry Lee would have favored more cautious measures in the First Congress had he not been certain that "the same ship which carries home the resolutions will bring back the redress." Inspired among radicals partly by the feeling that so just a cause could not fail, the conviction was chiefly grounded upon information sent home by Americans residing in England. If Congress is unanimous, wrote Franklin in September, 1774, "you cannot fail of carrying your point. If you divide you are lost." Josiah Quincy, sent to England in order to get first-hand information, wrote letter after letter to men in every part of America, assuring them that the oppression of the colonies was an affair of corrupt ministers who were not supported by one in twenty of the inhabitants of Great Britain. "Corruption and the influence of the Crown hath led us into bondage," is the common cry here. "To Americans only we look for salvation." But yesterday a noble lord had assured him that, "this country will never carry on a civil war against America; we cannot, but the ministry hope to carry all by a single stroke." Certainly, he assured his friends, the common opinion here is that "if the Americans stand out, we must come to their terms."

Above all, therefore, America must stand out; she must be "firm and united," waiting the day when England would come to her terms. But the difficulty was to be firm and at the same time united; for with every measure bolder than the last, conservative men grew timid or deserted the cause to swell the ranks of the Loyalist party. It was precisely to preserve the appearance of unity where none existed that the journals of the First Congress had been falsified; for this reason alone many conservatives had voted for the Association; and in the year 1775, after the battle of Lexington had precipitated a state of war, radical members of the Second Congress voted for conciliatory petitions, and conservatives voted to take up arms against the British troops, in the hope that if the colonists showed themselves unanimous in the profession of loyalty, and at the same time unanimous in their determination to resort to forcible resistance as a last resort, the English Government would never press the matter to a conclusion.

In February, 1775, Lord North had, indeed, offered resolutions of conciliation. The measure amazed his own followers and was greeted by the Whigs with Homeric laughter. Offers of conciliation could scarcely have arrived in America at a more inopportune time,—the very moment almost when the battle of Lexington came like an alarm-bell in the night to waken men from the dream of peace. And the resolutions themselves had all the appearance of being a clever ruse designed to separate the Middle colonies from New England and Virginia, in order to destroy that very union which Americans believed to be the best hope of obtaining real concession. Such the Whigs in England asserted them to be; and generally so regarded in America, they were everywhere rejected with contempt. In November, after the non-exportation agreement became effective, when an American army was endeavoring to drive the British troops out of Boston, Lord North declared in Parliament that whereas former measures were intended as "civil corrections against civil crimes," the time was now come for prosecuting war against America as against any foreign enemy; and with the opening of the new year it was at last becoming clear, even to the most optimistic, that the English Government was prepared to exact submission at the point of the sword.

As the vain hope of conciliation died away, the radicals, under the able lead of John Adams and Richard Henry Lee, pushed on to a formal declaration of independence. This was now, indeed, the only way out for them. The non-intercourse policy, injuring America more than it injured England, had proved a hopeless failure. During the year 1775 imports fell from, £2,000,000 to £213,000; and after the non-exportation agreement became effective, business stagnation produced profound discontent and diminished the resources necessary for carrying on war. So drastic a self-denying ordinance could not be maintained, for "people will feel, and will say, that Congress oppresses them more than Parliament." Unable "to do without trade," they were "between Hawk and Buzzard"; and on April 6, 1776, the ports of America were opened to the world. "But no state will treat or trade with us," said Lee, "so long as we consider ourselves subjects of Great Britain." A declaration of independence was therefore recognized, gladly by some, with profound regret by many more, as the only alternative to submission; for it alone would make possible that military and commercial alliance with France without which America could not successfully withstand the superior power of Great Britain; and at the same time it would enable the *de facto* colonial Governments, with a show of legality, to suppress the disaffected Loyalists and confiscate their property to the uses of the cause which they had so basely betrayed.

On June 7, 1776, Richard Henry Lee, in behalf of the Virginia delegation and in obedience to instructions from the Virginia Assembly, accordingly moved "that these united colonies are, and of right ought to be free and independent states; ... that it is expedient forthwith to take the most effectual measures for forming foreign alliances"; and "that a plan of confederation be prepared and transmitted to the respective colonies for their consideration." Debated at length, the final decision, already a foregone conclusion, was deferred in deference to the wishes of the conservative Middle colonies. It was on July 2 that the momentous resolutions were finally carried; and two days later the Congress published to the world that famous declaration which derived the authority of just governments from the consent of the governed, and grounded civil society upon the inherent and inalienable rights of man. In the history of the Western world, the American Declaration of Independence was an event of outstanding importance: glittering or not, its sweeping generalities formulated those basic truths which no criticism can seriously impair, and to which the minds of men must always turn, so long as faith in democracy shall endure.

V

The men who with resolution and high hope pledged their lives, their fortunes, and their sacred honor to the defense of these novel principles, could scarcely have foreseen the emotional reaction that was soon to follow; the profound disillusionment of those weary years when only an occasional victory came to lift the despondency occasioned by constant defeat: years when "the spirit of the people begins to flag, or the approach of danger dispirits them"; when "few of the numbers who talked so largely of death and honor" were to be found on the field of battle; when a febrile enthusiasm for liberty and the just rights of humanity seemed strangely transformed into the sordid spirit of the money-changer; those years of the drawn-out war when drudgery in obscure committee rooms was valued above declamation and the practical sense of Robert Morris counted for more than the finished oratory of Richard Henry Lee; the times that tried men's souls, when "the summer soldier and the sunshine patriot ... shrinks from the service of his country, but he that stands ... deserves the love of man and woman." Happily for America there were many who kept the faith, who fought the good fight, during these dark days. Yet one is apt to think that the Declaration must have proved a vain boast of rebels but for that Virginia colonel whom the Congress appointed, on June 17, 1775, to be "General and Commander in Chief of the armies of the United Colonies"; that man so modest that he thought himself incompetent for the task, yet of such heroic resolution that neither difficulties nor reverses nor betrayals could bring him to despair; that man of rectitude, whose will was steeled to finer temper by every defeat, and who was not to be turned, by any failure or success, by any calumny, by gold, or by the dream of empire, from the straight path of his purpose.

He had come, in June, 1776, fresh from the notable achievement which drove the British army out of Boston, to defend New York against the most formidable military and naval force ever seen in America. With a rashness born of inexperience or the necessity of making a stand, Washington carried his undisciplined farmers and frontier riflemen across to Brooklyn Heights on Long Island, to meet inevitable defeat at the hands of General Howe. A ship or two, which the slow-moving British commander might have sent up the East River, would have prevented the masterly retreat which saved the American army from capture. But Howe seemed bent only upon occupying New York, which thus became, and until the end of the war remained, the British and Loyalist headquarters. With a deliberation that enraged the Loyalist and non-plussed his subordinates, the general pushed the patriot army northward to White Plains, missing there a second opportunity to win a decisive battle. But the capture of Fort Washington on the Hudson opened the river to the British navy, and compelled the American forces to retreat through New Jersey, and across the Delaware River at Trenton into Pennsylvania. Half a year had not passed since the Declaration of Independence when the cause of America seemed already lost. "We looked upon the contest as nearly closed," Major Thomas assured his patriot friends, "and considered ourselves a vanquished people." The indifferent populace of New York and New Jersey came in crowds to swear allegiance to the victorious army. No one doubted that Howe would cross the river and take Philadelphia. The jubilant Loyalists of the capital city awaited their deliverance.

Congress, bundling its records into a farm wagon, scrambled away to Baltimore. And even the steadfast Washington, with his tatterdemalion army reduced to three thousand effectives, wrote that if new troops could not be raised without delay "the game is nearly up."

Of Villeroi, a general in the army of Louis XIV, it was said that he had "well served the king—William." It might be said of Howe that he shares with Washington the merit of achieving American independence. He never quite deserted the patriot cause; and now, at this critical moment, instead of pressing on to Philadelphia, he retired his main army, leaving only some Hessian outposts at Trenton and Bordentown. This arrangement enabled Washington to revive the waning enthusiasm of the country by executing one of the most daring and brilliant strokes of the war. Amidst the snow and sleet of a bitter December night, he ferried his forlorn little force through the floating ice of the Delaware, and on Christmas morning of 1776 surprised and captured Colonel Ball and one thousand Hessians. Cornwallis, on the point of departure for England, was hastily recalled to recover the lost ground; but he was out-generaled and defeated, and Washington occupied Morristown Heights, where he would indeed have been "left to scuffle for Liberty like another Cato," had he not been, to his great amazement, allowed by the British commander to remain unmolested there until the next spring. "All winter," he writes, "we were at their mercy, with sometimes scarcely a sufficient body of men to mount the ordinary guards, liable at every moment to be dissipated, if they had only thought proper to march against us."

If the conduct of the British general in the winter of 1777 amazed Washington, his management of the next campaign was even more inexplicable. The army of Burgoyne was then moving slowly southward from Canada by way of Lake Champlain and the Hudson River. It was the intention of the ministers that Howe should coöperate with the northern army; and Washington supposed that the purpose of the campaign was to effect a complete separation of New England from the more Loyalist Middle and Southern colonies. As this was thought to be precisely the most fatal circumstance which could come to pass, an army, far larger than that of Washington, was gathering to check if possible the advance of Burgoyne. But Howe neither moved north to the relief of Burgoyne, nor sent any part of his troops until it was too late. Wasting the early summer in fruitless maneuvers in northern Jersey, he finally carried his army by sea to the Chesapeake Bay, where he arrived on the 21st of August. The general had sailed three hundred miles, and had now to march fifty miles more, in order to reach Philadelphia, which was ninety-two miles from the point where he first embarked; and the army of Washington, the very army which he had sailed so far and wasted so many precious weeks to avoid, still lay across his path. At Brandywine and Germantown he fought, and easily won, the battles which could no longer be avoided. The way to Philadelphia was indeed open; but the fate of the northern army was already sealed. Caught in the difficult forests of the Hudson Valley, with supplies exhausted, unable either to retreat or to advance, on October 17, thirteen days after Howe won the battle of Germantown,

Burgoyne lost the battle of Saratoga and surrendered his entire army to General Gates.

The loss of Philadelphia was almost forgotten in the general rejoicing that followed the victory of Saratoga. And the surrender of Burgoyne was indeed a decisive event; for it inspired Americans with new resolution and was followed by the formal alliance with France. For months Franklin had been in France preparing the way for a treaty. The very presence of the man on the streets of Paris was an influence in favor of the American cause. To the Frenchmen of that day, when Voltaire and Rousseau and Fénelon had come into their own, this sage from the primitive forest, already famous as a scientist, this homely preacher of the virtues of frugality, with his unconventional wisdom and his genial tolerance, was the ideal philosopher of that state of nature which they had in imagination set over as a shining contrast to the artificial and corrupt society in which they lived. The enthusiasm of the nation for an oppressed people gave support to the Government when war was once declared, but it cannot be said that it had much influence in inducing the king to agree to the alliance with England's rebellious colonies. Bringing to bear all the resources which native wit and long experience had placed at his command, Franklin had already, encumbered as he was with unwise colleagues, procured much secret assistance. And it was probably the intention of the French Government not to depart from this policy; but after the surrender of Burgoyne, French agents in London assured Vergennes that the colonies were on the point of making peace with England, and of joining her, as the price of independence, in an attack upon the French West Indies. Since war seemed inevitable, it was manifestly better to have the assistance of America than her opposition. Vergennes therefore signified to Franklin his willingness to negotiate a treaty without delay; and there was signed under date of February 6, 1778, at Versailles, a defensive and offensive alliance between the United States of America,—recently founded upon the revolutionary principle of popular sovereignty, and His Most Christian Majesty, Louis XVI, by Grace of God King of France and Navarre.[2]

In spite of the resource and tenacity of Washington and the convenient inactivity of Howe, it is difficult to see how the Revolution could have succeeded without the assistance which now came from France. Contrary to expectation, French troops and even the French navy were of little direct aid until the battle of Yorktown. But French gold financed the war. In the winter of 1778, when Washington's heroic remnant of barefoot soldiers lay starving at Valley Forge while Pennsylvania farmers sold provisions to the British and Loyalists who were comfortable and merry at Philadelphia, the Continental Congress was already a discredited and half bankrupt Government. Confiscated Loyalist property was sold for the benefit of the new State Governments; and Congress, unable to collect its requisitions, was forced to rely upon ever-increasing issues of paper money. In this very year $63,000,000 were added to the $38,000,000 already in circulation, and in 1779 the printers turned out $143,000,000 more. Laws fixing prices were without effect, and the value of paper fell to 33 cents on the dollar in 1777, to 12 cents in 1779, and to 2 cents in 1780. When a pound of tea sold for $100, when Thomas Paine bought woolen stockings at $300 a pair and Jefferson brandy at $125 a quart, General Gates could with $500,000 of paper get a hundred yards of fence built in which to guard British prisoners, but arms and munitions of war were forthcoming only so long as drafts on Franklin were honored by the French Government.

But if the French alliance brought assistance to the Americans, it induced the English Government to undertake a more vigorous prosecution of the war. The ministers had doubtless thought that the policy of conducting the war with the olive branch and the sword in either hand would prove successful. Certainly Howe had so interpreted his instructions. He had fought only when it was necessary to fight; easily accomplished everything he seriously attempted; never pressed any advantage; had supposed that by occupying the principal cities, affording protection to the loyal, and by moderation winning the lukewarm, the flame of rebellion would burn low for want of fuel and in good time quite flicker out. Too faithfully followed by half, this policy had ended in the humiliation of Saratoga and in the added burden of a war with France. News of Burgoyne's surrender scarcely reached England before offers of conciliation, embracing more than every concession the colonies had originally demanded, were hastily pushed through Parliament and entrusted to commissioners sent to America to negotiate peace. It was now too late. Once before, just after the battle of Long Island, General Howe, declaring himself authorized to discuss terms of conciliation, had induced Congress to send a committee to meet him at Staten Island. The conference came to nothing; and the only effect of the episode was to create a strong suspicion in the mind of the French Minister that the Americans would abandon their Declaration at the first convenient opportunity. It was above all necessary that the ardor of France should not again be damped by any further dallying with English offers. The commissioners were therefore coolly received, and the attempt of Johnstone to bribe Washington and Reed, published by Congress in August, 1778, only furnished new fuel to the patriot flame.

Aroused by the French alliance and the flouting of its offers of conciliation, the English Government now set about to wage war in earnest. General Howe had returned to England in May, 1778, to stand a Parliamentary investigation; and when General Clinton who succeeded him evacuated Philadelphia, and, barely escaping disaster at the battle of Monmouth, carried his army back to New York, the olive branch was thrown away and the war took on a new character. Ignoring the patriot army, the British general resorted to the policy of ruthless raids against the prosperous Northern coast communities, burning their towns and their shipping, destroying their industries, and carrying off their provisions. In 1779, Virginia, which since 1776 had quietly raised tobacco, and the provisions which had so largely subsisted Washington's army, was laid waste all along its easily accessible river highways. Savannah was taken late in 1778, and at the close of the next year Clinton himself commanded an expedition which in May, 1780, captured the city of Charleston and forced General Lincoln to surrender his army of 2500 Continental troops. "We look upon America as at our feet," wrote Horace Walpole. And in fact the occupation of Georgia and South Carolina was regarded by the English, by the American Loyalists, and by many patriots, as the prelude to the conquest of the entire South and the end of the rebellion.

Little wonder if in these days of constant defeat and declining enthusiasm Congress too often fell to the level of a wrangling body of mediocre men. After the first years the ability that might have given it dignity was largely employed in the army, on diplomatic missions, or in the establishment and administration of the new State Governments. The particularism of the time is revealed in the belief that a man's first allegiance was to his State; to construct a constitution for Massachusetts was thought to be a greater service than to draft the Articles of Confederation; to be Governor of Virginia a higher honor than to be President of Congress. The political wisdom of the decade is therefore chiefly embodied in the first state constitutions and the legislation of the new State Governments. The constitutions gave formal expression to the philosophy of the Revolution, but in their detailed arrangements followed closely the practices and traditions inherited from the colonial period; popular sovereignty was everywhere declared, but everywhere limited by basing the suffrage upon property, and often half defeated by adopting an administrative mechanism in harmony with the prevailing belief that good government springs from "power balanced and cancelled and dispersed." The new régime was not altogether such as Patrick Henry or Jefferson would have made it, but it marked a safe and conservative advance toward the "establishment of a more equal liberty" than had hitherto prevailed.

The erection of stable State Governments greatly diminished the power and the prestige of federal authority. Insensibly the Congress and the Continental army found themselves dependent upon thirteen sovereign masters. The feebleness with which the war was supported sometimes strikes one as incredible; but the amazing difficulty of maintaining an army of ten thousand troops for the achievement of independence, in the very colonies which had raised twenty-five thousand for the conquest of Canada, was due less to the lack of resources, or to indifference to the result, than to the uncertain authority of Congress, the republican fear of military power, and the jealous provincialism which had everywhere been greatly accentuated by the establishment of the new state constitutions. Washington's army naturally looked with contempt upon a Government that could not feed or clothe its own soldiers. Congress, jealous of its authority for the very reason that it had none, criticized the army in defeat and feared it in victory. The State Governments, refusing to conform to the recommendations of Congress, alternately complained of its weakness and denounced it for usurping unwarranted power. Each State wished to maintain control of its own troops, and was offended if, in the Continental forces, its many military experts were not all major-generals. The very colony which gave little support to the army when war raged in another province, cried aloud for protection when the enemy crossed its own sacred boundaries; and, with perhaps one eighth of its proper quota of men at the front, with its requisitions in taxes unpaid, wished to know whether it was because of incompetence or timidity that General Washington failed to win victories.

After all the wonder is rather that Congress accomplished anything than that it did so little. A Frenchman, asked what he did during the Terror, replied that he lived. It was no small merit in the Continental Congress that it held together and maintained even the tradition of union; a higher merit still that in the midst of war it fashioned a federal constitution which the thirteen States, more divided by jealousy and their newly won authority than they were united by a common danger, could be induced to approve. Yet this task the Congress with difficulty got accomplished. In 1777, after months of debate, it adopted the Articles of Confederation. Leaving political sovereignty in the several states, they provided for a federal legislature with a very limited authority to make laws, but no federal executive to enforce them. Hopelessly inadequate as this constitution was to prove, the small States, notably Maryland, refused to approve it until the larger States ceded their Western lands to the common Government. Virginia, possessed of the most extensive domain, held out longest, but finally renounced her claims January 2, 1781; and in March of that year it was announced that Maryland had ratified the Articles of Confederation, which thus became the first constitution of the United States.

In 1779, while the States were wrangling over their Western lands, a little band of valiant backwoodsmen won a victory which gave substance to their claims and made their cessions something more than waste paper. Throughout the war the frontier communities were most loyal supporters of the Revolution. Their expert riflemen, organized in companies, of which that of Daniel Morgan is perhaps the most famous, served in the army of Washington, helped Gates to win the battle of Saratoga, and were of indispensable service in driving Clinton out of North Carolina in 1780, and Cornwallis in 1781. The borderers of Pennsylvania and Virginia, and the little settlements at Watauga and Boonesboro, maintained a heroic defense against the Indians, who were paid by General Hamilton, the British commander at Detroit, to wage a war of massacre and pillage on the frontier. Against intermittent Indian raids the backwoodsmen could defend their homes; but so long as the British held Detroit and Vincennes and the Mississippi forts, there could be no peace in the interior, and even if the colonies won independence, it was likely that the Alleghanies would mark the boundary of the new State. Under these circumstances, George Rogers Clark, trapper and expert woodsman and Indian fighter, set himself, with the confident idealism of the frontiersman, to achieve an object which must have seemed to most men no more than a forlorn hope. It was in 1777 that he crossed the mountains to Virginia, secured the secret and semi-official authorization of Patrick Henry, the Governor of the State, and raised a company of one hundred and fifty men with which to undertake nothing less than the destruction of British power in the great Northwest.

In May, 1778, the little band floated from Redstone down the Ohio, at the falls built a fort which they named Louisville in honor of the French King, and finally, on July 4, reached Kaskaskia. Guided by some hunters who had joined them, they took the fort by stratagem. The Indians, for the moment a greater danger than the British, were overawed by the skill and the masterful personality of Clark; and the Creoles, conciliated by his moderation, gladly joined in the capture of Cahokia. Not until February, 1779, was the intrepid commander ready to march on Vincennes. General Hamilton had recently come there with a small force, and there he proposed to remain until spring before marching to the recapture of Kaskaskia and the destruction of the settlements south of the Ohio, never dreaming that men could be found to cross the "drowned lands" of the Wabash in the inclement winter months. This fearful challenge was what Clark and his men accepted; marching two hundred and thirty miles over bogs and flooded lowlands; without tents, and sometimes without food or fire; as they neared Vincennes breaking the thin ice at every step, often neck-deep in water; yet succeeding at last, they took the fort and sent Hamilton to Virginia a prisoner of war. Detroit remained in British hands; but the possession of Vincennes and the Mississippi forts probably saved the Kentucky and Tennessee settlements from destruction, and doubtless had some influence in disposing England to cede the Western country at the close of the war.

Yet in spite of this signal victory, in spite of the French alliance, the darkest days of the war were yet to come. In the year 1780 the Revolution seemed fallen from a struggle for worthy principles to the level of mean reprisals, a contest of brigands bent on plunder and revenge. That it had come to this pass was partly due to Clinton's policy of detached raids; but the policy of raids was a practical one precisely because in nearly every colony there was a large body of active Loyalists, a larger number still who were indifferent, wishing only to be left alone, ready to submit to whichever side might win at last. Driven from their homes, plundered by British or patriot raiders, they in turn organized for revenge, sought plunder where they could find it, caring not whether they served under Loyalist or Revolutionist banners. In South Carolina, laid waste by the light troops of Tarleton and the partisans of Marion and Sumpter, in all the regions round New York, in the Jerseys, on Long Island and in parts of Connecticut, even the semblance of government and the customary routine of ordered society disappeared. The issues that had once divided men were forgotten while bands of Associated Loyalists and bands of Liberty Boys plundered the inhabitants indiscriminately, hailed each other as they passed in the night, or agreed, with the honor that prevails among thieves, to an equitable division of the spoils.

And few victories came in this disastrous year to cheer the remnant of tried Americans. Clinton's invasion of North Carolina was, indeed, a failure; and at the close of 1780, after the frontier troops had overwhelmingly defeated General Ferguson at King's Mountain, the British were forced to evacuate that strongly revolutionary colony. But Washington could do little more than hold with the desperation of despair to West Point, where his army had lain helpless and almost passive since the battle of Monmouth. Congress, barely able to hold together, could not maintain even that "verbal energy" which had once distinguished it. In this year as never before men served their country with one hand and with the other filled their pockets by manipulating the currency which had fallen to be a worthless scrip. And it was in this year, when fidelity seemed a forgotten virtue, when men enlisted in the army and deserted to the enemy with equal indifference, that Benedict Arnold, entrusted at his own request with the command of West Point, forswore his trust and wrote treason across the fair record of a patriot's achievements. Well might Washington write, "I have almost ceased to hope"; and Laurens, "How many men there are who in secret say, could I have believed it would come to this!"

Yet at last a happy combination of circumstances enabled the American and French forces, for the first time operating in complete accord, to bring this disastrous war to a most successful conclusion. Well aware of the importance of the Southern campaign, Washington had procured for Greene, the ablest of his generals, command of the forces which were gathering in North Carolina to resist the advance of Cornwallis in 1781. Defeated at the Cowpens and checked at Guilford, the British commander was forced to retire to Wilmington; but instead of returning to Charleston he moved into Virginia to join Arnold, convinced that the conquest of the Old Dominion must precede that of North Carolina. In May and June he carried ruin to all the prosperous towns of the province; but in July, when the American forces under Lafayette had been greatly strengthened, it was no longer safe for the British commander to divide his army. Acting under orders from Clinton, Cornwallis accordingly retired to the coast and fortified the neck of land at Yorktown. Washington had scarcely been apprised of this circumstance before he received a letter from the Count de Grasse, commander of the French naval forces in the West Indies, proposing joint operations in Virginia during the summer, and promising to bring his fleet to the Chesapeake sometime in August. The opportunity was a rare one. Abandoning the projected attack on New York, Washington and Rochambeau joined their forces and marched rapidly through New Jersey, entering Philadelphia the very day that De Grasse appeared at the mouth of the bay. They had already joined Lafayette before Admiral Graves arrived from New York with a British fleet to rescue the British general. Had Graves been a Rodney or a Nelson he might have given a different issue to the American Revolution; but he was not the man to win against great odds, and after an indecisive engagement he sailed away, leaving Cornwallis to his fate. Hemmed in by 16,000 American and French troops, the unhappy general, who never met Washington but to be defeated, surrendered his army of 7000, men on the 19th of October, 1781.

"It is all over!" cried Lord North when Germaine told him of the surrender of Cornwallis. The loss of 7000 men was not in itself an irremediable disaster; but the effort of the king and the "King's Friends" to establish the personal rule of the monarch had alienated the nation, while their attempt to subjugate the colonies had embroiled England with all Europe. In armed conflict with France, Spain, and Holland, opposed by the "armed neutrality" of Russia, Sweden, Denmark, the Empire, Portugal, the Two Sicilies, and the Ottoman Empire, never had the isolation of the little island kingdom been more splendid, or British prestige so diminished. The demand of the nation for peace could no longer be resisted, and the Whig party came into power over the king's will, and entered into negotiation with the enemies he had made. The American ambassadors were instructed by Congress and bound in honor not to make a treaty without the knowledge and consent of France. But in spite of Franklin's protest, Jay and Adams, who suspected, not without some show of reason but contrary to the fact, that Vergennes would oppose the extension of the United States beyond the Alleghanies, broke their instructions as readily as Jay broke his pipe, and without consulting their faithful ally arranged the terms of peace with England.

Independence was acknowledged as the indispensable preliminary to negotiation. John Adams declared that he "had no notion of cheating anybody," and it was agreed that British creditors should "meet with no lawful impediment to the recovery of all ... *bona fide* debts heretofore contracted" in the colonies. The skill of Franklin and the resolute persistence of Jay and Adams, together with the desire of the English Government to make a peace without delay, enabled the Americans to gain, in every other disputed point, all they could hope for and more than they had any reason to expect. It was conceded that they should enjoy the customary right of fishing in Northern waters. The best effort of England to secure a restoration of property and of the rights of citizens to the Loyalists was unavailing, and the compensation of that unhappy class fell to the Government whose losing cause it had supported. But of all the provisions of this Peace of Paris, the most important, next to the acknowledgment of independence, was the one which gave to the new State that incomparably rich woodland and prairie country extending from the thirty-first, degree of north latitude to the Great Lakes, and as far west as the Mississippi River. With these as its main provisions, the definitive treaty was signed on September 3, 1783, and ratified by Congress January 14, 1784.

Before the treaty of peace was signed, the cessation of hostilities had been formally declared and announced to Washington's army on the 19th of April, eight years to a day after the battle of Lexington. British troops occupied New York until November 29, when the evacuation of the city was finally completed, and the United States of America entered the company of independent nations, the exhausted and half-ruined champion of those principles of liberty and equality which were soon to transform the European world. With the British troops there sailed away, never to return, a great company of Loyalist exiles; part of the thousands who renounced their heritage and their country in defense of political and social ideals that belonged to the past. America thus lost the service of many men of ability, of high integrity, and of genuine culture; clergymen and scholars, landowners and merchants of substantial estate, men learned in the law, high officials of proved experience in politics and administration. The great achievements of history have their price; and American independence was won only by the sacrifice of much that was best in colonial society. Something fine and amiable in manners, something charming in customs, much that was most excellent in the traditions of politics and public morality disappeared with the ruin of those who thought themselves, and who often were in fact, of "the better sort."

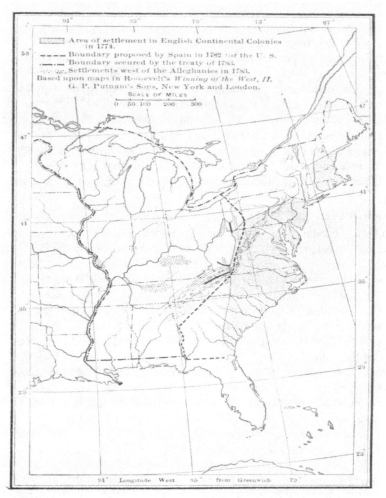

Area of Settlement in 1774; Boundary proposed by Spain in 1782; Boundary secured by Treaty of 1783; and Settlements West of Alleghanies in 1783

Happily for America not all of the "better sort" deserted their country. On the 4th of December, five days after the last British ship cleared New York Harbor, a little company of officers was gathered in the Long Room of Fraunce's Tavern. They were waiting to bid farewell to General Washington. No sign of rejoicing greeted the entrance of the familiar figure; and this masterful man of proved courage and inflexible will, this self-contained soul who endured calumny in silence, who accepted victory in even temper and defeat with high fortitude, was now strangely moved as he looked upon his beloved companions. Lifting a glass of wine he said simply: "With a heart full of love and gratitude I now take leave of you, most devoutly wishing that your latter days may be as prosperous and happy as your former ones have been glorious and honorable." When all had taken the general's hand and received his embrace, they walked together through the narrow street to Whitehall Ferry, where a barge lay waiting. As the oars struck the water Washington stood and lifted his hat; and his comrades, returning the salute in silence, watched the majestic figure until it disappeared from sight. Less than two years before, in the spring of 1782, the army would have made Washington king. He was now on his way to Annapolis, to present himself before Congress in order to resign the high office which eight years before he had accepted with so much diffidence, and to claim the indulgence of retiring from the service of his country. This, as it happened, came to pass on the 23d of December. On the day following he rode away to his home at Mount Vernon, a private citizen of the Republic which he had done so much to establish; a citizen of the Republic, and of the world's heroes one of the most illustrious.

BIBLIOGRAPHICAL NOTE

A good brief account of the Revolution is in Smith's *The Wars Between England, and America* (1914), chaps, I-VI; a fuller and better account in Channing's *History of the United States*, III, chaps. I-XII; all things considered the ablest summary is Lecky's *The American Revolution*. An able and suggestive work is Fisher's *The Struggle for American Independence*, 2 vols. 1908. Sir George Otto Trevelyan, with wide information, strong Whig sympathies, and great charm of style, has written the most fascinating work on the subject. *The American Revolution*, 4 vols. 1905. The best study of British measures which precipitated the struggle is Beer's *British Colonial Policy, 1754-1765*. 1907. For bibliography and summary of contemporary literature, Tyler's *Literary History of the American Revolution*. Selections from newspapers and contemporary documents are in Moore's *Diary of the American Revolution*, 2 vols. 1860. For the Loyalists, see Tyler, in *American Historical Review*, I; Van Tyne, *The Loyalists in the American Revolution*. 1902. For the attitude of the clergy, and the influence of religious and sectarian forces, see Van Tyne, in *American Historical Review*, XIX; Cross, *The Anglican Episcopate*. 1902. Thornton (*The Pulpit of the American Revolution*. Boston, 1860) reprints a number of contemporary sermons by New England clergy. For the Western settlements see Roosevelt, *Winning of the West*, 4 vols.; Alden, *New Governments West of the Alleghanies*, in *Wisconsin Historical Bulletin*, II; Turner, in *American Historical Review*, I; Thwaites, *How George Rogers Clark Won the North West*. 1903. The opposition between the interior and the coast regions, and the bearing of this on the formation of radical and conservative parties in the Revolution, are well brought out in Lincoln's *The Revolutionary Movement in Pennsylvania* (University of Pennsylvania Studies. 1901); and Henry's *Patrick Henry*, 3 vols. 1891. The letters, journals, and papers of leading Americans in the Revolution have been very fully printed. The ablest of the radicals was John Adams (*Works of John Adams*, 10 vols. 1856); Franklin became increasingly radical with the progress of events (*Writings of Benjamin Franklin*, 10 vols. 1903-07); Dickinson was the ablest of the conservatives who joined the Revolution, but with great reluctance (*Writings of John Dickinson*, 3 vols. 1895); the extreme conservative and Loyalist view is best represented by Hutchinson (*Diary and Letters of*

Thomas Hutchinson, 2 vols. 1884). For the period of the war perhaps the most illuminating writings of all are the letters of Washington (*The Writings of George Washington*, 14 vols. 1889-93).